Finch Books by Britt Cooper and Erin Dulin

Chronicles of Fayble
Queen of Shadows
Mistress of Blades

I0607522

Chronicles of Fayble

MISTRESS OF BLADES

BRITT COOPER & ERIN DULIN

Mistress of Blades
ISBN # 978-1-80250-991-5
©Copyright Britt Cooper & Erin Dulin 2022
Cover Art by Kelly Martin ©Copyright October 2022
Interior text design by Claire Siemaszkiewicz
Finch Books

Published in 2022 by Finch Books, United Kingdom.

Finch Books is an imprint of Totally Entwined Group Limited.

MISTRESS OF
BLADES

Dedication

To all our family — the lovers of our chaos who manage to keep our cups filled to overflowing. We could never do what we do without you!

Preface

A kingdom from stone and steel will soon rise,
Preserving their kin from fated demise.
A foolhardy curse she is born to break,
Alongside a soldier with equal stake.
Two souls and one heart unite royals lost,
Inscribed upon flesh, true love is the cost.
The war will be won in a tower high,
As centuries foretold, the time is nigh.

Chapter One

Try as she might, Rory couldn't bring herself to trust Artyrus. Suppressing her misgivings, she ignored the brigand, though every rational impulse within her told her to turn and run the other way. Merlin had sent him — or at least, that's what he'd claimed — and he'd stolen away with her, dragging her back to her duties in Chamelaute.

It wasn't as if she wouldn't have gone anyway. She was well aware of her obligations and the needs of her people. She'd have made her way home regardless, but the bastard was so *insistent*. Even now, her aggravating companion led the way astride his midnight-black horse, who was every bit as colossal as he was.

Resentfully, she eyed the back of his half-shaven head, the ash-blond hair sprouting from the top of his skull forming a short tail that bobbed in time with the beast beneath him.

Rory groaned. There were worse ways to travel through Wylewoode. There had to be, though she was hard-pressed to think of any at the moment.

"We're stopping," she shouted to her escort several yards ahead, slowing her horse. Her civility was a courtesy Artyrus didn't deserve. She offered her compliance out of the goodness of her heart, despite her disdain for her supposed guardian.

"No." Artyrus continued onward without sparing her a glance, his broad shoulders as stiff and unyielding as his ornery disposition.

Tempering her rising fury, she followed him, willing herself to be reasonable where he refused. Someone had to behave like an adult if they were to survive their trek, and that would be a monumental undertaking.

Now she understood the plight of her former sidekick Ric, the newly crowned king of Llundyn, for she had done the very same thing to him. She'd joined him by force and very much against his wishes. That arrangement had worked out better than she'd hoped, but she was under no illusions. Lightning wouldn't strike twice.

"Mind your pace," Artyrus added, his tone dripping with condescension. "We're still days behind schedule."

Rory tugged the reins, her horse rearing as she came to an abrupt halt. "Who put you in charge?"

"Aurora—"

"No!" Her steed turned in an anxious circle beneath her before she met his gaze, her eyes burning with unrestrained anger. "I'm through taking orders from you. I'm hungry, I'm tired and I want a break. We'll get there when we get there. Why all the urgency?"

He turned to face her, his patience apparently waning. "I was more than generous with you and your friends in Llundyn, and we stayed far longer than was reasonable, given your circumstances."

"Ah. How benevolent of you." Rory took a fortifying breath, all the while reconciling the little she knew of Artyrus with the seemingly endless knowledge he possessed about her. She smiled brightly, steeling herself for the inevitable battle of wills. "You may go at your own pace, but I'm going to set up camp. You'll make excellent time without me."

Trotting away, she eased her horse into the tree line, aiming for the stream that ran alongside the roadway. To her satisfaction, she didn't hear her captor tailing her. Perhaps he'd seen sense after all.

At last.

For the first time in days, she began to recover herself, reveling in the peace their rare separation afforded. It would undoubtedly be short-lived, but she wouldn't let that ruin the moment.

So what if she was a bit petulant?

Running away from Artyrus was childish, a far cry from the commanding manner in which she typically acted, but she'd had enough. He'd destroyed her restraint.

"Well, that's better," Rory sighed, patting her mare, Briar. Doubtless, she was temperamental like Rory was. Only somehow, *she* managed to get away with it. For even Artyrus, God's steadfast gift to bravery, was apt to steer clear of Briar's moody escapades and snapping teeth.

Throwing her leg over the mare's broad back, Rory dismounted, guiding Briar toward the stream for refreshment. The familiar thrum of rolling waters soothed her stormy spirit, the crystalline flow deceptively languid as she plunged her canteen into its depths. Briar wasted no time, easing in at Rory's side and quenching her thirst.

To any onlooker, the pair made for a hapless duo. But they were all they needed, making the ubiquity of Artyrus an utter nuisance.

Drying her mouth on the arm of her sleeve, Rory reached into her satchel, feeding Briar a handful of oats and taking care not to catch her fingers in the overeager horse's mouth. "This will do, will it not?"

Her newfound freedom was intoxicating, bringing a small, satisfied smile to her face. Why it had taken her so long to assert herself, to demand control of the situation, was beyond reason. Perhaps it was Artyrus's unsettling reticence that had unnerved her — that, or his sullen disposition. Somewhere along their journey, she'd decided not to poke the bear, unwittingly leaving the brute in charge of their odyssey.

She wouldn't make that mistake again. Better yet, she'd simply rid herself of him altogether.

Or perhaps not.

From beside her, Briar started, spooking only a moment too late for any resistance. Swiftly secured from behind, Rory was swept away from the tranquil waters, thrust headlong into the relentless embrace of her most formidable nemesis.

Rory thrashed about like a beached fish, arching and kicking furiously to no avail. "You've got to be kidding! Leave me alone!" Wielding her heels as a weapon, she struck, her foot whacking its target with vicious accuracy. Artyrus's sharp intake of air was little consolation, however, as he managed to hold her fast.

In one quick motion, he released her, but not before he'd somehow managed to capture both of her arms, deftly securing them before her with a leather thong. He stepped away, doubling over for one precious moment to catch his breath. "You're *ridiculous*," he wheezed, regaining his composure.

"You're playing a game you cannot possibly win. This is child's play," Rory snapped, holding her bound hands in front of her. He was sorely mistaken if he thought a simple leather strap would bring her in line. She wriggled her wrists, maneuvering one against the other to free herself. He'd gone too easy on her, leaving the band with plenty of slack. Twisting her wrists, she gave them a final tug.

Artyrus only smiled, an evil little smirk that had Rory itching for all-out war as he'd merely given her the means to entrap herself. He stepped toward her, plucking her sword from its sheath, seemingly unfazed by the hatred surely evident upon her face. "Your cooperation, if you please," he urged, his dark eyes meeting hers. "I do not wish to report such juvenile behavior to Merlin. Certainly you'd like to prove yourself worthy of your obligations."

Rory scoffed. "Tattling as if we're a pair of children. Why am I not surprised?"

"You are, indeed, behaving like one." Artyrus folded his arms across his chest before raising a single eyebrow.

A challenge.

Infuriating.

His assertion was annoying in its own right — but making matters worse was the sinister truth that he'd somehow hit a mark she hadn't realized existed. Her life had been one trial after another, with duty ever looming in the back of her mind and obscuring every facet of her future.

Perhaps some piece of her did crave the freedom of youthful irresponsibility, and being held to account was the last thing she needed. Rory closed her eyes, the fight she'd been harboring within her suddenly dissolving. Her sentiments hadn't changed, but taking a stand in the middle of a booby-trapped forest wasn't good headwork.

Artyrus nodded, wordlessly turning to lead the way back toward the roadway. Sighing, Rory grasped Briar's reins, guiding her along as she followed in Artyrus's shadow.

The man was at least aware enough to maintain a healthy distance, quickly reaching his horse where he awaited Rory, who was traipsing toward him slowly. "Up you go." Clasping his hands before him, he indicated his monstrous midnight steed with a bob of his head.

"No, thank you." Rory raised her bound wrists. "I can manage my horse well enough, even without the full use of my hands."

His grim features softened as he bent at the waist, beckoning her forward. "Nonsense. And besides, traveling together should help prevent any further detours."

Rory huffed, willing herself to ignore his provocation, finally having tired of the ceaseless back and forth between them. Making her way toward him, she mounted the devilish stallion without protest, settling into the saddle.

Clasping her boot as he rose, Artyrus extracted a dagger before moving around the front of his horse. Rory eyed him with growing suspicion as he reached for her other one, plucking a second dagger from its sheath. She was still armed to the teeth. Losing a pair of blades was of no consequence.

"Are you through?" Rory asked. "For one so concerned with making good time, you're certainly wasting enough of it."

Artyrus ignored her, instead jamming his foot into the stirrup before swinging his leg over, seating himself behind his unruly passenger. He retrieved two more daggers with maddening calm, which were concealed beneath a thin layer of linen, set between her shoulder blades.

"In case you wish to slit my throat," Artyrus gruffed, urging his steed onward with Briar following at his heels.

Rory fumed, even as she refused to acknowledge — at least outwardly — that he'd succeeded in disarming her almost entirely.

His ability to annoy her was truly unparalleled.

Their journey proceeded without disruption, providing Rory with an opportunity she'd always loathed — time to think. With Artyrus firmly in command of their route and horses — and even greater control over her from where he sat with his arms encircling her form, though he dared not touch her — she allowed her mind to wander for the first time since she'd left Chamelaute.

Planning had never been a strong suit for the wayward woman, taking on each obstacle only as it arose and never before. It was a way of life and not a bad one, though it sometimes led to a close call now and then. Rory eyed her surroundings, eager for a distraction.

The woods themselves were nothing special. Indeed, they were no different from any other woodland terrain. But their ordinary nature bred complacency, leaving one vulnerable to all the perils within Wylewoode. Deadly plants, quicksand and creatures that defied the imagination all resided within the confines of the forest. And though it was difficult to fathom, there were people there, too.

Rory had no interest in them, for only a loon would remain in Wylewoode by choice.

"Perhaps it's time," Artyrus said around a yawn after a time, guiding his horse through a gap in the foliage toward the water's edge. Lifting his arms, he shielded Rory from the tangled mess of branches as they ambled through to the nearby bank.

At first glance, the riverbank was pleasant enough, though the poisonous brambles lining the opposite shoreline reminded them that they were not in friendly territory. Soft light from the fading sun filtered through the canopy of greenery overhead, bringing a chill to the early evening air as shadows veiled the warm glow of day.

"Very well," Rory replied, reflecting an indifference she didn't feel. She was bushed and ready for a break. Artyrus dismounted first, turning to assist her as she did the same.

"Your hands." Pulling a blade from his breeches, Artyrus gestured toward her bound wrists. She offered them, palms up, avoiding his steady gaze as he cut cleanly through the strap in one slice, his brusque manner never failing to peeve her.

Artyrus excused himself then, striding into the brush and out of Rory's eye line. He had disappeared periodically to relieve himself, but it had never lasted long enough for Rory's liking. In truth, he could continue his trek and vanish altogether and there'd be no complaint from her lips.

She set to work, unpacking their meager belongings from each of their horses before sending them to the water's edge to graze. Minutes later, she'd gathered more than enough fodder for a fire and had a small blaze underway.

The burgeoning flames crackled as she prodded them to life, and before long, she had the makings of a tolerable meal, none of which she had any intention of sharing. Rory looked up, suddenly mindful of the blessed solitude in which she'd completed her tasks. How long had it been?

Rising to her feet, she stretched, casually surveying her surroundings as she worked to hide her concern. Artyrus's stallion, Magnus, remained nibbling the bracken creekside. All his possessions sat untouched, neatly laid alongside her own.

Much as she wished to ignore her unease, Rory knew something wasn't right. Recovering several blades from among his belongings, she wandered in the direction of her absent chaperone. Leaving him to survive the ills of Wylewoode was tempting, of course, but the havoc it would wreak upon her conscience wasn't worth it.

Creeping through the boughs, Rory moved quietly, following the sporadic traces of Artyrus's presence. He was somewhat ghostlike—his ability to obscure his tread leaving her reluctantly impressed, particularly in light of his size.

She hadn't gone far when she sighted him, the whole of his body suspended mid-air from where he hung by his ankle. Gently swaying in the mild twilight breeze, he issued curses too numerous to count as he contorted his body, attempting to grasp the rope as he folded himself in half.

Being too top-heavy for success, he heaved one final obscenity, collapsing as he seemingly conceded defeat, swinging like the tail of an irritable cat. The spectacle was equal parts pitiful and humorous.

Rory laughed, giving herself away as he twisted to meet her gaze. "Maybe a little help, if you wouldn't mind," he muttered, his face becoming a concerning shade of red.

"Poor fellow!" Glancing up at her captured keeper, Rory placed her hands on her hips, relishing a moment of fortune. She wasn't about to let the occasion end without a bit of chiding. "I imagine this is what you deserve, in light of your ridiculous strong-arming earlier. The pitfalls of these woods are vast. You'd be wise to allow me the lead."

After a brief deliberation, he merely sighed. "As you wish. Now, *if* you *please*." Gesturing at his ensnared ankle, he was nothing short of resigned from where he swung in an interminable arc.

And while Rory should've been reveling in her minor victory, she was oddly dissatisfied. Unsheathing her reclaimed dagger, she made for the tree that anchored her companion in the heavens. "Tuck and roll," she advised before severing the rope.

Like a sack full of bricks, he plummeted to the earth, his strapping form landing with a wicked *thud* as he turned to his back, exhaling in a mighty burst that twisted Rory's insides. Flopping an arm across his eyes, he lay in the dust, recovering himself. "My thanks," he managed.

"It's nothing," she uttered, backing her way through the path she'd come by. Shaking her head, she dismissed the entire episode, refusing to allow empathy to bloom, instead returning to her forgotten meal.

He reappeared slowly, plodding through the foliage as he made for his belongings, and it was no surprise that Rory found herself suddenly preoccupied with her feast, though her appetite had since expired.

The weight of her hefty cloak melted over her shoulders, providing warmth she hadn't realized she was in want of. She glanced up at Artyrus, who offered only a shrug in acknowledgment. "It's getting cold."

"Here," Rory replied, proffering her plate as he seated himself nearby. "Eat."

He took a hearty bite, gagging slightly as he forced piece after piece down his gullet. "Whew. Let's hope you lead better than you cook."

"Forgive me," she scoffed. "Culinary arts are among the least of my priorities." Scowling, she turned away, though not before she caught a hint of a smile upon his face.

Chapter Two

She had to be testing him, unless perhaps, by all mercies, she had died in her sleep. At rest, her visage was peaceful, with slender, calloused hands forming a pillow atop a bed of fallen pine needles and cool earth beneath her.

Artyrus knew better.

The woman was querulous. *Deranged.*

He readied himself, giving Rory a nudge with the toe of his boot.

He'd barely seen her move when her dagger slashed the thick leather shielding his ankle, and before he could step farther out of reach, Rory was on her feet, the knuckles of her hand blanched as she clutched the hilt of her broadsword.

She was quick, her stance more polished than many Artyrus had trained beside. Light eyes surveyed the woods, her gaze cutting through the morning mist and the low-hanging branches of ancient oaks. "I'll warn you once not to try that again," she sneered, slipping the dagger back into her boot.

Shoving a scant bowl of oats into her hands, Artyrus ignored her threat, leaving her alone to brood while he rearranged the remaining supplies that had to carry them through the remainder of their travels. While he respected her accomplished way with the sword, he was not about to let a delicate, raven-haired scourge intimidate him.

"Are you always this unpleasant?" she persisted.

"*Me*, unpleasant?" He found amusement in her inability to see the irony of her question. "Every word you speak is steeped in venom. It may come as a surprise, but no part of me yearned to be sent on a mission to fetch a smug runaway."

"I never ran away," she grumbled before seemingly becoming self-conscious, her focus falling to the ground. "And there's little to be done, at any rate." Turning on her heel, she moved away from Artyrus, setting her uneaten breakfast on the woodland floor. Instead, she began preparing for departure.

Her sudden eagerness to avoid him was jarring, but the day was already wasting. She made no effort to repress her loathing of their arrangement, so he thought it likely that she'd determined compliance the quickest way to be rid of him.

So be it.

Before long, they were on their way once again, forging through the never-ending morass within the heart of Wylewoode. The spongy bog was one of many reasons the territory was sparsely inhabited and widely avoided by even the most wayward of wanderers.

Artyrus had urged Rory to ride ahead of him, if not to quell her insolence, then to prevent her sneaking from his sight. His plan had failed miserably, however, as she huffed and cursed, weaving through draping conifers with Artyrus trailing closely at her rear.

"We need globe thistle," Rory observed, tugging the reins. Briar slowed at her leisure, as headstrong as her rider. "Come see for yourself if you don't believe me."

"We've run out of time for your games, Aurora." Artyrus's patience had been dwindling since the moment he'd received his charge. But, as was true when facing wild beasts, he could show no sign of weakness.

She shrugged. "Very well, then. I'll catch up once I've acquired what we need. I, for one, do not wish for this day trapped within a marshy hell with you to be my last."

"You don't want me to treat you like a child, yet you cannot cease behaving like one," Artyrus gruffed, with every ounce of his being fighting the urge to disarm and immobilize her once again.

"If we weren't mere paces from a large mound nest, I might agree with you, but that crocodile won't be far from her eggs." Pointing a slender finger at the offending roost, Rory refused to back down.

It was hard to distinguish from their lofty positions but impossible to deny upon further examination.

Sighing, Artyrus gave a curt nod. "We'll re-route."

"We need to mask our scent," Rory insisted. "It's just as much for your sake as mine."

A groan of defeat was the only response Artyrus could muster, and it was accepted without hesitation as a victory. Rory had her mare deftly maneuvering through the unpredictable terrain with a cluck of her tongue.

Given no other choice, Artyrus reluctantly followed. Even worse, Aurora wasn't wrong. Globe thistle was pungent enough to frustrate any predator pursuing them. Still, the subtle smirk she'd worn as she'd turned from him was almost enough to tempt him into risking it.

The detour had cost them an hour of progress, but Rory had, by and large, ceased complaining—a genuine blessing in Artyrus's mind. And if the sentiment that she was right was all it took to accomplish some sense of harmony, he would simply have to bear it.

"There. We'll break for water just ahead." Picking up her pace to a gallop, Rory followed a shallow stream until she approached a small clearing packed with globe thistles. The water pooled near the easternmost edge of the glade where she dropped from Briar's back, patting her cheek as she released her.

Sphere-shaped flowers in shades from lavender to cornflower blue bordered the clearing—enough globe thistle to ward off every crocodile dwelling amongst them and any distant relatives they might have lurking deep within the swamp.

"Be quick about it. We still have a lot of ground to cover." Artyrus dismounted, dropping his reins as their horses began lapping the water before them. Kneeling beside his steed, he cupped his hands and splashed his face, the restorative chill bolstering his wearied spirit.

Rory knelt opposite him, repeating his motions. The water ran down her face in shimmering rivulets, and she smiled brightly, undoubtedly feeling as refreshed as he.

With the sleeve of her tunic, she continued her preening, drying herself before pushing dripping strands away from her eyes. Falling to her back with interlocked fingers, she cradled her head as long, onyx hair fell into a dark halo around her.

She was *distracting*. And worst of all, she had to know it.

"I'll be gathering your weeds," Artyrus muttered, indicating the purplish flowers. He tied a small satchel to his belt, eager to put some distance between himself and the woman. "Stay here and be ready to press on when I return."

"I won't lie here and be told by some brute what I'm to do," Rory bit out, propping herself on her elbows. "Besides, you don't know these lands as I do. I'd hate to see you strung upside-down by your ankles again," she added with an infuriating laugh, extending her hand to Artyrus.

Biting the inside of his cheek, Artyrus held his tongue. No good could come of permitting her to bait him this way. Their travels would be at an end in short order, so he need only stay focused. Taking her hand, he hoisted her to her feet, and without waiting to see if she would follow, set out toward the edge of the thicket.

The earth underfoot had softened since he'd begun this errand, the promise of springtide proving fruitful as ever, with bountiful blooms and viridescent shades of new life flecking the woods around them.

Artyrus and Rory had worked well together once before in Llundyn, where their lives had been very much at stake. She'd earned his regard that day as a cunning warrior, but that respect had yet to be reciprocated. That, he believed, was indeed a low priority for her, given the resolute defiance with which she flourished.

Yet, in the clearing, they found a tolerable stride. Rory had stalked after him, slicing through globe thistle stems with her blade or pulling some from the root while Artyrus collected and stuffed the flowers into his satchel. They worked in silence, amassing more than they needed, but it was wise to be prepared.

"The root and stem are edible," Rory explained. Tossing her sword aside, she beat some remnant soil from the root. "Here, try." Retrieving the dagger from her boot, she sliced through it. Using the tip of her knife as a fork, she popped a sliver into her mouth, offering what was left to Artyrus.

He took it, only to tuck it away with the rest of their stash. He was, in fact, well aware of the flower's other infamous property—regularity that would have him doubled over deep within the bog expelling everything he'd eaten in the past day. "Thank you, no."

"Very well," Rory sighed, a small smile playing on her lips as she slipped her dagger away. "Let me take a look at what we've got." When she stepped toward him, a loud *crack* shattered the stillness of the forest.

"What—?" Before Artyrus could utter a thought, Rory collapsed into his chest as they were swept off their feet. His thrashing limbs only brought the pair closer together, suspended high above the earth. Artyrus growled, his anger peaking as Rory struggled and kicked, both attempting in vain to free themselves. "Is this your idea of a twisted jest?"

He couldn't see her fighting the vines that had trapped them together in this vulnerable, miserable state, but he could *feel* her—first, her elbow like a chisel to his spine, then the heel of her boot grinding into his shin.

"Your stupid hair keeps getting in my mouth," Rory spat, furiously plucking the rogue strands from her tongue.

"*You don't know these lands as I do,*" he intoned in a snide impression, his nose scrunched in ridicule. "We have more significant problems than your discomfort, wouldn't you agree? I may be able to reach your dagger if you would just hold *still!*"

"You don't think I thought of that?" Rory snapped. She slipped in a futile effort to shift her weight away from him. Artyrus grunted from the pressure of her back hitting his chest but took hold of her wrists to calm her, his arms snugly crossed over her stomach. "It dropped from my boot when we got caught. Now *let go of me!*"

"I don't want to hurt you, but everything you're doing makes this worse. Stop fighting me, and I'll let go," he leveled, his tone cool and even.

But Rory showed no sign of relenting, using all her strength to resist his hold. She was at a vast disadvantage between the net and Artyrus's vigor.

"*Stop,*" he whispered, feeling her frustration and fury as he voiced his plea.

And finally, she did.

"I'm sorry..." Finally quieting within his embrace, Rory's back pressed firmly against him. Her warmth settled into him, and he loosened his grasp. Silence fell over them, blanketing them in companionable calm as they each caught their breath.

"I never intended to steal you away from your new life," Artyrus said, his voice low. "I gave you time that was not mine to permit for you to say goodbye."

"I know." Rory cleared her throat as her voice broke. "I was never meant to stay. I know that. You're only doing what's required of you, just as I did when I was sent away."

Scoffing, Artyrus replied, "How certain are we that he's not mad?"

"Who, Merlin?" Incredulous at his implication, Rory dropped her voice as if the animals of Wylewoode might somehow bring word of their musings to Merlin, or worse, the king himself. "You mustn't speak like that."

"Don't tell me you believe all of the purported foresight."

"Has it not always come to pass?" Glancing over her shoulder, she quickly dropped her gaze.

"One way or another," Artyrus admitted, shrugging under her petite frame, their faces startlingly close. "I daresay I'm not convinced he's as arcane as those near to him boast he is. At some point or another, we've all seen the truth lurking behind a magician's tricks."

"I'm not surprised to hear you say so." Sighing, Rory disregarded his skepticism. "It's not easy to blindly believe as his gifts demand."

"On the contrary, little Valkyrie, I believe in many things I've never laid eyes on, just not an old man who delights in preying upon obedient henchmen to do his bidding."

"I trust it was not your intention to insult me, for I'm neither Merlin's henchman nor Odin's servant," Rory asserted, though there was no animus in her reply.

"Perhaps not." A wry grin formed on his face. "But you'll not so easily convince me you're undeserving of your new moniker."

To his great surprise, she laughed, her small frame cradled within his chance embrace. "I quite like it, in truth."

Somewhere nearby, the brush rustled. The disturbance was too concentrated to be due to the breeze alone, sobering the duo into silence. There, slung high above the ground, Rory and Artyrus were nothing more than quarry to a predator unknown.

"You'll fit through that hole above us," Artyrus breathed into Rory's ear. "Use me to gain your footing."

Nodding, Rory pushed against him, maneuvering herself into a better position. The noise drew nearer still, encroaching upon their aerial prison, with neither of them able to see the threat prowling beneath. Undeterred, Rory pressed on, reaching for the small opening Artyrus had spotted as he hoisted her higher yet.

A gritty cackle filled the air, but from where, they could not tell. Rory continued to climb, the net unforgiving as she clawed at the snare entangling them.

"Can you make anything out?" Artyrus hissed, drawing a sigh of resignation from Rory.

A creature skittered up the back side of the tree that held them captive, and Rory shuddered, dropping into Artyrus' lap once more. "Would that whatever is up there might chew through the rope and deliver us to freedom."

"Stubborn, aren't ye?" an aged voice crowed, only this time far too near. Cackling once more, her face came into view. Wrinkled and timeworn, a gray-haired woman swung one of her legs over the branch from which Rory and Artyrus dangled at her mercy. More spider than human, the wizened stranger straddled the branch, scooting her hunched form farther across the limb toward them.

Her jaw was clenched, holding a long knife between golden teeth, some blackened from decay. The blade glinted, struck by errant sunlight that had managed to slip through thick verdure — a beacon that would aid in either escape or ruin.

"We don't want any trouble," Rory began, her words thick with anxiety. When the old woman ignored her, taking hold of her knife, Rory's words rang with urgency. "Begone! We don't need your help."

The ancient curiosity guffawed, a horrible caw that set Artyrus on edge. If only he could reach his dagger, pinned beneath him out of arm's reach.

"And miss out on dinner?" Sawing through the rope, she grinned wickedly at her prey. "I should think not."

Fibers sprouted from both sides of the blade with each labored slice the crone made, putting them ever more at risk of a painful reunion with the forest floor.

After another slash, the rope *snapped*. With little time to react, Artyrus pulled Rory into his arms, the whole of his muscular body enveloping hers like a human casing as he braced for impact.

Only they never hit the ground.

Mere inches from the earth, they hovered breathlessly, Rory firmly within Artyrus's protective hold. The trap had caught as they'd plummeted, doubtless by the stranger's duplicitous design.

She made her way down the tree in haste. Inaudibly, nimbly, she moved in a way Artyrus had never seen, especially for one so ancient. But once again, the hag stood before them, securely planted in the soil just beneath them.

Picking at her rotting teeth, she flicked something into the air before snapping her fingers. Dark figures emerged at her behest, five or six surrounding them, from what Artyrus could tell.

Striking a casual pose, the old woman stared, her sage eyes appraising her hostages. "The name is Mimi. We'd be much obliged if you didn't try to run."

Chapter Three

Being captured wasn't part of the plan—not that Rory ever *planned* in the first place. Thus was the life lived in the moment, free from careful strategizing and dedicated to focusing only on the most urgent circumstances. Some would likely accuse her of irresponsibility, and perhaps they'd be right. She wasn't meant to rule—one certainty in her life for which she harbored no doubt.

And, if exigence were required to earn her attention, she had long since fulfilled that demand.

She silently cursed herself for succumbing to the same folly that had ensnared her chaperone. A *net*. A crudely concealed trap made effective by the unobservant, not so unlike the ankle trap that had bound Artyrus, and she'd given him hell for that. Shame consumed her, the absurdity of her failure causing her to tremble with fury.

It was a mistake for amateurs, something she decidedly was not and one she wished desperately to amend if for no other reason than to simply prove she *could.* She'd demanded to lead, intent upon demonstrating her mastery of the wilds and the man accompanying her. The latter portion of that truth was a startling realization that she quickly repressed in favor of ignoring its validity.

It didn't matter anyway.

Traipsing through the backcountry of Wylewoode was eye-opening. She'd never ventured much beyond the rudimentary roadway or the creek running alongside it. The rumors of sinister realities lurking within the forest were enough to have her steering clear, even though they were undoubtedly overblown.

She eyed her various escorts, marching in triplicate on either side of herself and Artyrus. None of their keepers were particularly attentive, giving the pair a wide berth as they chatted freely amongst themselves. Their lack of diversity did not go unnoticed. Some were older, some younger, but all were strikingly familiar in appearance. Namely, they were all of Penzellian origins, both a heartening revelation as well as a stark reminder of Rory's unfulfilled duty.

"Why the long faces, ye? We've no intent to cause you harm." Mimi grinned, treading backward without a hint of hesitation as she spoke, striding agilely over the terrain. A gravelly laugh escaped her as she picked up her pace, turning her back on them. The woman was impressive if a little unnerving, given her seemingly endless physical capability, despite her age.

Artyrus merely grumbled while Rory narrowed her eyes, biting her tongue. She glanced behind, catching Artyrus's gaze as she indicated the foreground with a quick bob of her head. He raised a single eyebrow, silently acknowledging that he, too, had noticed the faint lights in the distance.

Onward they pressed, reaching the outskirts of a camp so vast that it nearly took Rory's breath away. Tucked within the boughs of Wylewoode, the grounds were packed with tents and structures, thoroughly disguised with all the camouflage of nature—vines and leaves, mud and moss. Were it not for the subtle glow of the numerous campfires dotting the outpost, it would have been impossible to detect the encampment before stumbling headlong into it.

"Welcome to our humble enclave," Mimi lilted, offering nods and waves of greeting as she paraded her prizes along the pathway dividing the camp. Curious onlookers appraised the duo, who were sat atop Magnus, a sight in his own right.

Artyrus huddled nearer, his large frame shrouding Rory. "We're not to remain with these captors, I imagine."

Rory's first inclination was to jab her ally heartily in the ribs, his comment harkening back to a peculiar directive she'd been given by Merlin for her exploits in Llundyn. But upon further examination, namely the grim set of his mouth, she was certain Artyrus meant no insult.

Whispers from the gathering villagers followed in their stead, their chatter largely consumed by her presence and growing minute by minute.

Rory wasn't ready. Far from it.

And while she would have loved to have written off their interest as, perhaps, mere attraction or revulsion over her appearance, she knew better. Her age, her bearing, her features… Each attribute worked against her in her unending attempt to conceal her identity.

"Is there something you'd like to share with me?" Artyrus asked, his mouth brushing her ear as his bitter words met the day. It seemed that he had noticed the unsettling attention being heaped upon Rory. Leaning away from her, he grew rigid, leaving her unexpectedly chilled. "Was this all some sort of elaborate trick? All these minions doing your bidding?"

"You think me so cunning?" Rory bit out, his accusation settling over her with all the subtlety of a dozen millstones. *The utter nerve.* All at once, she found herself wishing that she had indeed been the conniving wench he alleged she was.

"I'm not the one who attempted to feed you globe thistles to inflame your bowels," he hissed, the low rumble of his voice reverberating through to her core as his mounting anger poured from his lips. "You've been aiming to cripple me from the very outset of our journey, tying my hands, my authority at every turn. Yes, I *do* think you capable!"

"If only!" Rory fired back, putting as much distance between herself and her closest adversary as was physically possible, given their current arrangements. "I had no inkling that any of this was here, if that's what you mean to imply."

"Nobody does," Mimi asserted, showcasing her golden teeth as she grinned with satisfaction. "An outpost of the damned, we are—not that you'd ever guess it. We will rise again!" Pumping her fist, Mimi reveled in the whoops of assent resonating from her contemporaries, though they all quickly returned to their business.

It was impressively run, each citizen seemingly knowing their place and completing their tasks. It did Rory's heart some good to see her kinsmen so dedicated and productive, despite the tragedy of their heritage. Further, the secrecy with which they operated deep within the heart of the woods brought her an inexplicable spark of hope. Her people were alive and well. All was not lost.

"We're here." Mimi stepped before Magnus without an ounce of fear, bringing the hulking creature to an abrupt halt. Mimi's lackeys fell in around her, securing Magnus's reins to a hitching post. Beside him, Briar was also tied, her manner remarkably docile as they explored the gear tied to her back. She never liked strangers.

Rory and Artyrus watched as their belongings were investigated, held captive atop Magnus until the miniature army had completed their duties. It was altogether strange being taken hostage by those she was supposedly destined to lead, but also somehow fitting. For Rory had never fulfilled her role, and if she were honest with herself, she had no desire to do so now.

"Down with you," Mimi ordered, siccing one of her enormous goons on Rory as she went to dismount.

"I've no need of your assistance, sir." Rory gently swatted the man's hand away as she landed on her feet. Artyrus followed suit, eagerly taking to Rory's side as they awaited their fates. It was ridiculous, really, the ease with which the pair had been overtaken. But then again, nothing about their adventure through the boondocks of Wylewoode had been simple.

"Don't let them separate us," Artyrus breathed, clasping Rory's hand in his. She glanced his way, surprised to find how essential his presence suddenly felt to her.

"Oh, you'll be separated. I'm afraid you've no choice," Mimi interrupted, her canny hearing proving to be a continuing nuisance. The ancient lady was a walking contradiction, appearing as old as time itself yet also as fit and agile as they were.

With a sharp whistle through her teeth, Mimi summoned another of her loyal guard. Shooing a beautiful woman their way, Mimi scurried about, hustling as she commanded her ilk.

The woman moved to Artyrus's side, and she had tawny skin and long, wavy hair not so unlike Rory's, apart from the color. "Don't worry. I'll take excellent care of your strapping gentleman here," she purred, her lucid eyes locked on Rory's as she reached for Artyrus's free arm. "I'm Adelyce, by the way."

"Well, *Adelyce*, he's not my gentleman, and he can take care of himself," Rory growled, readily ignoring the woodland vixen's adoring gaze, which was cast upon her chaperone. Adelyce merely shrugged, and Artyrus just...*stood there*. Would it have killed him to wrench his arm from her overeager grasp?

On second thought, Rory didn't care. Stars knew she was better off without him.

"Where am I to go, Mimi?" Rory wrested her hand from Artyrus's hold, taking a step away. The man bristled, plainly irritated that she was taking matters into her own hands yet again, though he said not a word.

"Ah, yes. Through those flaps behind ye, just there." Mimi indicated the tent with a vague flick of her wrist, seemingly uninterested in joining Rory for whatever interrogation would occur once inside. "And, Adelyce, get this fella some grub and a seat before the fire now, will ye?"

"Aurora—" Artyrus lunged for Rory, only to be dragged away all the more quickly by Adelyce, who appeared to be stronger than she looked.

Rory waved him off, making for the doorway. "Please. I'll be fine."

Of that particular sentiment, she was far from certain. Still, she doubted very much that she was in danger, given the intense interest that had followed her arrival.

She watched as Artyrus was hauled away, finding some satisfaction in his earnest effort to keep his sights upon her, even as additional bodies were required to move him off. He took his duties seriously, for better or for worse.

Steeling herself, she drew back the flap of the canvas tent, stepping into the dimly lit shelter. From within, it was far more spacious than she'd imagined from the outside. A small fire burned at its center, the silvery smoke curling upward where it wafted through the sunlit vent above. Adding to the warmth of the chamber were numerous fur rugs and throws and fluffy pillows seemingly made from the same hides that adorned the floor.

Yet the most unusual details were the gauzy curtains, drawn and bound in what felt to Rory to be a most haphazard way with golden, tasseled ropes. Sheer wisps of fabric draped from above with a canopy of colors in turquoise, amethyst and crimson shades, lending the space a royal air and an unexpected feminine touch.

"Hello."

Rory flinched, reaching at once for the dagger sheathed upon her belt as she spun toward the source of the voice. But she was entirely disarmed, with Mimi and her bevy of soldiers having done a fine job of ensuring that both she and Artyrus would be left to their mercy.

What Rory saw was every bit as surprising as her very surroundings. Emerging from the gossamer layers was a woman, slight of build and keen of eye. Her dark hair was pinned in a simple coil at the nape of her neck, with salt and pepper streaks that hinted at her advancing age, though her skin was silky smooth. Her stark white tunic enhanced her deep olive skin, which was crisp and strikingly flawless, given the filthy environment in which she dwelt.

But perhaps even more surprising were the numerous piercings. From the tips of her earlobes to the cartilage of her helix she was adorned with tiny precious gems and delicate chains, while a small silver hoop looped through the flare of her nose.

She was exquisite.

Panic swelled within Rory's chest. While it was a rare occurrence, nothing about her sudden captivity had gone as expected. Squaring her shoulders, she adopted the arrogant posture of her new companion. "Hello. What is your intent for my chaperone and myself?" Clasping her clammy hands behind her back, she hoped to appear indifferent. "As I see it, we've done no wrong."

"You are everything that I anticipated and then some." The woman took a step nearer, studying Rory as she did so. "That's saying something, you know. The expectations for royalty are frequently poor...and with good reason."

Rory balked, shaking her head. "You're mistaken—"

"I am not," the woman persisted. "You are the lost princess of Penzelle." She stepped nearer still, her fierce gray eyes surveying Rory with the intensity of a predator.

Rory refused to wither under her gaze, even as her resolve wavered. "That's absurd. Everybody knows the little princess perished in the attack. Chamelaute would never allow a threat to their rule to survive."

"But survive she did, and she's no longer so little." Smiling, the woman bowed. "I'm Mal—and you are?"

Rory stood in silence, neither bowing nor looking away.

Mal scoffed, putting some much-needed distance between them as she wandered toward a small table laid with tea and biscuits. Pouring herself a steaming cup, she began to laugh. "No, no. You're not royal at all!" She prowled in a circle, staring over the porcelain teacup, seemingly analyzing her prisoner from a new angle. "I believe the answer to my question is scrawled up the length of your spine. Tell me, dear. Would you like to show me?"

Taking a deep breath, Rory schooled her features. She did, indeed, have indelible ink running from the top of her backbone to the bottom—an intricate design scratched over skin and bone that had been a part of her christening. The years had come and gone, but the pattern remained, growing alongside her and becoming ever more lovely over time. It was miraculous.

"I will not." Rory stiffened as the tenacious woman continued her appraisal. She was intimidating in an understated way, a manner which suggested that she'd be gentle as she slit her adversary's throat.

"The prophecy is coming to pass at long last," Mal continued, her countenance filling with hope. And while her mutterings made no sense to Rory, that didn't make them any less creepy.

The tent's flaps rose, ushering in a swift gust of wind and a bedraggled Artyrus, who moved quickly to Rory's side, grasping her by the shoulders as he took her in. "Are you all right, Aurora?"

Mal gasped, dropping her teacup to the arid earth beneath her. It shattered, splintering into a mess of jagged shards at her feet as she seized the small credenza for support. "Everything has changed," she murmured. "The time is nigh."

If her visage had before been that of one with some secret knowledge, it had fractured alongside the broken vessel on the ground. A sense of wonder seemed to overcome her, at once perplexing the reunited duo as they held one another in confusion.

"You must go now to Merlin," Mal continued, the insistence in her voice further complicating the sense of bewilderment already consuming Rory. She stepped toward the pair of travelers, her gaze fixed upon Artyrus. Moisture filled her eyes — a startling departure from her earlier iciness until she suddenly hardened again. "Go!"

Rory grew cold, stumbling back through the doorway where her horse awaited her. Briar appeared to be packed down with all the gear she'd carried in. The urgency gave Rory whiplash.

Artyrus quickly followed, dashing from the tent without question and mounting his steed. Together, Rory and Artyrus bolted, fleeing the covert camp almost as quickly as they'd arrived.

"What was all that?" Artyrus asked, slowing Magnus to a canter when they'd covered some half dozen miles. "That woman seemed utterly mad."

"Perhaps," Rory agreed, though one facet of their time amongst the Penzellian refugees had her on edge. "But also far too shrewd. I wonder what she knows of Merlin. I'll not deny that her orders gave me pause."

Artyrus laughed, though entirely without humor. "Indeed. I do believe it made me trust the mystic man even less. I've half a mind to change our course entirely." He paused, smiling when he saw his charge roll her eyes. "Are you sure you can trust him?"

"Without question." Rory was pleasantly surprised to be consulted on the matter. Artyrus *never* consulted. Still, something about him ate away at her blossoming trust. The way Mal had looked at him…

"You are hiding something from me, I think," Rory alleged, her suspicion growing by the moment. Artyrus feigned shock, a spectacle so unexpectedly silly that Rory nearly cracked a smile.

"I? Perhaps I'd say the same. The way those people looked at you was a sight to behold, and I cannot imagine it had anything to do with your Valkyrie warrior princess status…or your charming personality."

Touché. At least half of his assertion was true. Rory softened slightly. He was observant. She had to give him that.

"Maybe we are both keeping things from one another." Rory glanced at her companion, who pondered her words with great deliberation.

"Naturally," Artyrus agreed. "Only I've no clue what my secrets are. But I've no doubt that you are well aware of your own."

Chapter Four

Artyrus had known she was valuable, for Merlin would never have sent him to retrieve Aurora were she not a cherished pawn in his ceaseless manipulations.

Irritation ruled Artyrus's thoughts, though distraction was the last thing he needed. "Had it crossed your mind during any of our time together to tell me?" When she remained silent, happily ignoring him as she so readily did, he pressed. "Well?"

The steel of their blades clashed together as they sparred, Rory brushing loose strands of hair from her brow before deftly maneuvering out of his reach. At the moment, it was not her enigmatic genesis that disgruntled him so much as her fleetness of foot.

"Tell you *what* exactly?" Blowing the same fallen tendrils from her eyes, Rory dodged another strike from Artyrus before unexpectedly taking a seat. She sheathed her sword, ending their engagement without warning.

He shook his head, suppressing a longsuffering sigh. It was the standard entitlement he'd grown familiar with, but he was intent on never allowing compliance to become his pattern.

Still, she had drained him. Proficient, to be sure, her athleticism and willfulness were beyond that of most men. Grateful for the respite, Artyrus sank the end of his blade into the earth. Retrieving an apple from his satchel, he casually tossed it into the air before plucking the stem from its center. Piercing the fruit's skin, he took a bite, savoring the burst of sweetness.

Rory eyed him, her gaze brimming with famished envy.

Artyrus groaned. "You'll be the death of me." Throwing the apple into her eager hands, he proceeded to dig a neatly packed cloth from his pouch, the exterior stained from the berries within. "So, let's hear it then."

"There's little to share," she replied around a mouthful of fresh provisions. "As I told *her*" – Rory nodded toward the thicket from which they'd come – "I simply survived."

"You've told me exactly nothing." Combing calloused fingers through his hair, he decided to try again, his impatience ever surging. "If we're to work with one another, we have no choice but to achieve some level of trust, do we not?"

"What is it you wish to hear?" She drew herself to her feet, seemingly avoiding his gaze.

"Tell me why all those people revered you as a savior. I heard their whispers, Aurora. I saw their souls brighten when we arrived at their camp. Do not take me for a fool."

Patting Briar's mane, Rory fed her what remained of her snack. "Very well." Her eyes met his at last, and she took a fortifying breath. "They are my people, and I am their hope. I'm the lost princess of Penzelle."

Rumors of her, he had heard, but never had he believed the princess to have been lost. He'd thought her to be as dead as the rest of her sovereign kin.

Princess.

The title didn't suit her in the least.

"You're no princess," Artyrus scoffed, the words sounding harsher than intended, hanging in the air between them like an impenetrable mist.

Rory gathered herself, adopting an arrogant mien as she crossed her arms. "Believe what you will or don't. It makes no difference to me. You wanted to know why they all but fell at my feet, and that is why. I'm the one they call 'curse breaker', the first female heir born to Penzelle in centuries. That is, if you wish to believe all the musings of the so-called prophecy."

Silence fell between them as Artyrus considered her claim, unable to make sense of it though the admission elucidated more than it confused.

"I may not be what you expected," she continued, "but I'm also no liar."

Artyrus couldn't help but smirk. "You're right. You're *not* what I expected."

Rory glowered, resembling the customary pouty princess so often present amongst royals. "I'm not because I couldn't be. I had no choice but to flee my home and leave my people behind."

Perhaps he could see it after all.

And if she were, in fact, the lost princess, she had endured more heartache in her years than most soldiers. The woman in front of him had escaped the sword of Chamelaute as it cut down her whole family in her childhood. The tale had circulated throughout his region, but only now did he begin to consider its validity.

The people had watched her as if she were the manifestation of untamed reveries.

In a way, she was.

"Why do you reveal yourself now?" There was no accusation lurking in the question, only intrigue, for she was not one to wither under expectation or pressure.

"Back there?" Rory indicated the encampment, rolling her eyes. "She knew. They all knew. What was I to do?"

"*Lie,*" Artyrus nearly cut her off, surprising even himself with his urgency.

"I couldn't." Her voice broke as the admission poured from her lips. "You saw their faces. You saw the way they brightened when they discerned my identity. Cowering is not my way, *overseer.*"

Doubtless, that was so. Aurora was no princess. She was a warrior. Her confidence had not wavered, even as they had been led into the unknown, outnumbered and ignorant of their escorts' intentions.

"I suppose not." Artyrus turned from Rory, considering her words and alleged title. "I'm afraid you'll have gravely disappointed them, however. You look nothing like a royal and boast the gentility of a low-born scapegrace." With a hint of a smile tugging at his mouth, he waited for her response, uncertain if he'd gone too far.

Her somber countenance gave way to laughter. In truth, Artyrus had never heard such genuine amusement from her and certainly never due to anything he'd volunteered.

"Am I to bow to you now that you've made your truth known to me?" he pressed, encouraged by her previous response.

The familiar rasp of steel grinding over leather served as her only reply. This woman, it seemed, would continue to confound him.

Facing her, he prepared for her attack. With a mischievous smile upon her face, she lunged toward him. Quickly, he reached for his blade, only to catch the fading light of day glinting off its whetted edges, taunting him as it stood just out of reach.

"Little cheat." Narrowly dodging Rory's pursuit, he chuckled as her broadsword grazed the bracer shielding his forearm, preventing it from being diced to bits.

Her graceful steps were always one move ahead, and she knew it. Cleverly pivoting away from Artyrus's influence, she taunted him. "Perhaps. But effective, no?"

Before he could anticipate her objective, she rushed him, sliding in his direction and knocking his shins from underneath him with a stiff boot. "To answer your question," she continued, felling Artyrus to his knees, "I'd rather see you kneel."

Turning on her heel, she tucked her sword away with a victorious sigh as Artyrus scrambled, repositioning himself. From the ground, he tripped her, throwing his leg into her path and catching her off guard. She collapsed onto him, robbing his lungs of air with the sudden impact. But as quickly as she fell, he threw her to her back. Pinning her to the soil beneath them, he gently held her wrists as she caught her breath, laughing under his powerful form.

With their faces mere inches from one another, Artyrus quickly sobered. He had avoided looking upon her striking visage as much as possible so as not to become distracted, but she was effortlessly diverting.

At that moment, she had seemed as lost to her focus as him. She studied his features as if she'd never seen him before, perhaps not unlike his attempts to disregard her.

"I win." Artyrus pushed himself off Rory, resting on his back beside her, and the growing tension between them evaporated the instant he spoke.

She chuckled once more, sparing him a glance. "You're right, you know."

"Such is the standard."

Clucking her tongue in feigned offense, the princess shook her head. "I'm no royal. While my lineage may proclaim otherwise, that station and future have passed away. It's never been my fate to be set apart in the manner my title demands."

There was little Artyrus could say. It was all true. When Penzelle had been overrun, he had been merely a child with no recollection of it himself. But he had heard many accounts from those who'd lived it.

"Yet, strangely enough," she continued, "I still find myself betrothed to your king's firstborn." She scoffed, though he found no humor written on her features.

The revelation jarred him, even as he refused to let her know it.

He'd begun to warm to her against all odds during their travels, and these harsh truths brought him back to his senses. His assignment had never been meant for pleasure but served a distinct, albeit cryptic purpose that he would not muddle.

While Artyrus put no stock in Merlin's supposed gift, he knew his place, and it was not beside a pledged princess, lost or present. Collecting himself, he forced a smile. "So, you're a promised woman then?" He elbowed her as her brow creased with distaste.

"An easy promise for King Luther to make when everyone believed me to be dead. I had no parents left to object to his wiles, courtesy of his evil machinations. But I will never marry Philippe."

Luther's intent was obvious, like dangling sustenance over the heads of ravenous wolves.

Unrest amongst the surviving Penzellian people had been ongoing for as long as Artyrus could remember. To quell a full-scale insurrection would've demanded a significant act of empathy. Penzelle was small but lethal in their vengeance. By all appearances, it seemed the high king had been made aware of the risk they might pose to his reign and gave them a reason to hope.

Artyrus had never heard of an existing betrothal, likely for the very reason Aurora had revealed. Luther didn't know she had escaped the siege ordered by his father before him, yet he sought the same victims' favor.

It was no matter. Regardless of His Majesty's motive, the princess was promised to the heir of Chamelaute.

* * * *

Artyrus awakened to the faint rustling of Rory gathering her belongings. *Strange.* In the weeks he'd known her, she'd not once been the first to rise. Perhaps she was eager to see Merlin.

"Your morning rations." Aurora scrunched her nose, extending a generous portion of soppy oats to him. "They're not as good as yours. My stepfather was always the one to prepare them when I was growing up, so I'm afraid I don't have much experience."

Propping himself onto his elbows, Artyrus accepted the gesture with a nod. "Ah, a princess and a cook. My thanks."

His bland spirits had nothing to do with Rory's cooking but everything with the day that lay ahead of them. He was mere hours away from fulfilling his task to return her safely to the great Seer, only to be at war with himself. Their encounter with the woman, Mal, and her minions had left him with nothing but questions, the most pressing of which was the motive of Merlin himself.

Rory was as capable as she was headstrong, but what did he require of her? To deliver her into Merlin's hands meant sacrificing the only surviving heir of Penzelle to his whims.

Thoughts of her safety had consumed him the night before. Restlessly, he'd considered alternatives, but to what end? He could keep her to himself no more than he'd allow Merlin to use her as an instrument for his ascension to greater renown.

"Are they that bad?" Rory asked, her fingers busy with the braiding of her long, dark tresses. "You don't have to eat it, you know."

"It's not that." Artyrus scooped more oats into his mouth, swallowing the thin feed and forcing a smile. "I was only contemplating our route today, and I think it best we journey around Brystole rather than through. There has been a great deal of tension spreading in those parts, and I'd rather steer clear of it."

Awaiting her challenge, not a word of objection arose. "It's just as well. I fear I've grown quite fond of being away. Would that we might sojourn until Merlin himself drags us back to Chamelaute." The princess giggled at her thoughts of subversion, calming the tumult of Artyrus's musings. It brought him peace to know that she was no more eager to see the mystic man than he was.

Together, they prepared for the journey ahead. Their final day of travel meant that Artyrus would be free to return to his previous life by sunset, but the allure of home had unexpectedly melted into apprehension.

The sun warmed them on their passage, and Rory beaming up at the sky as golden rays kissed her tanned skin. Despite his best efforts to disregard her, Artyrus couldn't help but steal a glance here and there. And while his futile regard would remain unanswered, he would, nevertheless, abide by Aurora's side until her security was assured, whether by the Seer or her people.

They approached their destination midday, prepared to meet Merlin within the small settlement. Although he knew with certainty that it was occupied mainly by Penzellian refugees, Artyrus wondered if the wise man was embraced amongst the citizenry or had been effectively vilified for disloyalty, given his accord with King Luther.

The road leading into town was eerily tranquil, setting Artyrus on edge as Rory spurred Briar to a gallop. Following her lead, he fell into step beside them, noting her troubled mien.

"It's too quiet." Cracking Briar's reins, she surged toward the hushed community without warning.

"Wait!" His plea fell on deaf ears, his own steed picking up speed as he chased after her.

Rory dismounted ahead of him, coming to an abrupt halt, her figure hovering over a heap on the ground. She dropped to her knees before it, gently shaking what

Artyrus made out to be a human form, lying limp atop the pebbled earth.

"You don't know what befell him. Back away." Leaping from his horse, he ran to her, taking her by the shoulders and prying her away from the inanimate mass as it rolled to its side, revealing a young man's face.

Rory turned into Artyrus's arms, her arresting eyes wet with tears.

"His flesh is still warm." A small cry escaped her as he drew her head to his chest, weaving his fingers absentmindedly through her loose braid.

The boy looked no more than sixteen, with a strong build like most Penzellian men. But the glow of life had not yet paled.

Rory gathered herself, wiping the moisture from her cheeks with the sleeve of her tunic. She withdrew from Artyrus, taking a step toward the figure. Before she could be stopped, she reached out to him, placing slender fingers just below his jaw.

"He's alive!" The relief in her words turned quickly into urgency. "We need to find a healer. *Now*."

Artyrus rushed to her aid, looking the young man over for any apparent wounds, but he only took long, deep breaths, much like one lost in slumber. Lifting him carefully from the ground, Artyrus fixed him to Magnus, his body listless and entirely unconscious.

They made haste, entering the village to find that the town was wholly, chillingly still. Only the leaves of the trees whispered to one another, the serenity unsettling. Rory and Artyrus stayed their horses, only to be greeted by silent chaos. Bodies littered the path on which they stood, as if having fallen to the dust underfoot mid-step.

"No. It cannot be, not again." Aurora dropped clumsily from Briar's back, scarcely regaining her footing when she bolted heedlessly into the nightmare. Again, Artyrus ran for her, cursing her recklessness.

Surrounding them was, by all appearances, a massacre.

Aurora had survived that same fate once already, but at what point would her fortune run out? Whoever had authored the heinous scene they'd stumbled into could yet be drafting an epilogue.

Checking each figure as she'd done with the first, her features knit with confusion.

"Stay back from them, Aurora!" Catching her by the arm, Artyrus had her attention at long last.

"Unhand me!" she cried, thrashing within his grip, her strength never failing to catch him off guard.

"Come with me away from here." His tone was calm despite the anger of his sentiments. "There's no blood or evidence of force. It could be plague."

Rory nodded in response, sucking in a shallow breath as she ceased resisting.

"We need to find water for the horses. Once we do that, we'll consider how to proceed." Gently, Artyrus tipped her chin up to meet his gaze. "We will find a way to help them."

"Yes," she uttered, the pain of that one little word slicing Artyrus to the bone as he shared in her grief.

Finding an area tucked away from the confusion, they left the young man they'd brought back with them and promptly set off. The well was easy to find, only a short ride west of the village. It would have been a welcome sight if only it had been deserted.

A lone silhouette stood at the travelers' destination as if expectantly awaiting their arrival. Artyrus took the lead upon their approach, tugging on his reins as the man came into view. He was tall and dark-skinned, with eyes that wrinkled at the edges when he smiled at them.

"Merlin is waiting for you. You must come with me at once," the man said as he bowed. "Archimedes at your service, Your Highness."

Chapter Five

Seeing Merlin for the first time in several months brought about a flurry of mixed emotions. It wasn't so much that Artyrus' biases had influenced Rory, though she'd be lying if she weren't to admit that her guard was slightly raised.

Rather, it was the shock born of a decimated town, the tragedy of a slumbering people. Rory couldn't wrap her head around the phenomenon—a baffling occurrence wherein nobody was truly dead and gone, though, for all intents and purposes, they might as well be.

Further complicating matters was the condition of Merlin himself. The man was frantic, out of sorts. Never had Rory seen him so glassy-eyed. The disheveled nature of his hair would've been laughable had it not been an indicator of their severe circumstances. He looked as though he'd only just rolled out of bed, the furrowed ends of his silver-white beard splayed like the sprawling roots of an aged tree while the nest of unkempt hair atop his head looked prepared to support a family of blue jays.

He moved about the dingy cabin, overflowing with all manner of experiments and concoctions, books, beakers and vials, seemingly unseeing. Dust settled upon more dust, the layers so pervasive as to become clouds with the lightest wisps of his movement. His long amethyst robe brushed over the surface of the floor, stirring up motes as his footprints settled into the filth of the wooden beams beneath.

It was a disheartening state of affairs. So distracted was he that their very presence had not registered.

"I've returned, Merlin," Rory ventured, stepping from the darkened corner where she'd been observing the haggard mystic.

He jumped, spinning around to take her in before nearly stumbling into a table laden with crockery. Archimedes dashed to his side, righting Merlin before he could further damage himself. "Aurora," Merlin uttered, straightening his tunic. "Thank goodness you've returned! There is much to be done."

"What's happened?" Rory moved closer to the soothsayer, taking care not to trip over any of the volumes littering the floor. "How is it that the pair of you managed to avoid the fate of our kinsmen?"

"I'd like to know how this happened at all, if you are the visionary man you claim to be." Artyrus did not mince words, folding his arms across his broad chest as he launched himself into the conversation. "Indeed, I should think the whole scenario averted if you are capable of such feats, yet here we are."

Rory paused as Artyrus's assertion sank in. It was an uncomfortable truth, complete with stunning implications. Her gaze met that of the man who'd mentored her, the one who'd been her guide, leading her through the complicated reality of being a princess in hiding with no kingdom, no advisors. "You knew… You knew, and you sent me to Llundyn?"

Merlin's reticence gave him away as he merely sighed in acknowledgment. At the same time, Archimedes' face fell, his own guilt plainly written in his slumped posture. Neither possessed the courage to glance up.

Artyrus scoffed, shaking his head as he began to pace the small quarters, his presence like that of a penned beast about to ambush its prey. "I knew I didn't trust you—"

"I did!" Rory cried, her anger cutting through the swelling tension. The isolated cabin was quickly becoming unbearable to be within. Taking a deep breath, she composed herself, smothering the sense of rising betrayal before she continued. "I did, Merlin. And now I'd like your help in understanding what *exactly* your angle was, for all I am now is the lost princess of a hibernating citizenry!"

She wouldn't allow the tears stinging her eyes to fall, nor would she lose her temper. Neither would do her kin any good. Neither would bring her people back from the brink of a curse she could not possibly comprehend without an explanation. Yet the old man only stood there offering nothing but his silence.

"Tell me," Rory growled, her patience thoroughly depleted. "Make me understand why you removed me from my people in a time of desperate need. You could've spoken to King Luther, demanded his assistance!"

Finally, Merlin met her gaze, his features resolute and calm in the face of her fury. "It was his doing. There was naught to be done but keep you safe, and you were safest far, far away."

"Oh yes, of course." Artyrus snapped his fingers with faux amusement. "King Luther simply put thousands of people to sleep. And how on earth, may I ask, did he accomplish this?"

Rory's chaperone was seemingly unprepared to accept any explanation that originated with the treacherous counselor to the king. In truth, he seemed dangerously close to losing his composure, not that she could blame him. While she'd been readily accepting of Merlin's exposition in the past, she, too, was struggling mightily now.

"Answer him, Merlin," Rory demanded. "How does a king accomplish such a feat?"

"They've been poisoned, each from the well you nearly sampled earlier," Archimedes said, though he still hadn't the nerve to look their way. "The compound is a derivative of the thorny brambles of Wylewoode — the ones with the blood-red flowers." He fumbled toward a small table, retrieving a vial filled with clear liquid, not unlike fresh water. "It was several days before it had reached the entire Penzellian settlement. They've been out for about three days and counting."

"Time is of the essence," Merlin added, his mien as unassuming as that of an ordinary villager going about their day-to-day business.

Rory detected no remorse, his flippant attitude fostering a growing irrationality as she observed him. She glowered at the old man, working to restrain her ire. "King Luther listens to you. He *trusts* you. Did you even try?"

Merlin folded his hands before him, serene and self-assured. "It is a delicate balance, Princess. He trusts me, yes, but he must believe me to be on his side. I couldn't risk losing his confidence."

"Making you complicit in the crisis now facing her people," Artyrus charged, his voice laced with danger.

Rory stepped in front of him, placing a conciliatory hand upon his chest. He was remarkably troubled, and that on her behalf brought her a welcome reassurance as she faced the specter of Merlin's disloyalty anew. "In doing nothing, you've endangered everyone. You know things that others do not, making it your duty to share." She moved toward her erstwhile mentor, her gaze meeting his as she attempted to flesh his motives out. "You could've prevented this, warned us all without being caught, but you chose not to. Or is that it? Did you see yourself being caught?"

Merlin shook his head. "Of course not."

"Then you are nothing but a coward, for you have chosen your service to a man who is not your king over the needs of your people." It angered Rory, the bitterness she felt sinking bone deep. She'd wished desperately to believe him, to believe in his purpose for her, but her assurance was rapidly fleeing.

Artyrus took to her side, his steady presence an unexpected comfort to Rory, even as he burned with indignation. "What's to be done, now that you've seen fit to feed your nation to the wolves?"

"We're working on an antidote," said Archimedes, seemingly the more verbose of the pair, else the only one willing to divulge any information, truth or otherwise. "The compound is most unfortunate, made in part from the flesh of the Alpina Variegata, a flower native to Sundsvaile. Even if we could reach their shores in less than a month's time, we would struggle to harvest the quantity necessary to wake everybody.

But its blooms are similar to the iris, and with any luck —"

"*Luck!*" Rory pinched the bridge of her nose, clenching her jaw in righteous fury as she gathered herself. Her anger was of little use. It was time for action. "Is that all? Is there no other way? Give me *something!*"

She glanced at Merlin. For one who had once been so positive and forceful, he had suddenly become utterly feckless. Huffing, she returned her attention to his counterpart, raising her eyebrows as she waited in silence. Archimedes withered under the weight of her gaze.

"There is word amongst Luther's courtiers that it's possible to awaken your people from within the dream, but we've only scant evidence to that effect," Archimedes offered, his hands cupped around the poison that had delivered her people to their present nightmares. "With the little time and effort spent by the king's men before they enacted their ploy, I've no confidence in any of their assessments."

Rory reached for the vial, holding it aloft as she examined it from various angles in the pale light of the cottage. "Fortunate, then, that I've no such concerns." She brought the bottle to her lips, tipping the flacon with a wrinkle of her nose, for the contents were malodorous.

"*Stop!*" Merlin cried, stirring from his contented stupor at last. "The full measure of that would surely see you die!"

"Relax. I'd never consume an unknown substance, though goodness knows I don't need your blessing," Rory groused, eagerly assessing the little bit of intelligence she'd gained while the three men around her sighed in relief. She placed the vial on the table before her, amused by the looks of horror on each of their faces. And when she spied a broken spindle amongst the rubbish littering the surface, an idea struck.

Clutching the splintered rod, she acted without another thought, her movements lightning fast as she dipped the barb into the poisonous fluid. With her next breath, she stabbed the soft flesh of her inner elbow. The resulting wound was immediate as the punctured skin welled with blood, trickling over the swell of her forearm in ruby-red rivulets. It wouldn't be a lethal dose, and she only hoped it was enough.

"*Aurora*," Artyrus breathed, his words but a murmur amidst the ensuing chaos as he reached for his charge, wrapping her in his strong hold as she faltered.

"What have you done! This was never part of the plan!" Merlin howled, stumbling over the rubble of his dwelling toward Rory only to be thwarted by Artyrus, who shrugged the man away as he approached.

"Oh, great Seer, did you not see this coming?" Rory muttered, her words coming slowly to her lips as Artyrus swept her into his arms, moving to a decrepit cot in the corner of the den. He laid her down, fanning away the cloud of dust that billowed about her before tearing a strip of fabric from his tunic to bandage her damaged arm.

"You're to save your kingdom!" Merlin sputtered, venturing toward his protege, though he dared not get too close. "How can you possibly do so if you're comatose?"

"What difference does that make to me now? I'm no further from a solution than you, and perhaps I'm even nearer. It's one thing I *can* do for my people." Rory's words became ever more slurred, her eyes fluttering as she fought to remain conscious. She stifled a yawn, patting Artyrus's shoulder as he fussed over her wound. "You darling man... I shall miss your companionship in my dreams. Please, do remind me of my purpose when I wake. If I do..."

Rory's hand fell from Artyrus's shoulder, lying palm down upon her chest as she was overcome by sleep. Her breaths were slow and even—as tranquil as one could hope, given the uncertainty of her circumstances, and a contented sigh escaped her parted lips. The dark coils of her hair splayed across the pillow in silky fingers, framing her face like a thorny halo.

She appeared peaceful in slumber, but what had her reality just become? Artyrus tied the bandage off, suppressing a cocktail of sentiments that threatened to drive him to the edge of sanity. The woman was uncommonly reckless, acting without a care or a thought for herself, for her safety. Her impulsive nature had made his life a living hell for weeks, but that hadn't changed his level of devotion.

Artyrus was struck, then, by two conflicting alternatives. Protecting her was his aim, but where did the truest threat ultimately lurk? Glancing at the charlatan known as Merlin, he was confident that the man was a buffoon but not a danger—and Archimedes even less so. That left him with one choice, the least clear-cut of the two. He reached for the vial of poison, swirling the broken spindle through its contents. Ribbons of red spun from the splintered end of the shaft, the remnant blood of a woman both maddening and brave.

"What is the meaning of this?" Merlin crowed, though he made no effort to approach. Beside him, Archimedes bowed his head, seemingly resigned to the potential outcomes of Artyrus's foolish machinations.

Artyrus raised a warding hand, halting any more dissent from the soothsayer, the fibers of his patience finally having snapped. "She has done what you have not, willing to sacrifice herself for the sake of her kingdom. I know not what horrors we will meet within the dreamscape. Hell, I don't even know if we shall wake, but I will not abandon her to face it alone."

Archimedes folded his hands, his gaze meeting Artyrus's. "I beg you to reconsider."

"I will not."

"Very well," Archimedes replied, his quiet words earning a derisive scoff from his companion Merlin. "But I wish to offer you a warning." He held up a finger, staying an emerging protest from Artyrus. "To die in the dream is to die in reality. You must stay alive."

"Thus, my impending journey into dreamland. I swore I'd protect her," Artyrus bit out, glaring at the mystic who had brought him into the mess that had become his life. "It's what I vowed to do when you found me, and I've no intent to change that now."

Seating himself beside the cot, Artyrus took a moment more to process all that had occurred. It was stupid, perhaps even futile, to do what he was about to do, but his mind was made. He watched Aurora, her features serene in slumber. Would that their journey together through the dreamscape be as peaceful as she.

He could only hope.

Ignoring the thunderous voice of self-preservation echoing through his mind, he lay beside her. Raising his arm, he prepared to strike, the barbed rod clutched within his sweaty fist. "See to my wound."

Chapter Six

Aurora stood alone.

Gently brushing her fingertips overtop of the flesh where she'd punctured herself, she found that there was no discomfort or wound, only the phantom memory of the spindle driving into the tender tissue of her arm alongside blinding pain. What remained was an echo, subdued into a faded sensation of reality.

It seemed she'd done it.

Her surroundings had not changed—or not much, at least. The walls around her had lost the stench of mildew, and the air no longer smelled of Archimedes' experimental compounds. None of Merlin's trinkets or brews were anywhere to be found, but there was still plenty of clutter, nonetheless.

Most notably, Artyrus was gone and so were the others.

As was typical, she had fallen prey to the specter of injustice without considering the challenges that might greet her at the edge of her recklessness.

It was possible, even likely, that she might never awaken from her forced slumber. Grave consequences, to be sure, but so be it. She was born to lead Penzelle. It was high time she started acting like it.

Doubtless, her guilt had inspired her haste, for she had maintained anonymity throughout the days of her youth. Veiled only by unmitigated audacity, Rory grew up the daughter of Chamelaute's most acclaimed bladesmith. And while Drustan was not her birth father, he had graciously taken her into his home after the slaughter of her family. She'd been brought to the honorable man by her nursemaid, Isolde, who had saved her life when she'd slipped out of Penzelle under cover of darkness. Together, they'd become a family, living freely right beneath the nose of the king.

Drustan and Isolde had kept her safe, giving her the best life for which any Chamelautean child could have hoped. But in doing so, the confidence of Penzelle had dwindled. Without the assurance of a living heir, readily visible and making moves within the kingdom, her people were thrust into subjugation under King Luther's oppressive reign.

And now they all slumbered, unaware that they might never return to the life they once knew.

Rory would never allow the despot of Chamelaute to win.

Slipping into this unsettling dream, she had sought a resolution for every soul she'd seen at rest, lying defenseless on the streets of Caerleon—but where to begin?

Underfoot, the broken spindle scraped across the cool stone floor. Rory bent to pick it up, examining it for blood but finding nothing—only the same splintered wood that had delivered her to this world of subconscious madness. It was all rather odd, with the unblemished pin now serving as a reminder that time was not a luxury she or her people could afford in this alternate existence.

Spurred to action, Aurora searched the cabin, her movements brisk and determined. She scoured the room, finding that it was at once familiar as well as disorienting. Her surroundings felt as authentic as they had awake, but something she couldn't put her finger on was altogether different.

Here, her vision was veiled with a subtle haze, lacking the clarity to which she was accustomed. Colors were muted but decipherable, and everything she touched lacked its anticipated texture. Even the knotted wood of the table before her felt like...*nothing*. Smooth? Flat? She expected a rough surface, or perhaps the acquisition of a splinter as she stroked the oakwood, given the appearance of the tabletop, but it was entirely unremarkable.

Scents seemed only to exist when she forced their memories, willing herself to perceive familiar aromas. Sniffing a nearby vial, she discerned no scent at all, likely because the substance was unknown to her with no memory to recollect. It was all somewhat unnerving, her missing senses frustrating her pursuit of normalcy. With each exploration, the princess grew increasingly troubled over the daunting task that lay ahead.

She had to start somewhere, but there was no way to know what might greet her on the other side of the cabin door. With little to scavenge in the disorderly hovel, Rory quickly looted anything of value.

After a bit of scrounging, she came upon a waterskin. She removed the cork, and the water burst forth, flowing freely from the mouth at an absurd interval. And what should have thoroughly drenched her tunic instead left her altogether spotless, with nary a drop of moisture to wring from her garment.

Laughing aloud at the inanity of this strange state of being, Rory threw the braided strap of the waterskin over her shoulder. While she wasn't sure if she would ever need it, it felt better to have *something*. Rory obtained a small satchel with a few more moments of searching, filling it with a spare tunic — ill-fitting though it was — a length of fishing line and a half-dozen farthings.

It wasn't much.

Further complicating matters was the inconvenience of her aching stomach. She hadn't had much of a meal, having idly nibbled to pass the time before she'd reached Merlin's village. Heaving a sigh, she cursed herself for dumping the remainder of her oats from breakfast. Would that she might hunt something up, though the cottage had thus far proven relatively useless where provisions were concerned.

In the next breath, a small wheel of cheese appeared on the table in front of her. With a mere thought, it had materialized before her eyes. She studied the subliminal favor, turning it over in her hands. It smelled like any other cheese once she focused her efforts, calling to mind the recognizable scent as she took a taste.

Bite after bite, Rory ate, soon forgetting how famished she had been after her wearisome day. The meal was less than satisfactory, but it would have to do. There was no flavor to speak of, nor any real sensation of fullness in her stomach as she sank her teeth into it, but it seemed enough to satisfy her perceived needs, at any rate.

"Weird," Rory breathed, ignoring the blooming sense of dread that formed in the pit of her belly alongside the fictitious cheese.

She finished the cheese, noting for the first time a sliver of brilliance cutting across the cobbled brick at her feet. Following its trail, Aurora wandered over to a small window, the bleeding light pouring through a crack in the closed shutters.

Skimming the weathered wood with light fingers, she went to push them open but sensed she was no longer alone. Rory reached for her sword instinctually, her awareness shifting to the rear of the room.

It was gone.

Of all the items that had re-appeared in this forsaken place, her blade had been the one she needed most. She had assumed it remained securely at her side, so accustomed to carrying it that her sword had become as essential as another limb.

Instead, Rory retrieved the splintered spindle from her tunic pocket—a laughably inferior means of defense against whatever had engaged her attention, but better than nothing. Turning, she prepared to rush whatever lay in her path, for speed and surprise had always been her strengths.

Artyrus.

Relief flooded through Rory at the sight of him. With his back to her, he'd not yet noticed her, but there was no mistaking his powerful presence. Wordlessly, she watched, curiosity staying her urge to run to him.

He surveyed the cabin much as she had upon her arrival, picking up items here and there, until, unsheathing his sword with deadly speed, he pivoted toward her, his stance ready to lunge.

He dropped his weapon the moment he laid eyes upon her, exhaling heavily. "It worked."

"Perhaps too well." Aurora tried without success to prevent a smile from forming, but Artyrus's arrival alleviated so many of her growing concerns.

"Have you lost your mind?" With his fists clenched at his sides, Artyrus stalked toward her. "Merlin is mad, of course. I'd expect these sorts of impulsive acts from him, but what you did, Aurora." He shook his head, his irritation evident. "It could have killed us both. Hell, maybe it still will."

The harshness of his words sobered Rory in an instant. Doubtless, he was right, but she'd never considered that he might follow her.

The relief she'd felt when first he'd appeared had vanished entirely, her ire growing by the second. "You've made your own decision."

"You need to be careful." His voice was low, pitched with uncharacteristic apprehension. "If something happens to you here—" Artyrus paused, retrieving his broadsword from the stone upon which he stood.

Rory caught her reflection in the steel of his blade, lonely no longer but very much alone. She was but one person, with the weight of an entire kingdom upon her shoulders.

What had she been thinking? It was suicide.

And yet.

"Why did you follow me?" The question slipped past her lips without sanction, demanding an answer.

Dark eyes with unyielding depth met her own as he moved toward her, the penetration of his stare stripping her of any callous sentiments. "Obligation." His gaze shifted to the canteen slung over her shoulder. "And where exactly do you think you're going?"

"I'm sure I'll figure it out somewhere along the way." Rory pushed past Artyrus, crossing the cabin for the exit, her shoulder colliding with his as she advanced toward the door.

"Must we?" A weary groan from Artyrus called her back to him.

"*I* must," the princess replied, the urgency of her words magnifying a harsh new reality.

She would succeed in awakening her people, or they were all as good as dead.

Rory's mind drifted back to the slumbering persons they'd seen as they entered the village. Each one would be left to the mercy of the pitiless king of Chamelaute if she failed. Firsthand, she had witnessed his ruthlessness. While she remembered very little, she had endured the guilt of survival every day since.

The king would go the way of all flesh before Aurora would see her people slaughtered again.

Her treasonous thoughts alone justified a sentence she could never outlast, but it was her truth. Artyrus was right. This immature and ill-advised pursuit could well mean her death.

And his.

As if anticipating her next move, Artyrus took her by the arm. His hold was firm enough to convey urgency, but he released her just as quickly. "How will we know where to find them? What can we possibly do to wake your nation?" Solemn resolve shone plainly in his features, his ardent devotion serving to further plague Rory's conscience.

"This is not your fight," she replied, her words sounding more like a plea, but for what? A dream was nothing more than a fantasy.

Still, every bit of her knew it was more.

"Maybe not." Artyrus ran his fingertips over the length of the honed blade in his hand, turning it within his grasp. "But I mean for us to prevail."

He shouldn't have been there, but his dedication ignited her spirit.

"*Your purpose is yet to be fulfilled, Aurora,*" her nursemaid had told her each night as she'd struggled over the plight of her family, her people. "*May your heart refine your goodness. Let wisdom be your counselor, and never allow circumstance to define your destiny.*" Isolde's words had taken root deep within her soul when she had still been a child, and they meant ever more to her now.

Destiny. Fate. They were preordinations that demanded Rory confront her past and seize her station. Both were less than desirable undertakings. Yet she would escape neither, no matter how far she ran or how well she hid.

"Then prevail we shall." Her words were bold and far more self-assured than she felt, but she'd will them to be true somehow. Meeting Artyrus's gaze, Aurora nodded toward his weapon as she stepped near the cabin door. "But first, we will need to find me one of those."

"I daresay I've not seen you without yours." Artyrus's mouth tipped at the corners in a reluctant smirk. "It appears we've entered into an Otherlande of horror."

Turning the handle, Rory sucked in a sharp breath. "We're about to find out."

Chapter Seven

Otherlande wasn't entirely unusual, though finding the balance between what was true in the world outside and the reality within their befuddling dreams was a trial fraught with error. It wasn't so much an inability to recall life before their galling trip into dreamland but the reconciling of all the utter absurdity that happened within it.

"It's now or never, I suppose," Artyrus muttered, gesturing toward the realm that lay outside their humble surroundings. While the cottage was nothing special, at least it felt *safe*.

Rory sighed, wishing desperately for her beloved sword, for a dagger — anything, really, with which to arm herself, though she wasn't sure what good it would do. "I don't even know where to begin."

"The only way out of this hellhole is through whatever that is." Artyrus indicated the faux village with the point of his broadsword, and Rory noticed that he had yet to return his weapon to its sheath. Indeed, he seemed every bit as anxious about their surroundings as she was, which was little consolation, given their predicament.

Further perplexing the pair was the lack of concern over all the chaos they'd witnessed from the narrow window of the dwelling. The townspeople went about their days in cheerful ignorance, with little regard for a disappearing neighbor or a flying barmaid. Nudity abounded alongside a plethora of animals not known or domesticated to the region. Some, Rory was certain, did not exist at all on the outside, further confounding her as she struggled to acclimate to her surroundings.

"I wish I had one of those," Rory groused, eyeing Artyrus's sword with bitter envy. "Why did your broadsword make the journey into this nightmare with you when mine did not? I've no dagger, no stiletto..."

"You have me," Artyrus replied, and the subtle smirk he wore was not lost on Rory.

Were she of a better humor, she might've been amused. But as their circumstances stood, his reassurance only served to further fan the flames of her petulant mood. She held up the blasted spindle, tucking it into her satchel. "Perhaps this sorry excuse for a weapon will have to suffice. It causes damage, at the least."

"You're quite a gentle woman," Artyrus mused. "And truly, you've no need of a weapon to protect yourself. Your mind will be your guide in here."

"We'll see."

Stepping through the doorway, they were greeted by an odd sense of familiarity. Aside from some of the typical curiosities in any dream, it wasn't altogether distressing. Side by side, they made their way down the broad roadway lined with tidy shops and merchants hocking their wares. It felt remarkably normal, at least as long as they managed to ignore the occasional ten-foot human being or sky-blue horse.

"Well…" Artyrus took a deep breath through his nose, seemingly in a bid to retain his ever-limited patience as he sidestepped a woman dripping in head-to-toe diamonds. "Lord help us."

Rory, on the other hand, was helplessly fascinated. Keeping her wits about herself proved to be a monumental feat as there were distractions around every bend. "What could that be?" She indicated a gathering of villagers crowded about a small dais, upon which the town herald stood. Picking up her pace, Rory strode within earshot.

"Hear ye! Hear ye!" he cried, his hand cupped beside his mouth. "The time of the trials is nigh!"

The crowd gave a cheer, eagerly pressing nearer to the platform, threatening to crush Rory. Artyrus moved behind her, efficiently blocking their advancement as he warded off their restless energy.

"The trials," Rory began. "As in the games for Excalibur?"

"I've not witnessed them since childhood." Artyrus shifted his weight, his annoyance with the jostling townspeople evident in his clenched jaw, the flexed muscles of his long arms. "And I'm not certain what good such sport will do in *here*, at any rate."

He was right, of course. The games occurred only every dozen years as a means of appeasement, giving the people of the oppressed kingdom of Penzelle an opportunity to wrest the sword Excalibur from the stone in which it had stubbornly remained for centuries. Throughout the years, each king of Chamelaute had vowed to step away from the throne in submission to the victor, effectively reuniting the at-odds nations in a peace unknown for many lifetimes.

It seemed that would never be.

For not only had the sword remained firmly fastened within the stone, but the leadership of Chamelaute had also become utterly virulent in their rule of the tiny nation of Penzelle, which was bordered entirely by the other kingdom on three sides and the violent waters of the deep on the other.

"It wouldn't matter anyway," Artyrus gruffed, his chest colliding with Rory's head as he righted himself once more, a muffled curse escaping his lips before he continued. "King Luther would never walk away, even if someone did manage to pull that forsaken sword from the stone. It would be all-out war instead, and we both know it."

Something in his tone gave Rory chills, her companion's disdain for the Chamelautean king nothing more than an open secret between them. His animosity toward King Luther was something of a curiosity, in truth. She didn't readily understand what had caused such latent anger in the servant to the Crown, and given Artyrus's penchant for silence, she would likely never know.

"The games will be three," the herald continued, his voice ringing through the assemblage as the peoples' excitement multiplied. "A dance of swords, a riotous melee and a joust of honor for me and for thee! Come one and all to sign your name, and in these games, we all will play!"

"*Ugh.*" Artyrus sighed. "A rhyming minstrel cannot be avoided in any realm, it seems."

"Let's go!" Rory grabbed Artyrus's hand, wasting no time as she made for the clerk, dragging her irritable keeper along behind her. "It's as good of a place to start here as any."

"To what end?" Artyrus pulled Rory to a stop, taking her by the shoulders as their gazes met. "The trials will endanger your life, and Archimedes warned me before I entered this misadventure that if you die in here, you will die in reality."

Aurora paused, giving his words a moment's consideration. "Then do not let me die." She stayed an emerging protest, covering Artyrus's mouth with her slender fingers. "I understand the stakes, I assure you. But this is the way forward. You wouldn't recognize this for the opportunity that it is. My people... We live for these games because it is the only means we have of recapturing any sovereignty for ourselves. For *me*." Dropping her hand, she could see that she had struck a chord.

"Again, to what end? I beg you, be reasonable." He was softening before her eyes, his voice calm and even as he negotiated with his charge.

"I can pull the sword from the stone," she asserted, scanning the horizon for would-be competitors. "It feels very much like my birthright, and if anybody should be stepping up right now, it's me—for my people, for my parents and also for myself. I have bided my time, wishing and praying for an opportunity to redeem my family, pretending to be someone that I am not my entire life. This is it! *Please*, see this through with me."

Artyrus groaned, and it sounded very much like victory.

"What is your triumph worth in *here*?" He gestured toward the chaos that had become their reality, but Rory merely perceived the word triumph, with Artyrus seemingly accepting her success as a foregone conclusion.

"My triumph means waking. What do we have to lose?"

"Only our lives." Artyrus raised an eyebrow, his countenance dry. "And winning doesn't mean that you will pull the sword from the stone—just that you will receive the opportunity to try."

Well, then. Perhaps his belief in her wasn't so implicit after all.

"Maybe there is something more for me—something like fate, given my heritage," Rory pleaded, her gaze earnest as she met his once more. "Maybe it is meant for me."

"Merlin said this wasn't how this was supposed to happen."

"Since when do you trust Merlin?" Rory grinned. She had him now.

"All right," Artyrus muttered, a ghost of a smile crossing his lips. "Consider me at your service."

* * * *

Signing up was a farce—a simple X upon the parchment was all that was required. But the parchment itself contained nothing more than a nonsensical grouping of letters and numbers, making the entire exercise unnecessary in the first place. Still, Aurora had done it, and Artyrus had as well.

Artyrus returned the quill to the clerk, eager to relieve himself of all the eccentric company surrounding him. "Shall we attempt to learn the ropes of our new world? I don't relish learning on the fly in the arena."

"Not a bad idea," Rory agreed, only to be struck by an approaching knight, his pauldron colliding with her shoulder as he passed. On his heels were several additional soldiers and another individual who was rather unexpected under the circumstances.

"*Prince Philippe.*" Artyrus watched as the pompous heir to the throne of Chamelaute made his way to the dais, his natural arrogance never failing to garner attention.

The crowd parted before him, stepping aside in either awe or unease as he strode past them. When he reached the dais, he wasted no time, ascending the stairs before addressing those gathered before him.

"You are fortunate to be in the presence of one such as myself," Philippe began, raising his palms in a manner that made him appear approachable, though Artyrus knew better. "I've given of my time and abandoned the comforts of my legacy to be here amongst the likes of you." Philippe offered only a disdainful sniff, his gaze passing over the crowd as if they were beneath his notice. "My father and I are sovereign. Having to endure these juvenile games at all is preposterous, and you've never managed to produce any competitors of note. That, if nothing else, tells me that we rightfully rule, despite your daily efforts to impede our authority."

The crowd around them grew agitated, their anger mounting with each fractious word spoken by the prince. But Philippe was undeterred, waving their hostility off as he continued. "Because my father is so benevolent, however, he has insisted upon fairness in these trials. He sends his assurance that he will, indeed, remove himself from the throne, should any of you succeed." He smiled, a maniacal twist of his lips that had Artyrus seeing red.

Philippe had always been a buffoon—an entitled, spoiled fool who traded upon his family's titles and profited off the backs of his subjects with no end in sight. They had ruled for centuries, this line of tyrants, having readily deceived the surrounding realms into accepting their reign through generosity and flattery.

By virtue of his service to king and kingdom, Artyrus was intimately familiar with the inner workings of King Luther's affairs. He'd frequently found himself troubled when carrying out his duties, burdened by suspicion and a nagging sense of guilt, with the Penzellian massacre ever-looming in the back of his mind. And though he'd played no role in the carnage, he'd always struggled to look into the eyes of the man with such detailed knowledge of that grave day.

Glancing at Aurora, he was amazed by how she had managed her life. He'd been raised without parents as well, but he had never known his. She had been there when hers had died, watched her people crushed under the weight of the oppressive Chamelautean boot. A small blessing, indeed, that she had been so young. Perhaps that made it all easier to bear...

His fascination was getting out of control.

"That possibility is of no concern to me," Philippe continued, his incessant droning regaining Artyrus's attention at last. "For I shall participate in these games and vanquish any notions of self-governance yet again. I believe Excalibur has been awaiting one such as myself." He gestured toward the vacant arena where the storied sword was nestled amongst a bevy of knights, whose sole purpose was to protect the integrity of the weapon from any random attempts.

"What a lovely husband you will have," Artyrus muttered, taking Rory by the hand as he led her away from the gathering.

She balked, seemingly caught off guard by her stormy companion. "How do you—?"

"Disposing of yourself with someone like *him*," Artyrus growled, his agitation running away with him. "The man is a despot on the best of days! You do realize—"

He stopped short, pausing mid-stride as he struggled to contain his tirade, his mouth pinched shut. Shuddering slightly, he gulped, forcing the words back down his gullet without much success. The treason he wished to speak was forceful, swelling within his chest as if it had a mind all its own. But revealing the inner workings of his head would come to no good, his mutinous thoughts every bit as unwelcome in their dangerous new dream world as they were in reality.

"I know he's pompous, but this is too much, even for you." Rory stepped nearer, nudging him with her hip. "Why stop now, though? Especially in here. You should be uninhibited. Do continue." Her eyes sparkled with humor as she observed him, his attempts to maintain his own confidence meeting with a giggle from the lost princess.

"He should be the leader of *nothing*," Artyrus spat, and try as he might, the words would not abate, pouring forth from him like a fount of honesty. "He is not to be trusted, least of all with any woman—and certainly not with a kingdom!" Thrusting his hand over his mouth, he slowed his diatribe. He forced a deep breath then another, sucking in air as he regained control of his wits.

"Why goad me into speaking treason?" he hissed through his fingers when he thought it might be safe. "There was no stopping it!"

"I couldn't help myself," Aurora lilted. "And you did say you wanted to learn the ropes here in this strange realm. I figured I might as well test some of the boundaries. It's a bit like a naked dream, really, you revealing all your unfiltered thoughts without any desire to do so."

Artyrus scoffed, despising the heat he felt rising in his cheeks. She was getting to him again, just as she always did. Her brazen nature never failed to garner a reaction. She teased and provoked him to within a hairsbreadth of insanity more days than she did not.

"You dislike being vulnerable, I think," she said after a moment more, offering a sidelong glance filled with something much like curiosity. "A wonder, then, that you've shared what you have with me. Maybe there is some hope for our partnership after all."

"We are agreed, so long as you refrain from mining my thoughts with any more of your prodding." He offered a half-smile, his irritation subsiding. For the truth of the matter was that it had not been so unsettling to share the depths of his mind with her.

And that was a heartening and alarming prospect indeed.

Chapter Eight

No weariness had come upon Artyrus or Aurora. No veritable hunger nor the humbling necessity to relieve themselves. These well-established requisites of the traditional circadian structure were only brought to mind by habit, or, rather, the recollection of these essential behaviors from before. It was jarring and surreal all at once.

Nighttime had fallen, the blackened sky above sprinkled with shimmering starlight. Enchanted, the princess watched as lustrous flecks of gold rippled across the celestial backdrop with effortless fluidity. As extraordinary as it was, something was chilling about the spellbinding current. It called to her, summoning her to join the seductive fantasy unreservedly, beseeching Rory to succumb to this effortless existence.

Forget, the wind whispered as a shiver ran up the length of her spine. It was a thought so comforting, so serene that she closed her eyes, allowing her memories and burdens to fall away, if but for one blissful moment.

"Come back to me." Artyrus waved a hand before Rory's eyes, demanding a shift in focus for which she was not entirely grateful.

She smiled tightly, acknowledging him. But Aurora's thoughts were challenging her will, attempting to draw her back into the tender vein of apathy.

Planting himself in front of her, Artyrus caught her gaze. He searched her eyes, questioning and troubled. "Are you all right?"

Cursing herself internally, she lied. "Yes, of course."

Rory's whole being yearned to lose herself in the way only dreams would allow. Since she'd been spared from the slaughter of her loved ones, dreams had been her escape. They meant freedom and the latitude to reimagine her life as someone, *anyone*, other than the lost Penzellian heir. She was a symbol of hope to others, even though many knew not if she had even truly lived.

Yet reality was oftentimes bleak.

Together, they wandered through the quiet streets, which had earlier bustled with unconscious souls. "Strange, is it not?" Artyrus began, remaining ever near to her side. "Even in sleep, we remain subject to the presumed confines of the mundane. Do you think they've all turned in for the night, convinced of fatigue?"

It was true that due solely to the presence of the moon and the veil of eventide, Aurora had begun to consider where they might lay their heads until sunrise. "You've not grown tired either, then?"

"I confess that I did briefly lose sight of the minor detail that we're already at rest in body." Artyrus sighed, followed by a hint of a smile tugging at the edges of his mouth. "But no, I'm not tired."

Rory worked through her braided tresses, removing the cord keeping her dark strands fixed at the ends. She ran her fingers through the waves, sweeping them to her back. Artyrus inhaled as she tucked the loose pieces behind her ears, chuckling when the princess peered up at him through thick lashes.

"Did you just *sniff* me?" Aurora raised a brow in amusement.

"Your hair…" Artyrus's stare remained fixed upon her, his cheeks flushed. "I've appreciated the scent of it during our time together. I hadn't smelled anything since I set foot in this dreamscape, but I identified that." He laughed, discomfiture plain in his features as he averted his gaze.

While she was not unaccustomed to notice from the opposite sex, she was caught off guard by his admission. Warmth crept from her chest, up her slender neck to her face, and she was thankful he had turned from her, for she had rebuked herself more than once for observing him with favorable regard.

He was largely insufferable, and she refused to allow lust to muddle her senses. If anything, it was slumber-induced madness, and she would entertain it no longer.

Without so much as a backward glance, Artyrus began toward town. Rory hustled along behind him, joining him at his side as though no tension had passed between them. They walked amongst the peaceful village for some time, observing the oddities of their new surroundings in companionable silence.

It was all terribly ordinary, save for a faint melody playing in the distance. Sung softly in a tongue Rory didn't recognize, she found that against her better judgment, she was intrigued. "What do you suppose?"

"I don't suppose," Artyrus gruffed, determinedly carrying onward.

His lack of adventurousness confounded Rory. Indeed, she saw no harm in a bit of exploration. "We're looking for a way out of here, are we not? The key could be anywhere."

It was a pathetic argument, and both of them knew it, but that wasn't about to stop Rory. She took off toward the source of the sound with nary a warning. Artyrus quickly followed, a longsuffering sigh escaping his lips.

Following the melody, they drew closer to the eerie refrain that seemed to echo around them with no escape until suddenly, the tune ended.

"I've met not one who can resist the lure of that song."

The princess and her guardian stiffened in their tracks. With one hand firmly gripping the hilt of his sword, Artyrus stepped before Rory, his broad shoulders creating a nearly impenetrable shield between her and whatever lurked in the shadows ahead of them.

"Would you so quickly cut down a child, warrior?" No more than fourteen years of age, a boy emerged, revealing himself within a fragment of cerulean moonlight. Artyrus moved nearer to him, keeping a steady hold on the steel at his side.

The boy persisted despite Artyrus's threatening presence. His countenance was earnest as he cautiously stepped forward with his hands closed timidly over his heart. "I only wish to show you something."

Sheer curiosity drew Rory to where her chaperone stood, his powerful form rigid…obviously wary.

"Stay where you are." Artyrus's tone was guttural and foreboding, even to Aurora. It was less a warning than it was assurance that the child would breathe his last should he advance any farther in their direction.

The boy moved quickly then, slicing the flesh of his palm with a small dagger he'd concealed within the sleeve of his moth-eaten tunic.

Aurora gasped, moving headlong into Artyrus's extended arm as he held her back. "He's injured! Let me through!"

"He injured himself, if you hadn't noticed — with a *concealed* weapon, no less," Artyrus growled, seemingly desperate to keep the princess subdued.

Dropping the knife to the ground, the boy raised his arms, yielding to the pair without incident. Blood from the wound dripped onto his boots in crimson streaks absorbed by seasoned leather. "I'm going to reach for something," he uttered, his movements slow and deliberate. He held his bleeding hand balled into a fist in the air as ribbons of shining fluid fell to the dirt underfoot.

"We need to help him." Rory ripped a thin strip of cloth from the garment she wore, shoving her way past Artyrus at last.

"No need, milady." The child turned to face them, pinching a vial of murky liquid between his fingertips. His features brightened as he flicked the cork out with his thumb. Tipping the bottle, he crumpled the hem of his shirt as he soaked it with the clouded substance.

"Here. Please, let me." The princess stepped closer, taking the dampened material from him.

"Aurora, *stop!*" Artyrus reached for her, but she shrugged him away, ever dismissive of his directives.

Tenderly, she took the boy's wounded hand in hers, turning it over to examine the fresh cut. "What is your name?"

"Ffion, milady."

With a gentle smile of acknowledgment serving as her response, Rory used the moistened material Ffion had prepared, carefully blotting his injury.

"Now, look." Ffion pulled away, holding out his hand. "Good as new, it is."

The princess snatched him by the fingers, drawing him nearer as he stumbled toward her. She studied his palm, and there was no cut, no blood, not even a scar where he had sliced his skin before their eyes. "How did you do that?"

Ffion yanked his arm from her grasp before wiping his hands on his tunic, his face beaming with pride. With earnest eyes, he extended the vial to her by way of explanation, leaning nearer to her as he spoke. "I have more, and goodness knows you're going to need it."

She shoved him, and he cackled, cocking his head to one side. "How 'bout you, Hercules? A concoction that heals instantaneously, or perhaps something to help you sleep better at night? I offer a fair price. All you need do is pick your poison."

"A potion to meet all your nonexistent needs, he says." Artyrus nudged Aurora without amusement. A baleful sneer formed upon his face when he turned to Ffion, curling his lip with disdain. "Do not speak to us again, boy. Don't even so much as look in our direction if you happen upon us in the street or it will be your final act."

Britt Cooper & Erin Dulin

Ffion squinted, meeting Artyrus's gaze. "What did you say? How could you possibly know…?" He shook his head, running a hand through his coarse hair as he blew out a sharp breath.

Rory was, admittedly, fascinated by Ffion. He was brazen, to be sure, and perhaps a bit rude, but his behavior didn't warrant her guardian's wrath. "Leave him, Artyrus."

Her plea fell on deaf ears. Neither Ffion nor Artyrus backed down from the other, her words evaporating like vapor.

"You should be more vigilant, you know." Ffion kicked the dirt at his feet, a cunning glint in his large eyes. "The consciously unconscious won't be pleased about two Penzellians sharing their awareness."

He had Artyrus's attention now. "What do you mean 'consciously unconscious'? And do not trifle with me."

"There are others here like you who know they are sleeping." Daring to close the distance between himself and Artyrus, the boy's voice dropped to a whisper. "Here on behalf of the high king himself." He stepped away, seemingly measuring the impact of his words as he watched the pair. "That's all I know, I swear," Ffion continued, his speech no longer hushed. "I'm here for my reasons, but I've learned to keep my head down."

"Why *are* you here?" Rory couldn't help her curiosity. "You've maintained awareness as we have, but for what reason would you deliberately choose this?" Indicating the false world around them, she watched Ffion's confidence waver as he squared his narrow shoulders, as though he wished to maintain an air of nonchalance.

"I'm not here for myself," he began, and there was no detectable manipulation in his statement. "I've only been asleep a few days, I think, but it's hard to tell here. Nothing is predictable, like the elephant stampede through town yesterday and the man who flew past me as I went to draw water. Nothing about this place is correct. You can't feel, taste, see or think the way you can when you're awake. I've learned some tricks to help me get by, but everything about this is unnatural." Frustration dominated Ffion's tone as his nail-bitten fingertips massaged where he'd cut himself mere moments past.

Rory's fascination with him increased with every word he spoke, as did her questions. "If you know nothing is real, why waste your efforts trying to earn money from slumbering strangers?"

"It's easier for someone to give me something that's already real to them than for me to conjure anything at will. Sometimes it works, others not." Sighing, Ffion gathered his dwindling collection of tonics. "I've ached with hunger since I got here. I haven't found anything good enough to satisfy my empty belly, but I keep trying anyway." He scoffed at himself, shaking his head.

Aurora's heart sank with his admission. She, too, had come into this fantasy with an empty stomach, hungry and unsettled. But there was little she could do to help him, if anything at all.

Slipping his vials into a well-worn satchel, the boy nodded his farewell.

"Wait." Artyrus grabbed Ffion's arm before he took his leave. "Give me one of those stimulants you've just demonstrated. Two, if you can spare it."

Rory looked to Artyrus, endeavoring to read the motive prompting his unexpected compassion. His posture had eased as Ffion untangled the warped efforts behind his puzzling behavior, but her chaperone's irritability remained unaltered.

The child's brow creased, uncertainty coloring his profile. "But—"

"Before I change my mind." Retrieving a fist full of coins from the pocket of his trousers, Artyrus offered the silver to him.

Aurora, indisputably, had much to ask her companion as well.

Ffion pressed two glass bottles into Artyrus's palm, hastily snatching the coinage. The steadfast gleam of the moon illuminated each metallic piece as they clanked together, dropping into the abyss of the boy's bag.

"Thank you, sir." Ffion offered only a quick bow, seemingly risking not one second more in their presence. Turning on his heel, he retreated into the shadows from which he'd materialized. Nimble strides soon accelerated into a sprint down the alleyway, his form fading into blackness.

Aurora watched as Artyrus popped a cork from one of the small containers, dipping his pinky into the clear liquid. He touched his finger to the tip of his tongue before spilling the remainder of the fluid onto the ground, his countenance drawn with annoyance. "Water."

Ffion had been wise to run.

Chapter Nine

The boy was a creep and a nuisance, but something
about him called to Rory — the depths of his cynicism or
a level of desperation that matched her own, maybe.
She didn't understand the sentiment, only that she felt
a kinship with the lad. Without warning, she ran for
him, leaving Artyrus behind. There was no doubt in her
mind that her companion would disapprove, his
irritation with the urchin unnecessarily combative.

But Aurora knew he thought her impulsive. There
was no harm in proving him right.

Artyrus reacted as she'd expected, following on
Rory's heels with a grunt of effort and an exasperated
mien. Still, she was quick enough, avoiding her hulking
guardian as she made for the shadows to which the boy
had retreated.

Rory quickly took in her surroundings, noting the
darkness of the narrow alleyway and the lack of escape
routes. Perhaps Artyrus was right after all. It was a
terrible place to be even in the real world, and this place

was even more unpredictable. But her curiosity was overtaking reason.

"Ffion!" Rory shouted, reaching the other end of the passageway that opened into the center of a few humble cottages. It was deserted, save for the three semi-conscious individuals entering the quiet courtyard. She paused by a fountain set within the center of the dimly lit garden, watching as the young man deliberated, his back to her.

His hands were clenched into fists at his sides, and Rory briefly wondered if there was any pain to be had from his self-inflicted wound. Indeed, it seemed he was as suspicious of them as they were of him, though neither had been given reason for their concerns. Well, other than their entirely dubious encounter in the village.

"How did you do it?" Rory demanded, slowly making her way toward the boy. "Your hand. I saw it bleed one moment, and in the next, there was nothing. Yet all you had was water..." Her words trailed into silence, all her thoughts coming in a rush to her lips.

Artyrus joined her, taking to her side, his annoyance evident in the tight set of his jaw. His silence was typical but slightly unnerving given the circumstances.

For his part, Ffion seemed relatively unflappable, calmly turning to address his acquaintances. He ran his palm over his cropped hair, the faint light of a nearby torch highlighting its ginger tones. "All I had to do was want it. Nothing more than a cheap parlor trick," he said after a few moments more, a sly glint to his eyes. "There's really no point in my deceiving you, milady. In truth, it's rather a relief to speak to someone who understands this place for what it is — a fallacy of your innermost thoughts."

"How, then, did you have those coins?" Rory demanded, turning her attention to Artyrus. For she knew very well that she had herself maintained all their funds throughout their journey, and she'd entered the dreamscape with not a single one.

Artyrus frowned, his brows furrowed as he pondered her question. It seemed he had not given it much consideration.

"It's simple. He's not as mean as he wants me to believe he is." Ffion grinned, relaxing his posture slightly as he continued. "Compassion is what manifested those."

Rory nodded as if his absurd explanation made rational sense while Artyrus sneered. The pair were slowly acclimating to the chaos of their unified dreams, even as what remained of their wits felt perilously close to breaking.

"You're knowledgeable here," Rory began. "Or at least comfortable in this hellhole. Be our guide, and we'll pay you."

"Are you out of your mind?" Artyrus scoffed, throwing his arms up in defeat. "We can't—"

"We will," Rory cut in, placing a hand upon her guardian's chest to stay him, a fiery glare passing between them as she narrowed her gaze. "*I* will."

"A lovely thought, but your coin is of little use to me here." Ffion smiled sadly, his mind seemingly elsewhere.

"I'm not talking about here," Rory continued, determination coloring her features. "When I wake us from this nightmare, you shall be the first to benefit."

"Why make such promises to him?" Artyrus huffed. "He already tried to scam us once. How in the world could you possibly trust him?"

Rory ignored her sullen partner without missing a beat, eager to strike an accord. Ffion was an unknown, but no more so than any of the other oddities to which they were already adapting. Where was the harm in one more? "Consider my offer. A guide through this bedlam would be most beneficial, and for some reason I can't quite understand myself, I trust you."

The boy flushed, his ruddy cheeks aglow as he considered her offer anew. But the faint sound of hooves in the distance drew his attention away. Placing a finger to his lips, he motioned Rory and Artyrus into the shadows, his gaze pinned to the passage.

A trio of horses galloped past the end of the corridor. The rider in the lead wore armor as dark as coal, his minions donning suits of silver. Cloaks lined with blood-red velvet whipped in the breeze behind them as their steeds rumbled onward, the echoing of their strides thundering through the quiet town and resounding off the crumbling walls surrounding them.

"The hunters," Ffion whispered when they'd passed. "Word has it they're hunting a rogue royal." He brushed his hands over the length of his overworn pants, the stiff set of his shoulders relaxing as the chaos subsided. "There are rumors enough that if the black knight looks you in the eye, you'll fall dead on the spot."

He turned to find Aurora sharing a loaded look with her guardian, the secrets they harbored laid bare upon their troubled faces. "What'd I say?"

"You can't compete," Artyrus gruffed, folding his arms across his chest. "It's too dangerous."

"If I'm not here for this, then what is my purpose?" Rory fired back, her indignation on full display. She refused to back down—not from Artyrus nor any challenge. She had run from obligation for long enough.

"*Hellfire*," Ffion breathed, taking a step backward as though he were in the presence of a dangerous predator. "You're real! You're the lost princess! The prophecy, it's—"

Rory sighed, feeling every ounce of the weight of the world upon her slender shoulders. "It's nothing—not if I cannot fulfill my duty, wake my people."

"So it's true!" Ffion's excitement was suddenly unparalleled, his exuberance overflowing as he offered an inept bow. "Well, then. Perhaps you need me now more than ever!"

"*No*," Artyrus growled, raising an eyebrow in warning as he glanced at Aurora. "We've enough to contend with without becoming nursemaids on top of it all."

"Follow me," Ffion said, effectively ignoring Artyrus once again. "There are plenty of places to hide in town while the hunters are on the prowl."

* * * *

Making their way through the borough, the trio stuck hard and fast to the shadows, creeping along the edges of the quiet cottages and semi-vacant marketplace. It seemed they were not the only ones interested in avoiding the vigilantes gallivanting about the town, though they likely had the highest motivation with Aurora in tow.

"The palace is right there," Ffion said, gesturing to a mammoth castle that was suddenly in their midst, just beyond the sturdy ramparts. The royal dwelling materialized seemingly out of nowhere, having remained invisible until the boy called their attention to it.

"Is that where our beloved Philippe resides?" Artyrus snapped, his animus for the spoiled royal ever-looming in the back of his mind. He glanced toward Rory, happily noting that she, too, seemed perturbed by the thought.

"In fact, it is not." Ffion edged away from the walls, his desire to put some distance between himself and the palace clear. "It's nothing more than a dragon's den, indwelt by a monstrous, iridescent wyvern. While some things are strange here, the nature of some beasts will never change. I stay as far away from that fire-breathing creature as possible."

The fear on Ffion's face was confirmation enough of that, for the boy looked stricken as they passed the vast residence. Beyond the ramparts was a field of thorny brambles, entirely obscuring the portcullis from view.

"Strange," Rory said. "The castle looks much the same as the royal dwelling outside this nightmare. I suppose its occupation by a dragon is fitting, given King Luther's presence within the palace in the world beyond."

"I've seen the creature before, once perched upon the keep and another time creeping from the window. She flew away, only to disappear." Ffion shivered with the memory, and Artyrus felt an unexpected spark of sympathy for the boy.

He didn't trust Ffion. He was a long way from that. Still, perhaps it wasn't the worst thing to have an ally or two, particularly one with a bit of inside knowledge about this Otherlande.

"How long will the black knight and his minions be marauding?" Artyrus asked, eager to get them all to a safer place.

"They're at it all night, which could be what feels like hours or days." Ffion frowned, frustration evident upon his youthful face. "I never know when it will be morning. I blink, and it's finally there."

"Do you hear that?" Rory paused mid-stride, closing her eyes. Without warning, she was moving backward, drawn toward the briery gates as if by force.

Pacing in reverse, Artyrus stepped in her path only to be trodden over by the entranced princess. "Aurora —"

"Let me go," she uttered, pulling against Artyrus as he attempted to draw her away, running her fingers over the smooth stone of the wall as though she could not get close enough. "The time is nigh."

"Couldn't agree more," Artyrus said, throwing Rory over his shoulder before making his way away from the silent siren call as quickly as he was able.

The boy led them to a clearing of sorts on the outskirts of town, surrounded by a very ordinary forest of vines and trees on one end and a rocky bluff overlooking the ocean on the other.

The deep waters beyond the cliff were illuminated by the light of the moon above, the lambent flicker of the surrounding stars dancing on the waves where they crested and crashed upon the jagged crags at the foot of the wall.

It was much too vivid to be authentic, again serving as a reminder that they lived on borrowed time in a foreign dimension.

Without the absurdity of the day, the encounters with creatures and circumstances that would ordinarily exist only within the confines of the imagination, the evening might've been mildly pleasant. But Artyrus had had it with the unconventional. Would that they might solve the madness of the dream world and make a swift exit back into reality. It was his most profound desire.

Compounding his dark thoughts was his concern over his charge. Aurora was nothing if not headstrong — moody, insistent, impetuous. The woman was driving him to distraction, her lack of respect for her safety and inability to consider the consequences of her actions having become the bane of his existence, both in real-time as well as this farce of a life he now led.

"So," he began when they took a moment to recover. "You'll not go running back to the palace now, will you?"

"Indeed, I will not," she agreed, offering a sidelong glance before indulging in a sip of water from her waterskin. "I don't know what came over me. Now, I—"

Artyrus turned, glancing over his shoulder to see what had so captivated Aurora's attention, her gaze pinned to something far beyond. Ffion, too, had joined the duo, his mouth agape as he watched.

A young woman sprinted from between the trees, her feet so quick they were blurring with each long stride. Lengthy locks billowed behind her, drifting in her wake alongside myriad leaves as she whipped through the low-hanging branches.

She wasn't alone, for not far behind was a posse of some twenty men, armed to the teeth with all manner of weaponry and rapidly gaining on the lone female. They emerged from the tree line like a tidal wave, pouring from between the sturdy trunks in an angry flood as they surged toward their mutual target.

Reaching the clearing, she dodged one dagger then another, zig-zagging her way across the broad meadow as the knives landed harmlessly amongst the sea of grass. She was agile, leaping over stout outcroppings of stone and lengths of fallen trees as if they were nothing more than pebbles in her midst.

"She's headed for the cliff," Artyrus breathed, as the three observed her predicament, with not one of them near enough to her to offer any aid.

The woman carried on, undeterred, racing for the precipice as though it were the most logical solution to the outrageous pursuit. The men were rowdy, taunting her with oaths of retribution and seemingly confident that they had her right where they wanted her.

"What do we do?" Rory cried, her hand itching toward her side though there was no sword to be had.

Shaken from his stupor, Artyrus took off. He had not a prayer of reaching the poor woman, but simply standing there in observance was no course of action. He glanced about himself, seeking a means of distraction, only to find he was armed with nothing more than his wits.

But before he'd managed to get anywhere near, she reached the edge, leaping gracefully into the heavens with her arms spread wide as though she expected to take flight.

Artyrus watched in horror as she instead began to plunge, right before she blinked out of sight.

"Did she just—?" Aurora bent at the waist, catching her breath as she came alongside Artyrus. Ffion wasn't far behind, his face a mask of confusion as they each attempted to come to terms with the scene before them.

"She didn't fall." Artyrus stepped toward the edge of the cliff, peering below to confirm with his eyes what he knew in his mind. There was no body, no gore, only the same pristine crags he'd seen before.

Farther up the bluff coast, the rabid men were reaching the same conclusion, cursing their luck as they retreated and offering not one glance in the direction of Artyrus and his companions.

"Perhaps we should regroup," he said, taking a deep breath.

"I think not," came a sharp female voice from behind them. "Stay where you are."

Chapter Ten

Ffion slumped to the ground just as Rory turned. A singular dart had felled the boy, a cardinal feather marking where he'd been hit. Directly behind him stood a feral-looking young woman, again taking aim with her mouth pressed firmly to the end of her pipe.

She released another bolt, this time sending it blazing toward Artyrus.

"Get down!" His warning echoed through the clearing, and Aurora dove for Ffion.

Artyrus threw himself out of the dart's path, directing the full force of his body toward the girl. Her eyes twinkled with a knowing glint as her form rippled like water before him, evaporating when he reached for her. His body hurtled forward with her disappearance, and he stumbled into the void left behind.

Aurora's heart lurched when she touched Ffion, his slight frame no more than a heap on the earth. Even knowing the little she did of him, this was a wholly undeserved strike and unprovoked at that.

"He's not dead," the girl began, materializing before Rory. "But you will be soon if you don't step away from him."

"And you will die if you so much as think about hurting her," Artyrus growled, the rasp of steel against leather ringing through the air as he unsheathed his sword.

"How valiant you are. So *fearless*," the wild girl mocked, the inflection of her words as serpentine as her leer. She clutched the blowpipe tightly, her slender fingers caressing the silver facade as if the easy strokes might prompt it to do her bidding.

"What do you want with him?" The princess shielded Ffion's limp body as he groaned. Meeting the woman's glare, she pushed further. "Do you know him?"

"I already warned you." Hair in the color of unfiltered sunlight swirled around her face, an unkempt mane with matted tendrils spiked with twigs and leaves. The girl drew the flute to her lips alongside a deep intake of breath, her movements swift and sure.

Artyrus made for her as the dart burst forth from the pipe. The sandy-haired devil remained intact this time, her lithe figure twisting away from the gleaming edge of Artyrus's blade.

Aurora evaded the shot, rolling out of the way and scrambling to her feet. She joined strides with her guardian, lunging for the girl. Fighting for every inch, Rory struggled to narrow the gap between them, falling shy when the woman's feet lifted off the ground, her fingertips skimming the heel of the woman's boot as she took to the air.

She was flying, ascending ever higher before their eyes.

Artyrus sprinted past Aurora, sheathing his sword upon his approach. His long arms extended just far enough as he grasped the nymph's ankle, effectively preventing her from gaining more altitude, even as her arms desperately clawed at the sky.

She was stronger than she looked, the crease of her brow set with raw determination as she writhed and jerked under Artyrus's hold. He heaved her out of the sky with unyielding strength while she flailed and kicked, her shoe making contact with his jaw. The guardian swore under his breath, his powerful muscles taut as he fought to subdue their thrashing adversary.

"Why don't you try that little trick of yours again?" Rory spat. She was fascinated yet terrified by the untamed creature before her. The girl rolled her eyes, conceding to Artyrus, though the fury in her stare suggested everything but compliance.

"Which one?" A wicked smirk formed on her lips, the words designed to bait. "The one where I brought down the little imp? Whatever he's told you to garner this level of loyalty is likely false. He's a beast in sheep's fleece."

Artyrus scoffed. He had suggested the same a thousand times since Aurora had convinced him that the boy might have his uses. It was a conviction that she held fast, regardless of her partner's wariness.

Grasped by the wrists and trapped underneath Artyrus, the woman eyed her captor. "I could take him off your hands, you know…for a small price."

"*No,*" Artyrus snarled, the finality of his refusal without dispute.

Rory couldn't stay her curiosity, no matter how vicious their new friend was. "Why *are* you still here?

If you can just vanish, why waste your effort struggling this way?"

"Perhaps I like the view." The girl raised a brow, indicating Artyrus, who still hovered over her, his knees firmly rooted on either side of her slender figure. He, however, ignored her entirely.

Ffion mumbled something nearby, drawing Aurora to him. "What do you want with the boy?" she demanded, fussing over his figure. His eyes were bright, standing in stark contrast with his condition. Again, he murmured something, but the effort failed.

"I already told you, he's fine."

"Fine and alive are very different things," Artyrus snapped, his focus shifting to the boy lying limply in the grass.

"Why else do you think I'd still be here, you halfwit. When the poison wears off, that boy will come with me one way or another." The woman's confidence never wavered, her chin set in defiance, even as she remained fixed to the earth.

"*Try* it."

Two simple syllables and Artyrus had sent a chill up even Rory's spine, but the girl never so much as flinched. Instead, she curled her lip in amusement, a taunt well-earned, given the unfathomable flair she possessed for giving them fits.

Loath as Aurora was to admit it, the woman would be an asset. The competent manner in which she'd evaded her pursuers and even the lethal prowess she'd unleashed upon Ffion through her uncommon means of defense were irrefutably valuable.

Rory swiped the blowpipe from the pocket of the stranger's tunic, turning the weapon over in her palm.

"Release her." She met Artyrus's stare, willing him to abide by her command.

He relented, loosening his grip on the woman's arms as a silent agreement passed between himself and the princess. The girl scrambled to her feet but did not attempt to run, instead rubbing her wrists, her face a mask of anger.

"If he doesn't recover, I'll kill you myself," Rory vowed, her pulse throbbing with each word as she nodded toward Ffion.

"*Petra*," Ffion moaned, his limbs slowly regaining mobility. He managed to prop himself on his elbows, his gaze landing upon the girl. With no evident fear in his face, he plucked the dart from his arm, tossing the bolt and its crimson quill aside. Relief flooded his features, his smile broad and eager.

Rory eased with his recognition of the girl, of *Petra*. Exchanging a glance with Artyrus, she noted his rigidity had not been affected. He stood with his hand upon the hilt of his sword, his stance communicating a fervid willingness to slice Petra into nothing more than scraps should the need arise. A storm raged within his eyes, matching those of their new acquaintance.

Aurora broke the heavy silence, kneeling beside Ffion. "It will be his choice. He will neither be forced to go with you nor remain at our aid. The boy can decide for himself."

Petra huffed a laugh. "Get on with it, then."

"I've come to help you home," Ffion managed, his familiarity, his warmth toward the contemptuous creature catching Rory off guard.

He knew her. That was clear, but was this spiteful monster why he dared venture into Otherlande? Rory was rocked by another thought then, realizing for the first time that if Ffion were consciously unconscious that the woman must also be.

"We're not going anywhere," Ffion croaked.

Petra studied him, her evaluation holding no enmity yet no palpable tenderness either. The duo was an enigma to be managed or perhaps manipulated if they could somehow discover the true nature of their dealings.

"Oh, but we are." Petra moved toward Ffion, and he wielded only a listless hand to stop her while nearby, Artyrus again drew his sword.

"Make no mistake, Petra. You will die where you stand if you don't heed their commands," Ffion warned. "I beg of you, don't fight them. Help us."

"We don't need her help," Artyrus growled. "*You*, boy, are burden enough."

"What do you know of the prophecy of Penzelle?" Aurora stepped between her guardian and Petra, ignoring Artyrus's upset over her question. Gently, he reached for her, a silent plea.

"Aurora—" His utterance was so grave and soft that he almost changed Rory's mind.

But she knew that caution was often the more consequential mistake. She would not defer to timidity for the sake of herself.

"*A foolhardy curse she is born to break...*" Aurora waited.

Watched.

Ffion's face shone with the same wondrous delight as when he'd first realized who she was, while Artyrus paled as the declaration tumbled from Rory's lips.

"I am she. It's not a role I've ever desired, but it is no less true." Exhaling, the princess closed her eyes as fractured images of her family's slaughter plagued her mind. She was here for them, to carry on their legacy. She could not fail.

Petra observed Rory with quiet contemplation, her nose scrunched as she carefully massaged her temples. Perhaps she had broken through the girl's hostility after all.

"I'm entrusting you with this because I need your help. If you are trapped as we are, we may be of use to each other," Rory continued. There was no use trying to hide her motives, and she knew it. And, truth be told, maybe she saw just a little bit of herself in Petra. There was wisdom and experience in her bearing that did not occur by happenstance. She could be an asset.

"Petra, please. They're to fulfill the prophecy." Ffion had regained enough vigor to steady himself, now standing upright. His earnest petition drew a small glimmer of concession from the girl.

"We mean to awaken all who were forced into this fallacy," Aurora added, ignoring how Artyrus stiffened more with each truth she divulged. But she was compelled by more than impulse where Ffion's friend was concerned, and by Aurora's estimation, in his silence, her companion understood.

"You'd deign to use my knowledge of this delusion for your gain, but your first mistake is assuming that I *want* to wake." Petra's eyes narrowed as she considered the offer.

Her allusions to reality's grimness were as vague as Ffion's, catching Rory off guard. She, too, had had struggles in her life, but never had it been enough for her to desire to leave the real world behind. She briefly wondered what their waking lives held. Would that there might be a way to bridge the gap—a means of helping them in consciousness.

Supposing they were all able to find a way out.

Ffion lifted his chin in opposition. "Whatever it is you plan to do, I will not be joining you. I followed you here to bring you home."

"*Home.*" Petra scoffed as if the word itself tasted of poison on her tongue. "There's no such thing to me anymore."

"Perhaps not to you," Artyrus cut in, his words brandished to wound if his blade could not. "It may come as a surprise, but others here still have families and lives ahead of them, people who deserve a future. Go ahead and reject our proposal. We'll find our way."

First light leaked through softly rustling leaves, the trees swaying gently to a sighing breeze. In the next moment, the dimness of early morning dissipated, like it had observed some hushed command through Artyrus's dismissal.

"We haven't the time for this," Artyrus added, his patience rapidly waning. "With the dawn, the tournament is set to begin."

In the distance, a collection of trumpets sounded, proclaiming just that. The timing of it all was mildly unnerving as if they'd awaited Artyrus's announcement.

Aurora met his gaze, a shared sense of disquiet passing between them before she decided enough was enough. Time was a strange commodity in this Otherlande, and she didn't wish to waste it any longer. She offered Petra her blowpipe. "Good luck to you."

"You mean to compete, then." It was more a statement than a question. Petra retrieved her weapon, suspicion marking her features. "You should, at the very least, embody your heritage. People are more apt to embrace what they know. But then again, you couldn't possibly understand Penzellian tradition having remained hidden all these years. Apart from your coloring, you bear every mannerism of a Chamelautean."

Rory's goodwill ran thin. It was an accusation, a condemnation of her very character. "You know *nothing*. Be on your way then." The princess set toward her companion, disregarding the hellion with a sweep of her hand.

"Then you do know how to present a regal air," Petra sniped, earning a withering look from Aurora.

Another blare of the trumpets reverberated through the glade, and soon, every warrior within hearing range would be pouring into the arena. It was time to do that for which she'd come.

"Enough of this." Artyrus's delivery was clipped and cold. Rory met his gaze, burdened as it was by the challenge that summoned them forth.

"Are you joining us?" Rory asked Ffion.

The boy glanced between the trio, a reflection of his past and his potential future laying before him. To say that he was bewildered was an understatement.

"If you wish for my assistance, let me begin here," Petra relented, her eyes fixed upon Ffion as she spoke. "I grew up amongst a faction of Penzellian refugees who'd found sanctuary in the heart of Wylewoode for a time. The prophecy was their very lifeblood. If you're to compete alongside them, *look* like you belong. They deserve at least that." Only then did she demand Aurora's attention alone. "Leash your attack dog, and I will get you ready before these first trials take place."

It was a bid for peace on its basest level, yet Rory was not so naive as to regard Petra's offer as anything other than self-serving. Still, it was better than going it alone. The girl possessed knowledge that neither she nor Artyrus could, new to the dream world as they were.

"Fine," Rory agreed. "But you'll follow my commands — and no more darts."

Petra nodded her assent, though the maniacal gleam within her eyes did little for Rory's confidence.

Artyrus kept a wary eye upon Petra's every movement as she worked her fingers through Aurora's long, dark tresses while Ffion sat, plucking blades of grass from the earth. He'd recovered as well as could be expected and seemed happy to have his friend along for their adventure, even in spite of her hostility.

With expert precision, Petra had formed an intricately woven braid down the center of Rory's head, a voluminous plait of inky strands. At her temples on either side, she twisted three parallel rows of hair, so tightly bound to her scalp that Aurora shifted with discomfort under the viperess' dexterous touch. She dared not complain, however, for fear that the woman might remove her hair altogether.

Petra had worked quickly, securing the remainder of the loose waves alongside the braid and coiled tiers with a strip of golden hide. Wrapping it closely to Rory's crown, Petra knotted the leather ribbon. Aurora's traditionally styled ponytail cascaded down her back, falling just between her shoulder blades.

Artyrus surveyed her appearance, the princess keenly aware of his gaze having been cast upon her. In the time she'd known him, not once had she preened — no more than a few seconds to rake through her travel-tousled mane.

She swore she saw his breath catch.

"Is it too much?" Aurora hadn't the faintest idea how she might look to him, apart from her pulsing temples.

"No, you're..." The guardian's words trailed. He swallowed hard, drinking in the sight of her. "You're perfect."

Chapter Eleven

Petra was going to be a problem.

Perhaps she'd set aside her misgivings for a time to assist them and maybe she even felt gratified to do so. Neither of those possibilities gave Artyrus any peace. The situation was tenuous at best, his partnership with Rory having become a quartet of doom in a matter of, well, however long it had been in what felt before like an endless night.

The only favorable development out of their plight was the princess herself. She was nothing short of radiant in her traditional Penzellian garb, her hair arranged in the intricate, lofty braids worn by her ancestors. Indeed, he felt not an ounce of regret over his private acknowledgment of her beauty, which effortlessly matched the bravery and determination of her warrior soul.

A raven-haired Valkyrie was she, and they would need every trace of her fortitude to survive.

It pained him to admit as much, having been accustomed to bending situations to his own whims for the whole of his life. He'd met his match in Aurora, a woman at once mighty and fierce, whose knowledge of her inner mind was more self-assured than anyone he'd ever known, including himself.

He was losing his judgment, damn him. Otherlande was messing with his head, rapidly eliminating his common sense. Releasing a harsh breath, he refocused, his attention landing on the calamity that was Petra.

Alongside Ffion, she wandered before them, dispensing her wisdom—if that's what it really was. For all Artyrus knew, she might simply be mad, delivering them all into some illusion of her foolish design.

"The rubes within this nightmare are manageable enough, asleep as they are in body and mind." Petra scoffed, briefly blinking from view before returning as if nothing had happened. "It's almost unfair, in truth. If only taking advantage of their folly had some bearing on reality."

Her mood immediately darkened, the mention of their real lives outside the farce they were trapped within too much to abide. Her temper was one thing, but her volatility entirely another. The unpredictable nature of her movements, her schemes, had Artyrus on edge, his hand ever poised to draw his sword, should it come to that.

"Then there're the ones who come and go," she continued. "I can only figure them to be sleeping naturally, arriving in the dream as they slumber and disappearing when they wake, the lucky bastards."

The potential for that had not yet crossed Artyrus's mind. Was there nothing about the confounded dream that was normal?

"Do you have any pointers for us?" Aurora asked, her uncertainty in their mission evident in the crease between her brows. For the first time since they'd taken their poisonous interlude, she seemed almost vulnerable.

"Do I have pointers?" Petra laughed, leading them to the broad cobbled road that traversed the center of the town. "Of course, I have pointers. Should I share them is the question."

"Share them, you little troll," Ffion said, giving her a hearty shove and drawing another raucous laugh from the half-mad woman. He'd been somewhat subdued since her arrival, but the amusement upon his face was indication enough that he was pleased to share her company.

Petra returned the favor, her shoulder colliding with his. "You dare to call *me* the troll." She grinned, their interaction like that of siblings and remarkably mundane. Turning, she met Aurora's gaze. "All right, look. Nothing here is usual. You must guard your back at every turn and be prepared for anything. Dreamers can do things you cannot, at least not yet."

"I've noticed that," Rory muttered, briefly catching Artyrus's eye. He shrugged, his lip twitching in amusement. Petra's warning would be obvious to anybody paying even the slightest measure of attention.

"You could be dead by the end of the day," Petra went on, her tone detached as though she were discussing breakfast rather than life and death. "Then where will we be?"

"We'll all be dead, too," Artyrus grumbled, having had enough of her babbling. "It's to your benefit to see this through. Otherwise, we've no need of you."

"Oh, I think I've proven my worth already." Petra gestured toward the gathering villagers, their faces awed as the foursome approached the arena.

All around them, the people stood, their mouths gaping, eyes wide, as they took *her* in, for every last one of them was focused on Aurora. Arrayed as she was in the clothing and finery of her people, she was a sight to behold, and Artyrus silently prayed that they wouldn't realize she was the queen they'd awaited in desperation since the fall of their kingdom.

The townspeople pressed ever nearer to them, with the various competitors arriving at the arena alongside their entourages of family and friends, each one hoping to be the heroic victor who would rescue the Penzellian refugees from their plight. It was bedlam, the sheer volume of people threatening to swallow them whole.

His misgivings over everything — the trials, the dream, the supposed *prophecy* — assaulted his mind anew. How would he possibly ensure Aurora's safety? It wasn't that she couldn't protect herself. He knew full well that she was capable of that, but this nightmare was a different story altogether. Suddenly, the fanfare of the impending trials felt fraught with danger.

And Petra had known *precisely* what she was doing when she'd done Rory up. How had he been so ignorant?

It was time to part ways.

Artyrus grabbed Rory's hand, drawing her toward himself. "This is a bad idea," he breathed into her ear. "There has to be another way." Slipping his arm around her shoulders, he turned, prepared to confront the deceptive little nymph who had launched them further into chaos through her exceptional handmaidenry, but she was nowhere to be found.

"What's wrong with you?" Rory shrugged out of Artyrus's hold before stepping toward Ffion, who was preoccupied with something in the distance.

Petra.

She'd climbed atop the railing encircling the arena amidst the disarray, standing beside the town herald, who also perched upon the wall. Her features were smug as she folded her arms across her chest. Morning sunlight filtered through her wild mane, her form illuminated for all to see as she began to speak. "You are fortunate, one and all, for today begins the journey to freedom. Many will compete, but one champion will emerge, and she stands in your very midst."

The crowd was rapt, the compelling deceiver before them on the brink of sharing a truth that was not hers to share. Whether she was simply ignorant or a willful saboteur, Artyrus didn't care. Her lack of judgment was infuriating.

"The games will be numerous, but the victory singular, all by the hand of she who was lost—your once and future queen!" Petra pointed in their direction, smiling as she indicated Aurora with the tip of her finger.

Understanding dawned, the gathering erupting in exclamations of joy. Much to Artyrus's relief, they did not advance any nearer, instead dropping back and falling to one knee to honor her.

"Well, I—" Rory placed a hand to her chest, her eyes welling with tears. She bowed her head, by all appearances humbled by their praise. The cheer that rose was deafening, with the people having found their strength and spirit at long last.

"That," said the town herald, "should've been my privilege." He calmed the pandemonium with raised palms, his ire for Petra over his stolen moment of glory evident as he struggled to regain his platform.

Petra leapt from the wall, making her way back to Ffion, who watched on in amusement as Rory was inundated with well-wishes and adoration.

But Artyrus seethed. "How am I to protect her now that you've revealed her identity?" he hissed at Petra as she strode past.

"I've done you a favor. For now, the eyes of everyone in this forsaken dream will be upon her. Nobody would dare to touch her." She walked away, evidently finished with her business.

Artyrus briefly considered her words. It was utterly counterintuitive. Hiding in plain sight had been his aim, but now...

"Did you hear?" Aurora stepped before Artyrus, drawing him out of his deliberation. "You're in the first group. It's time for battle." Her face shone with excitement, a satisfied smile forming upon her lips. Then again, she was always ready for combat.

He, however, could not have possibly been less so.

Rory fell in amongst her people, taking up a position in the gallery overlooking the tiltyard. Ffion had joined her, but Petra was nowhere to be found. The woman was capricious, yet Rory found she wasn't entirely unhappy with the abrupt revelations.

It was a relief. She'd hidden for so long, uncertain of her lot and unprepared to take the actions demanded of her lineage. Petra had left her no other choice, making the pathway before her much clearer than it had been mere moments before.

Her people's reception had heartened her — their tender regard, their enthusiasm bolstering her resolve to find a way through her unusual predicament, no matter the cost. She would not fail them.

She watched as the competitors took to the list field, twenty or so in all for the first round, and found that she had no trouble identifying Artyrus. With his broadsword hanging at her side, she worked to suppress her anxious thoughts. Despite her protestations, he refused to leave her without seeing her armed first. And while she was pleased to have the means to defend herself once more, it left him at a startling disadvantage. There was no way the provided swords would function as well as his own, though maybe it didn't matter, given their circumstances.

The participants were matched without much rhyme or reason, each brandishing a sword and shield as they were lined up opposite one another. Artyrus was amongst the most powerful in build and stature, for whatever that was worth, given the intrinsic unfairness of the tournament. Neither Rory nor Artyrus were capable of stacking the odds in their favor. They would have to rely upon instinct and skill alone.

The first match began, with the participants facing off in the center of the arena. Bout after bout, they sparred, the clash of metal ringing through the air. Their technique did not vary much at all, except from Penzellian to Chamelautean, of which there were only a few. That included Artyrus, who looked to be next up.

"God help him," Ffion mumbled, his eyes glued to the men on the field. His sentiment for her grim chaperone caught Rory off guard, with Ffion's sense of loyalty having blossomed, even in spite of Artyrus's surliness.

"You watch him. He's nearly as good as I am," Rory replied, nudging the boy in the ribs as he grinned at her.

"Perhaps I should be jealous," came a voice from over her shoulder. She turned to find none other than Prince Philippe, his handsome face mere inches from her own.

A shame that beauty was so often wasted on the ugly at heart.

"It seems," he continued, "that we are betrothed. I confess I had wished to ignore my father's edict, but it might be more tolerable than I'd imagined. Indeed, I've never known such an exquisite Penzellian." He took her hand in his, bending at the waist before placing a kiss upon her clasped fingers. "But then again, I could never waste myself on one either."

The wicked glint in his eyes had Rory ready to maim him. Yes, she was outfitted with a sword, but her fingernails might also do the job.

She offered only a disdainful sniff, her scorn for the royal without equal. "As if either of us has a choice in the matter. When push comes to shove, I know I will do so, no matter how distasteful it is." She turned from the brute and returned her attention to the arena, eagerly watching as Artyrus began his match.

"I see," Philippe uttered, stepping to her side. He rested his hands upon the railing, his gaze never leaving her face. "Yet I would never warrant your loyalty. That is obvious. You seem quite taken with that one." He nodded toward her guardian as his steel met the metal of his adversary's shield, each of the men resilient in their battle-born zeal. "Why?"

"We are all one another have here," she answered without hesitation, though she immediately regretted her candor. "And I quite imagine I would never claim your loyalty, either." Her eyes met those of her betrothed, a captivating shade of green filled with endless depths of secrets. There was bitterness there, alongside a healthy dose of ego—a combination certain to ensure a hostile union.

He raised a manicured eyebrow, his mouth set in a grim line. "Of course not. I could never devote myself to anyone fully, least of all some sort of Penzellian scum." He smiled then, his gaze dropping to her lips.

Aurora burned with anger, even as she refused to allow him to see it. She smiled in return, gazing up at him through thick lashes. "What a lovely marriage we will have."

With that, she walked away with Ffion on her heels, leaving the prince who seemed to be reluctantly intrigued in her wake.

Chapter Twelve

It was nothing Aurora couldn't handle. She'd observed substandard swordsmanship in the arena all morning and was delighted by what she had witnessed. Men of all shapes and sizes, both young and wizened, clashing steel against steel, lumbering about the ring like they owned it until, one by one, they fell.

Each loss was her triumph.

The matches did not end in death, save for one, with a severed head rolling through the arena's center. The dead man's opponent had promptly been disqualified and sentenced to a punishment fitting the crime. The offender was, unsurprisingly, Chamelautean.

The sight had awakened some grim sentiments that Rory wished heartily to ignore, but she would not let it rattle her.

Apart from the single horrifying display of bloodlust, most encounters had climaxed in reluctant surrender at the tip of a broadsword.

"Are you ready?" Artyrus sidled up to her without her notice, standing so close in the tightly packed crowd of onlookers that his breath rustled her hair. "With your speed, I cannot imagine you'll have much trouble, but be sure to keep your awareness about you."

"It should all get more interesting as people begin losing their grasp on normalcy," Petra said around a bored yawn, idly picking at her nails.

Artyrus shot her a warning glare. There seemed to be no natural bias for Petra, apart from vast self-interest. Upon their introduction, it had seemed that she harbored at least some sympathy over the plight of Penzelle, but any hint of pity she'd felt appeared to have disappeared.

"Perhaps Ffion has a potion to ensure my victory," Rory said, winking at the boy and earning a cheerful snicker in return. She was eager to change the subject, for both of their new companions had joined them at her insistence, and Artyrus's unease with the situation was evident at every turn. Would that Petra might keep her volatile tongue to herself. Stars knew their quartet didn't need any more tension.

At least Rory hadn't been wrong about Ffion. Not yet, at any rate, for he, with his wily charm, had managed to equip Artyrus with a new sword just before he'd battled, ensuring that neither she nor Artyrus would spend a moment unarmed. Never mind that the blade was impossibly worn. Still, Artyrus had fared well enough with it, despite the marred edges and wobbly hilt.

"Well—any further instruction or caution before facing my opponent?" Rory teased, turning to face Artyrus.

He ran his knuckles down the length of her forearm as if, for a moment, he'd forgotten himself. She shivered at the touch, light and reverent, so contradictory to the warrior she'd just watched dominate his outing in the arena.

"You need no instruction with a sword," he said, his flesh again brushing gently over hers when he spoke. "It's your unfortunate challenger I should counsel, though your filthy tactics are always diverting." His brow shimmered with sweat, the adrenaline from his fight still blazing in his eyes.

She wanted to stay where she was, wanted to explore the lines of his taut muscles with her fingertips. The flames flickering behind his gaze told her that he wanted her to do just that.

Distraction.

These desires were all distractions meant to cause their failure. The dream, strange as it was to acknowledge, was clever, toying with the princess as a cat plays with its quarry. For better or for worse, she was the mouse.

"I almost forgot," Ffion said, interrupting Rory's musings. "I found these earlier."

Two gleaming vambraces to protect her forearms. She couldn't have been more grateful for him at that moment. The boy was quickly becoming a treasure. Ffion beamed as Aurora accepted them, with pride emanating from his freckled face.

Artyrus's lips twitched at the corners, suggesting a smile, though Rory was sure he'd never reveal his full sentiments where Ffion was concerned. "Allow me," he said, taking one of the armored coverings in hand.

The princess slipped her arms through the cool metal. They fit closely to her skin as they should, and she rolled her wrists around in fluid movements to test her mobility just as she would mere moments from then in the ring. The craftsmanship was excellent and possibly rivaled even that of her dear friend, the blacksmith, John in Llundyn.

Rory bent, kissing Ffion's cheek. "Thank you. These will surely come in handy."

It was evident by the way Ffion's cheeks flushed from her praise that he was not used to his efforts being acknowledged. He nodded, his smile bright and broad.

"Watch your back, and try not to mess up your hair," Petra muttered impatiently. "I do not wish to tend to it again."

Aurora sniffed in amusement. "I'll make it my priority."

She glanced at her trio of companions, offering a nod in parting before making her way to the arena, though her gaze lingered upon Artyrus for a beat longer than it should have. There was something fevered in the way he watched her, something so primal and tempting that she had to look away.

She'd have to quell the ever-increasing interest before she made a fool of herself. The heat crawling up her neck was indication enough that she'd let her imagination run away with her, but no more. Mastery of Otherlande would be determined only by her willingness to resist its manipulations.

And win the Merit Tourney.

The princess and her chosen adversary stood alone in the dusty court, weapons in hand. He was Chamelautean and may as well have foamed from the mouth. Baring yellowed teeth, he began circling her, towering two heads above her in height.

It would be his most significant disadvantage.

"Be careful with my precious bloom," a mocking voice bellowed from the stands. Rory didn't have to look to know that it was Philippe. "My betrothed is an orchid amongst women, is she not?" he continued. "What a shame it would be if you scarred her exquisite face."

Instinct took over as Aurora burst into action, the prince's provocation the fuel that ignited her. Her footwork was precise and feather-light in an effortless dance of combat, leaving Philippe's minion fumbling for her with plodding steps. The man grew ever more frustrated as the dirt underfoot turned into thick mud beneath him alone, leaving her wondering if the dream might somehow be aiding her in the growing conflict between Penzelle and Luther's tyrannical order.

No favors.

Rory cursed the nightmare and its bias, for the trials were meant to separate one worthy from the rest. She was no better than the king, in all his devious ways, if she couldn't prevail without mystical collusion.

Instantaneously, the mud dried, crumbling off the soldier's boot.

The crowd erupted in the stands around them when Aurora's opponent lunged for her, having been freed from his earthen shackles. She evaded him smoothly enough, his height and bulk proving the downfall she'd hoped it would be. He recovered quickly, turning to meet her in a readied stance, waiting, teasing, baiting her to make the next move. The princess obliged, running straight for him, her grip firm on the ornate hilt of Artyrus's blade.

The brute curled his upper lip in a menacing sneer as his sword nearly doubled in size before her eyes. He would kill her, given the opportunity, his intent clear as the cloudless sky above them. She was being hunted in plain sight.

"You're no match, *Princess*," he barked, saliva sputtering out of his mouth when he spoke. Her foe was doing his best to shake her resolve.

"We'll see."

Aurora charged forward with unrelenting speed, feinting to the right before pivoting left as the man swung his blade. Bending her knees, she arched backward, his sword a reflective streak flashing over her face so close she felt it brush the tips of her lashes.

She had known Philippe wished her dead after their near encounter with the black knight, but she'd not anticipated the prince would be so bold as to stage her execution as a mishap of the trials. She'd already witnessed the brutality of one lackey at the expense of a green Penzellian fighter, perhaps to prime the audience for such *incidents*.

He had severely underestimated her.

The princess twisted, tucking her shoulder into her turn. She dropped to the ground, and, sliding off to one side of her opponent, Rory used every bit of force she could manage to bring him down. Rotating in place, the warrior raised his weapon, preparing to plunge it into her chest.

Before he could strike, Aurora drove her heels into his shins. He cried out, his body swaying before falling to the earth. Rory sprang to her feet, sword in hand, set to break his pride and watch him beg. Kicking his blade aside, she raised her own, slowly lowering the gleaming metal to meet the hollow of his neck.

Then he was gone.

She whipped around in search of Artyrus. He was nowhere. There was no one in sight and not a sound in the air. Panting, she wiped the moisture from her brow with the back of her trembling hand. Tremors coursed through her body as she took in the void surrounding her.

Her thoughts raced, desperate to make sense of the nothingness as she sank to her knees in the center of the empty arena. It was as if the dream had forgotten itself. Where leaves had gently rustled, there was only stillness and quiet. Even the sun had dimmed, like a veil shrouding what had been.

Aurora.

A whisper in the unearthly absence called to her. It came from nowhere and was nothing. No more than a passing thought, a murmur somewhere deep in her subconsciousness.

A kingdom of stone and steel will soon rise...

Alone. The princess was wholly and hopelessly alone.

Preserving their kin from fated demise...

The words thundered in her veins, beckoning her to *where* or *what?* She didn't know, and yet she moved. Her steps propelled her forward, away from the ring and toward the calling of her very blood.

It had to be another manipulation like before when the stars had tried to convince her to stay, when the night had asked her to join Otherlande for good. Or perhaps it was some sort of cruel punishment for disregarding the favor proffered during her battle.

With any good fortune, Artyrus and the others had all awakened, even if it meant she had not.

Aurora.

Once more, she heard her name called, the utterance rippling the air about her. She reached out to touch the subtle waves, her fingers curling around soft lines of arid space.

"Aurora!"

She knew the voice and had not imagined it, Artyrus tearing through the curtain of muted isolation. He shook her gently, folding her into him as she found her bearings. Otherlande, somehow more vibrant and alert than before, had been restored to its initial state if she was, indeed, still asleep.

"You looked... You were—" Artyrus pulled away from Rory to examine her. "What are you *doing* out here?" he managed, his features knit with confusion.

Aurora stumbled over her thoughts, trying to unravel what had happened but found no answer.

"I searched everywhere for you after you wandered off. Ffion said—"

"Where did you go?" Aurora demanded, cutting him off. "I almost had him, then everyone was gone. Everything was different, quiet. And it spoke to me. It spoke the prophecy."

"What are you talking about?" Concern shone on his face, his gaze locked with hers. "You won. Philippe was furious, though he tried not to let it show. You mean to say that you don't remember?" Artyrus tenderly braced her arms as if to hold her in place, and Rory didn't know whether his hold was intended to steady or to keep from losing her again.

Shaking her head, the princess could not comprehend how she'd seemingly been in two places at once. Their dreams had run concurrently yet entirely separate from one another. "Our dormant thoughts and fears can force us apart. When I was with you, did I seem at all different?"

"No." Artyrus's nostrils flared when he spoke, and his tone was dismissive, perfectly at odds with the gentleness of his touch.

They hadn't been forced to meet these subconscious machinations without each other, but if the tournament that day had revealed anything, it was that nothing was definitive—no timeline, no seemingly physical presence. They could trust nothing.

"We cannot rely on each other here," Rory uttered. It was an uncomfortable truth she wished desperately to ignore, but it would be to their detriment.

"You can take care of yourself. You've proven as much on several occasions in the brief time I've known you." Sincerity shone in his lingering stare as he took Aurora's slender hand in his, her limbs still clad in armor up to her elbows. "Forgive me if I sometimes fail to remember that you do not require me at your side."

"I'll remind you, should the need arise." She smiled, and Artyrus drew her toward himself, pressing his lips to her knuckles. Rory met his fervid regard, struggling to control the riotous rhythm of her heart.

"I've no doubt." Releasing her, Artyrus searched Aurora's gaze, residual worry branding his features. "You're all right then?"

She nodded, unwilling to risk speaking for fear that her voice might betray the desire rooted deeply in her bones.

"Well, then, we are late," her guardian breathed. "There is much to be done."

Chapter Thirteen

Dressing up had never been a favorite pastime for Aurora, particularly when it involved a skirt. The traditional garb of her people was elaborate—heavily adorned with leather and fur, laden with decorative metal plates and buckles, giving the impression they'd never be unprepared for battle.

It was cumbersome but, admittedly, fabulous and something that she hadn't worn in well over a decade as she'd hidden in plain sight amongst the Chamelautean population. The prospect gave her a small thrill.

"Try this." Petra launched a floor-length gown Rory's way, the garment landing with a *thud* at her feet as Petra dug through the wooden chest for more treasures. The vacant house at the edge of the borough had been just what they needed, with Petra assuring them they'd find proper attire for the evening's festivities.

Rory retrieved the dress, appreciative of the skill with which it had been designed. The woven leather plaits of the sleeveless bodice gave way to the full, airy skirt. Beautifully crafted, the corset was so thick as to be almost like armor itself. It was also much too small.

She held the garment to her chest. "A shame this will never fit."

"Put it on," Petra commanded. She moved toward Rory with a gold-gilded pauldron and chest plate in hand, seemingly ready to force the princess into her findings at any cost.

Rather than argue, Rory did as she said, stripping away her clothing before she stepped into the tiny dress. Shimmying the fabric up over her legs then her waist and chest, she was shocked to find that it did, indeed, fit—and quite like a glove at that—yet another curiosity in a dreamscape full of them.

Strips of tanned leather crisscrossed her torso at random angles, billowing into a gauzy nest of umber from the basque waistline to her feet. A subtle shimmer shone upon the whole ensemble as if it had been sprinkled with a dusting of golden flecks, giving the faint impression that Aurora was, herself, aglow. It was breathtaking.

Without skipping a beat, Petra made for Rory, embellishing her with the ornamental armor as she attached the pieces over her shoulders and breasts. The thin metal would do little in battle, but it did much for Aurora's state of mind. For at long last, she felt like the princess she had always aspired to be in her heart, prepared to make her debut in Penzellian society as their future, their hope.

"You look just like a bloody royal!" Ffion chirped from the doorway. Rory turned to find him beaming, his boyish face earnest as he appraised her appearance anew.

"She'd better," Petra groused, having set about fixing Rory's combat-worn hair, busily twisting and braiding the tresses in much the same manner as she'd done before. "You must make an entrance tonight at the banquet. Show them all that you mean to succeed, come hell or high water."

"I think she will manage that very well," Artyrus said, entering the humble room in which they'd been preparing. Rory turned to find her guardian bedecked in the traditional Penzellian fashion—a startling sight to behold but one that suited him better than she'd ever have imagined.

Attired in a woolen kilt in hues of mossy greens and browns, he was the picture of Penzellian royalty himself. Tall black boots left him exposed at the knee, while a thick bolt of the same patterned wool formed a sash from hip to shoulder, fastened in place over a matching vest and jacket. A white linen cravat was tied at his neck, knotted and tucked into his dark waistcoat.

He was…

"Ahem." Ffion cleared his throat, glancing with amusement between the tongue-tied princess and her chaperone. He jerked his thumb toward Artyrus. "I did that."

"Indeed, he did," Artyrus agreed, having found his voice at last. He brushed the woolen kilt with the back of his hand. "This appeared to be sized for a child. I thought, perhaps, it might fit my thigh, but he insisted I try it anyway."

"A wise choice," Rory said around a giggle. "I experienced a similar phenomenon." She indicated her dress, dismissing the oddity of the whole experience with a shake of her head.

Behind her, Petra offered only a sigh as she stepped away, having completed her hair once more. "This will do."

"Not quite." Artyrus stepped toward Aurora, looking down upon his charge, who appraised him with wide, crystalline blue eyes. From within his jacket, he pulled a delicate gold crown, inset with smoky quartz and sapphire gemstones on each gentle peak and smaller gems within the narrow channel encircling the band.

"I thought this might complete your image. I..." He paused, his brows drawn as he pinched his lips together in a manner that was altogether sheepish, measuring his words. "I was thinking of you when this appeared on the windowsill where I was dressing. While I do not wish to flaunt your title, I thought you would wear it well."

Rory nodded, ignoring the heat blooming in her cheeks when he slipped the crown onto her head. Smiling shyly, she took in her form in the standing mirror that conveniently revealed itself.

She was ready.

* * * *

The foursome entered the banquet to uproarious applause, and Aurora was amazed at the sheer volume of, well, *everything*. Held in a rather untraditional venue, the villagers had gathered in the meadows just beyond the forbidden, dragon-inhabited castle, though the creature was nowhere in sight.

The sky was bathed in unusual tones of blush and periwinkle where the sun hung low, with just a crescent of its radiance visible on the horizon. Echoes from the surf far beyond filled the air, with the light scent of salt and sea breezing through the gathering. It was all remarkably normal.

Set beneath a smattering of twilight stars, which offered their light alongside candlelit chandeliers suspended by nothing but the heavens themselves, the tables were laid with delicacies from the whole of Fayble.

Luscious fruits that Rory hadn't seen since her childhood were arrayed in all the colors of a rainbow. Platters of meats and cheeses were spread like a mosaic over the table's surface, spilling from the edges, intermingled with trays of crackers stacked as high as a man and tureens of sauces.

Pastries. Candies. Cakes. *Chocolates*. There was no end to the wonders provided for their feasting. It was as grand an affair as Rory had ever seen, and so it was to be for each night of the tourney. A shame that all the delights could not be savored with the same enjoyment to be had in reality.

"Till my heart's content, says I!" Ffion shouted, pulling Petra into the fray. The woman was less than pleased to be dragged away but followed along behind him nonetheless, her affinity for the boy evident.

"It seems we'll be celebrating like royalty." Aurora sampled a tart topped with a brilliant orange marmalade, sighing as she recalled the memory of its flavor.

"That's fitting for one of us, then," Artyrus replied, his attention captured by something in the distance.

Rory followed his gaze, spying a font of mead flowing like a river.

"Are you thirsty?" she asked, eager to know if some of his most basic senses were returning to him.

He shook his head. "It isn't that. Those men there." He indicated two individuals who stood beside the fountain. Unlike the vast majority of attendants, they were not clad in kilts, instead wearing the armor of Prince Philippe's men.

Rory inched closer, pitching her voice low, though it was much too loud to matter. "Who are they?"

"The men who raised me. Two of the three, at any rate."

She looked again a second time, taken aback by the revelation. For some reason, it felt more realistic for Rory to imagine Artyrus emerging from the woods a fully-grown man from the time of his origins, rather than having had any intervention from anyone, soldier or otherwise.

"Ector and Kaye, father and son," Artyrus continued. "And Lord Pelinore. The three of them shared responsibility for me. They're all I remember — nothing before them, not my parents. Pelinore took me in, little foundling that I was, my parents long since dead. Saved me from certain death on the street, in truth."

He glanced away, with his thoughts seemingly lost to another time. "I began as a page when I'd grown old enough for duty, and before long, I became Sir Kaye's squire. The three of them taught me everything I know, made me who I am — an unusual arrangement, to be sure, but I'm eternally in their debt."

"Raised by three men." Rory smiled, eying him sideways. "That explains a lot — but do go on."

A smirk formed upon his face, despite the solemnity of his sentiments. "From Sir Ector, I received the gift of perseverance, while Sir Kaye taught me the elements of cunning and artifice. And from Lord Pelinore, I obtained the gift of wisdom. Like guardian angels, they."

Rory couldn't have agreed more, for Artyrus was, indeed, firmly rooted in each of the principles he'd named. "Is Pelinore here as well?"

"I wonder." Artyrus shifted in place, searching the gathering and appearing somewhat bewildered. "Their presence here at all is confounding. They'd be here for him." With a nod of his head, he indicated the despicable Prince Philippe, who was surrounded by all manner of soldiers and a handful of women who had, apparently, never had the pleasure of encountering the real version of him that existed beneath his cool, captivating facade.

"Speak to them," said Aurora, pleased to facilitate a reunion. "Perhaps they can give us some clues if they're also consciously unconscious as we are." She raised a finger, staying his emerging objection. "I'll be here filling my belly with tasteless delicacies. What trouble could I possibly find?"

"Plenty," he grumbled, though humor filled his features. "Behave." He walked away, casting a warning glance over his shoulder.

Rory waved him off, making for the food and wishing that she could enjoy it with all her senses, but it was not to be. With each disappointing bite, she felt very much like sulking, just as she saw her opponent from her afternoon battle doing not far from her, though his attitude was likely due to his resounding defeat and not the flavorless buffet.

If only she could recall her victory.

"I thought it was you."

Rory glanced up, her gaze meeting that of an attractive man that she, too, recognized though she could not think how. Eyes so dark they were nearly black matched the inklike tone of his cropped hair, with both features shining like the moon above. His broad shoulders were clad in the armor of Chamelaute, and his lips...

"How are you, Gwen?" He smiled, showcasing a mouthful of straight, bright white teeth as she struggled to recover her beguiled wits.

"*Lancelot*," she breathed, a grin she could not hope to suppress forming on her overwarm face. "Why, I've not seen you for some—"

"Seven years, darling," he replied, moving nearer. "Since I moved from squire to knight."

"Yes, that's it."

"And I've not seen you since you were my Gwenivere, since before you were promised to a kingdom and a prince." His bold gaze stripped her bare, roving from her head to her toes as he attempted to make sense of her transformation.

"I've ever been promised to them both since birth," she replied, having, at last, overcome her surprise. "And I am no longer Gwenivere. I've embraced my destiny as Aurora. No longer must I hide."

"Indeed. And a princess at that. I admit I'd never have guessed your royal lineage in our youth as we practiced our swordplay in the mud or picked berries in the wilds outside of Hampshire." He held out his hand, the joy upon his handsome face making everything about the eventide banquet more compelling. "Dance with me?"

"I'd love to."

Memories from their youth flooded Rory's mind as Lancelot took her in his arms. He smelled faintly of strawberries — something she was certain wasn't real at the moment but a mere remembrance of their history.

Rory laughed when Lancelot extended his arm. She twirled beneath it, spinning into his embrace and back out again. Standing face to face, they moved, her hands held tightly within his as they followed the customary steps. All around them, the people kept in time with the music, merrily celebrating with a dance known to the whole of Fayble. "Your skills have improved."

"I should hope so, given that the last time we did this, we were fourteen." He pulled her closer, and she felt nothing less than desired — a sensation she'd had not for a very long time. It was in his strong hold, the curve of his smiling lips.

Silence fell between them as they continued their movements, though it was familiar. Effortless. She'd forgotten what it was to have the attention of one so direct, not having experienced his regard for nearly a decade. In her youth, she had imagined such things, cocky though he was and too busy about his boyhood to devote much effort to the pursuit of her.

But it was a far different encounter in womanhood.

"You're needed," came a brusque voice. Aurora was quickly separated from the arms of Lancelot, instead finding herself drawn along behind a sullen Artyrus, who made no effort to slow his retreat from the banquet.

Behind her, Lancelot stood, his lower lip between his teeth as if he were attempting to stifle a laugh. He offered a casual wave, a promise of more to come clear in his eyes as he watched her go.

Aurora followed Artyrus into the woods, anxiety muddling her mind. He seemed inordinately unsettled, and for one who rarely showed such levels of emotion, it was highly disconcerting. "What is it?" she gasped when they slowed. "Was your conversation with your guardians poor?"

Moonlight filtered through the trees, illuminating Artyrus's frame with fragmented light. "Think, Aurora!" he snapped. "You were making an utter spectacle of yourself! You are Prince Philippe's betrothed, whether you want it to be so or not, and your passionate dance with his right-hand man will do you no favors."

"Lancelot is —"

"Is the commander of his army," Artyrus continued, his tone heavily laced with resentment. "Philippe will not even blink before having you punished, betrothed or not. Hell, he very nearly ended your life this afternoon! And Lancelot." He paused, running a hand over his face in frustration. "Do not demean yourself with one such as he."

Without a thought, Rory's palm collided with his cheek, her swat causing his head to jolt sideways when her anger spiked. His response was instantaneous as he caught her wrists within his grasp, pinning them above her head upon the tree behind her. His hold was almost gentle, standing in stark contrast with the fury covering his face. "Do not strike me!"

"Don't speak to me like that!" She strained toward him, rising on tiptoe. Their faces were within a single breath of one another, her temper running away with her. "You act like I can't handle myself!"

"You act without thinking!" He dropped his chin, his gaze falling to her lips, and Rory shivered under his scrutiny. He was overbearing.

Arrogant.

"Oh." Ffion appeared beside them, eyes wide as he took in the scene before him. He smiled, wandering away as he cast a sly glance over his shoulder. "I figured as much."

Chapter Fourteen

Artyrus needed space, needed to separate himself from the distractions — everything that made him question his instincts, his sanity.

He needed away from *her*.

Aurora's inability to control her impulses and her damned attitude made him boil. But the worst part was how much he liked it. She would be his undoing.

Already, piece by piece, he felt her pilfering from him anything she wished. He'd allowed her extra time in Llundyn and followed her into the forsaken nightmare without so much as a second thought. Sure, he'd told himself it was his duty, that he'd vowed to protect her.

And so he had.

But he knew it was more. He knew the smell of spring was woven through her long raven tresses, the color dark as a moonless night. And then there was her flawless, tawny skin set against those fathomless crystal eyes that rendered him senseless as he considered all the sorrow, triumph and vulnerability stirring in their depths.

Yet none of it mattered, for she was Penzelle's sole heir and promised to another man at that.

Betrothed — even if Phillippe did want her dead.

Artyrus wandered into town away from Rory, hoping that somehow, mercifully, he could silence his thoughts. She'd been so close to him, so incredibly close. Otherlande possessed a cruel sense of humor, dangling before him the very thing he craved, the woman who hoarded every bit of his focus for herself.

He'd done well enough as he roamed, burying his unseemly regard for the princess until, from the shadows, a soft whistle sounded from before him. He knew it was meant for him alone as the quiet notes lilted his way, a trill from his youth established to alert when one of his trusted keepers was on his trail.

Only the orphan himself and his comrade-in-arms, his greatest confidant, knew that warning — the sound that at once made him flee without explanation from romantic interludes and drunken nights in dilapidated taverns when he'd thought he could sneak off unnoticed.

Kaye.

They were brothers in every sense of the word, apart from blood. He was four years wiser and stood three inches shorter than Artyrus, the latter of which the guardian never let his friend forget.

Deeper darkness than the blanket of eventide shrouded the warrior, his armor catching only a faint twinkle from the flames lighting a nearby veranda. Kaye's mouth tipped at the edges with a hint of a smile, which vanished as Artyrus approached, the urgency in his brother's shaded face unmistakable.

The guardian's eyes were just adjusting to the silhouette when recognition seized him — that armor. It was the same suit of silver that he had seen before when Ffion revealed Prince Philippe's violent intent through the trio of marauders.

"Don't say a word." Kaye's voice was barely above a whisper, his tone harsh and crisp as winter as he stood stock still with his helmet resting casually under one arm. He'd flickered out of sight with his father when Artyrus had last seen them.

"I...*please*, I can't—" The knight's features were pinched, concentration straining his watchful eyes. His form shuddered a bit where he stood in the shadows, not his unwavering bearing but his essence. The entirety of his frame blinked as if will and presence covertly warred for command over him.

Artyrus would have laughed at the theatrics had his brother's tone not been so solemn. He was always careful.

Ffion warned them of the three ominous soldiers sweeping through Otherlande atop unearthly steeds, unlike anything he'd ever seen in consciousness. And Kaye was one of them, clad in the same gleaming silver metal, now cautioning Artyrus against the lurking threat.

"So it's true." Artyrus kept his voice low as he watched Kaye struggle against himself. Was he in pain? He almost looked to be, but his words of caution rang through Artyrus, still unfamiliar enough with the dream to know whether it possessed the ability to turn a man, even as steadfast as Kaye, against himself and his family. His hand hovered near the hilt of his sword just in case. "The black knight and his men... *You* hunt a rogue royal."

Kaye's tight nod of confirmation was enough to make Artyrus's stomach churn. How far would the order to kill or subdue reach?

And yet, the knight had still come to warn him, no matter how vague or cryptic the encounter might be.

Kaye swallowed hard, like a thought or other utterances of caution were stuck to the back of his throat. When his voice finally broke free, it was not his but Philippe's as he said, "You will take them both, by whatever means. No risk shall remain standing."

He choked as if it had taken all his effort to expose what little he knew. If it had, indeed, been Philippe's direct command spoken through his friend's lips, then it was likely he was restraining himself against attack. "Trust no one," Kaye said, his words his own once more, hurried as they were.

Under traditional circumstances, Artyrus would never have imagined the possibility of their loyalty crumbling for any reason. Still, he didn't know what level of awareness, if any, the knight possessed. His actions and impulses were unpredictable at best.

"And Ector?"

Kaye's only response was a look of remorse that flashed through his eyes. His form flickered again, the muscles in his jaw clenched.

"Why are you doing this?" Artyrus could see the internal battle, a storm of purpose thundering beneath his brother's menacing exterior.

"They have Pelinore," Kaye heaved, the words bursting forth as he disappeared for a beat. Then two. He appeared again as the sheer force of determination beaded over his brow, sweat dripping down his temple. "You know him, the black knight. He's —" The warrior clutched his neck like the revelation might brand itself in his throat, the truth seemingly strangling him.

"Artyrus."

He heard her, breathlessly speaking his name. He and his brother may have been cloaked in shadows, but she was not. Aurora's countenance contorted into an expression of wary frustration as she attempted to make sense of the scene unfolding before her.

Why had she followed him?

Kaye saw her, too, a brief hint of mischief gleaming in his eyes. "Yet another reason for him to hate you."

Artyrus could only surmise his meaning. Philippe had always disliked him. He'd hated him as he'd proven his capability again and again in the Chamelautean ranks and even more as King Luther had acknowledged his prowess.

Movement caught his attention, a coal-black form reflecting against the mirrored armor upon Kaye's chest. It drew nearer, closing the distance between them. His brother saw it then, the black knight, and Artyrus was certain he read an apology in Kaye's pointed regard, noting the shift in his stance.

Kaye raised a brow in challenge, clenching his fingers into a fist before plunging it into Artyrus's stomach.

Rory gasped as her rapid footfalls drew nearer, her lithe figure only a blur in Artyrus's periphery when she rushed toward him. The hit had merely knocked the air from his lungs but hadn't doubled him over, though, under ordinary circumstances, Kaye would never hold back.

He couldn't hesitate, not with Aurora quickly approaching and unaware of the black knight's presence. Kaye had bought him time and an unpleasant moment of clarity. Artyrus went rigid, and he swore he saw his brother wince as he rolled his shoulders into position.

Drawing his elbow back, he threw his weight into the punch, his knuckles colliding with Kaye's jaw. It was hard enough to jolt his head backward, and he slumped, perhaps not entirely for show, but there was no time to find out.

The black knight was closing in on them. Without sparing another glance at his friend, Artyrus bolted for Rory, who was still charging forward with his sword firmly gripped in her hand. He could fight the assassin, of course, but it was too much to risk with the princess there. If he fell, she would be forced to face the midnight soldier alone.

"*Run!*" Artyrus roared. He very nearly slammed into Aurora, taking her by the elbow to alter her route. She sheathed her sword as they ran, easily matching his long strides with the speed and endurance of a trained fighter. Pride rippled through him, but the crunch of gravel behind them stayed his focus. He could hear the knight's ragged breath as he chased them, tracking them around corners and through dimly lit alleyways.

Together, Artyrus and the princess swerved through every passage and street toward the village center until finally, they broke free from their pursuer. Doubtless, he would continue searching, but for the moment, they'd found cover and a beat to steady their racing hearts.

"I think we lost him." Rory's voice was hoarse from exertion when she glanced behind them, tense relief flooding her paled features.

In a barn near the center of town, they found shelter. It smelled of wood rot and straw, even with Artyrus's muted senses, but it was a more than welcome hideaway. Aurora scrambled up a ladder, crawling into the loft overhead. It creaked softly beneath her as she made her way farther back, away from the edge and out of sight.

Pulling himself upward, Artyrus settled beside her in the small open space, with long yellow stalks of hay in mounds all around them. He'd barely caught his breath when he turned to look at Rory.

Part of him continued to seethe from their earlier quarrel, but still, she had followed him.

Her gaze was cold in return, and rather than the turbulent sea he'd grown accustomed to seeing in her eyes, all he saw was ice.

Good.

"You shouldn't have left us like that." Her sharp words hung between them, but Artyrus couldn't bring himself to apologize. Aurora sat there, waiting for him to respond, but when he didn't, she continued. "What if something had happened?"

He scoffed. "You always remind me how capable you are. I was only allowing you the room to prove it. Make up your mind, Aurora." His bitter words revealed more than he'd intended, and Rory seemed to grasp as much when her glacial gaze narrowed on him.

"What happened after my fight?" Her inquiry demanded a confession and one he wasn't ready to share. Certainly not then, and perhaps not ever.

"It's of no consequence." A lie. For Artyrus, it was.

"Do I not deserve to know? Should I not be aware of how I spent the remainder of my day when my *mind* couldn't be bothered to be there?" Fear threaded through her tone—a sliver of desperation that nearly weakened Artyrus's resolve.

"If you weren't permitted to see it, maybe it wasn't meant for you." The idea was not bred purely from his attempt at evasion, but he had considered the theory endlessly since he found her alone, lost within herself.

"Do *not* play me for a fool, Artyrus." Palpable anger dripped from each syllable, her petite form shifting toward him as if she might slap him again.

He felt the sting in his cheek like she had, at any rate.

But she did deserve to be informed, for what if she'd not been with him but Philippe instead? Or Lancelot? The princess braced herself, her body conveying every bit of resentment she bore.

"You were attentive and kind," Artyrus began, *disarming,* though he didn't dare say it. He paused, weighing how much of their time together he wished to recount.

Together, they'd wandered far off from where Petra and Ffion had settled, and he'd been wholly spellbound. He couldn't tell her how her fingertips brushed down his spine when she'd approached him and left a trail of flames in their wake.

"That's all?" Rory didn't soften with his scant report, but Artyrus saw that some distant part of her knew everything he wouldn't say. Or maybe he merely hoped.

"You took my hands, and you..." Her prodding had again challenged his will, the words he kept to himself slipping away one by one. "You wrapped yourself in my arms, and I held you."

When Aurora intertwined her fingers with his, he prayed that she would remember. Something about the satin flesh of her palm against his calloused hands dragged him deeper into the acknowledgment of what had transpired, wholly and unreservedly—a vain courtship of recklessness carved upon his soul.

"My breath rustled your hair, and when you looked at me, Aurora..." Her breath caught at his words, shattering any hope of restraint he'd maintained. "It was devastating."

It had wrecked him when her lips grazed over the line of his jaw, so gently that he'd shivered at the contact. She ruined him when she'd whispered a plea in his ear for only him to hear.

He cursed himself for the confessions that tumbled forth, truths he wished to keep all to himself. At last, he understood the pained look on Kaye's face when he'd spoken as he grappled for control. Doubtless, his friend wanted to tell him everything, fought to reveal what he knew of Philippe's schemes, but his subconsciousness wouldn't authorize it.

The dream wasn't at fault, nor did it have power over anyone. Fear and uncertainty, any vulnerability would be exploited unless suppressed. The guardian cursed himself for falling prey to impulse.

Rory studied him, her cheeks flushed with color, but when she opened her mouth to speak, he took his hand from hers. The admissions he'd laid bare settled between them, but he wouldn't wait to see how she might respond. Some piece of him felt it, the reciprocation of his yearning, almost as if she'd said it aloud.

"You're betrothed." Truth cleaved the silence into unmet desire, its influence more savage than whetted steel.

Aurora scrunched her nose in contempt, bewilderment evident in her gaze.

The prince may well hate him, but no more than she seemingly did.

Chapter Fifteen

There was really no proper way to prepare for a melee, least of all when it was taking place inside a world with a mind all its own. Rory had made it through her first bout by the skin of her teeth, having nearly been run through from behind with a pike wielded by one of Prince Philippe's minions.

Resting in one of the numerous tents designated for the competitors, Rory sat with Petra and Ffion, awaiting the next trying round of the tourney. Her nerves rollicked through her with all the subtlety of a stampeding herd, resisting every effort she made to bring them under control.

She was off her game, her thoughts distracted by, well...*him*. Her conversation with Artyrus hovered in the back of her head, diverting her attention as she dodged blows and jabs from her betrothed's stooges. The same could not be said for Artyrus, who sailed through his bout in the rotation before hers with all the agility of a seasoned soldier.

That only served to make her mood darker still. Had he not been affected at all?

"Given your lapses in the previous round, I wouldn't be surprised if you meet your end." Petra glanced in Rory's direction before huffing upon her fine silver blowpipe, shining it with the linen of her blouse's sleeve. "With your beloved putting a target on your back, you'll need more than luck to stay alive."

"Luck will have nothing to do with it." Rory worked to suppress her resentment for the blunt woman. "Only wit and skill can save you in the arena. And do not call that serpent my beloved."

"I've some pastry I stole away with last night. It reappears every time I think I've finished it, so I might as well share," Ffion piped up, ever the arbiter in the never-ending disagreements shared between the two. With a cheerful smile, he bestowed his gifts upon the women.

Rory accepted, idly nibbling the pastry, though it did little for her in terms of distraction. She appreciated his attempt at the least. A moment later, Artyrus arrived, his countenance inordinately grave. He glanced around the tent, his gaze landing upon Aurora.

"We need to talk." He jerked his thumb toward the entrance. The impatience with which he spoke had her on edge.

"What's wrong?" Rory rose to her feet, ignoring the way her heart accelerated with his presence. Her body ached, laden with heavy armor from head to toe that shrieked with her every step. Tucking her helmet under her arm, she followed him out, uncertain as to which version of him she would find — the man who was attentive or the one distant and cold.

"What's happened to you?" Standing face to face outside the tent, Artyrus reached for Rory before thinking better of it, instead running his hand across his stubbled chin.

Great.

This would be detached Artyrus, Rory decided, having become increasingly familiar with his mannerisms. Perhaps that was for the best, however, given her current state of mind.

"At the melee," he continued, holding her gaze. "You were out of sorts. More than once, I nearly intervened. You've got to get your head on straight before you lose it."

"*That*," Rory fumed, "is your fault! Everything you told me in the loft and the many things that I know you kept to yourself." She clenched her fists at her sides, incredulous that he could be so obtuse. "And you weren't distracted at all during your bout!"

"I thought of nothing *but* you!" he fired back, his dark eyes ablaze like a roaring pyre. "Everything I'm doing, Aurora, my sole focus is for your safety! For we've no real understanding of what may become of you should you perish in this fantastical hellscape."

"Oh, but we do." Prince Philippe stood just beyond the pair. He smiled, seemingly eager to use the information he'd gained from their run-in to his advantage. "I thought you were both a little too aware here to be simple dreamers. Still, being the benevolent future king that I am, I'll give you a clue—die in this *hellscape*, and you're done for in reality."

From the doorway, Ffion whistled through his teeth while Petra stared murderously at the prince. He was as unwelcome as ever, and now he was equipped with knowledge about the princess and her companions that was best kept under wraps.

"It was a stroke of luck that you ended up here with me in this place," Philippe continued, his mood unaltered by the onlookers. "Indeed, it is due to the prospect of your demise alone that I've welcomed your participation in the tourney. Stars know it's no place for a woman, though you've put on a better show than I'd ever imagined possible."

"And you," he added, turning to Artyrus. "Her good fortune is coming to an end. You seem rather attached, even as your loyalty should remain with *me*. Prepare yourself for her death."

"It goes both ways, you know," Ffion snapped. "You could die in the arena as easily as anybody else!"

Petra stepped around Ffion, making for the entitled royal without hesitation, and though she was a head smaller than he, her courage made the difference. "There are other ways to die here more painful than a sword to the gut or a mace to the skull. But if that doesn't get you, you'll lose your mind anyhow. Death in its own way, as you'll never be who you once were again."

She glowered at the prince as silence fell, her threat hanging in the stifling air as he absorbed her savage tongue lashing. Petra took Ffion by the hand without another word, escorting him away from the confrontation.

"Sunshine in a bottle, she," Philippe mused, backing away from Rory with a vicious little smirk before he turned, making his way toward the arena.

The trumpet sounded, summoning the competitors. Artyrus watched Aurora for a moment, concern written on the planes of his face. He seemed to understand, as only he could, that she was far from ready for the fight that lay ahead. She briefly closed her eyes, preparing herself to yield to the demands of their strange, unified dream.

"You've already won," Artyrus uttered, gently tucking her disheveled tresses behind her ear, his fingertips brushing the flesh of her neck. "Whether we awaken or slumber for eternity, you are hope personified. Your legacy will endure."

Awed by his unexpected sentiments, Aurora nodded, desperate to keep her tears at bay. Artyrus was a man of few words, but more often than not, his passion got the better of her. She made to go, only to be drawn toward him as he took her by the elbow.

"Bring them to their knees, Valkyrie," he growled. She shivered when his warm breath kissed her ear, her courage swiftly soaring.

The pair entered the arena, again finding an abundance of familiar weaponry. Hammers and flails, spears and clubs. It was a veritable treasure trove of death-dealing, but Rory was determined not to succumb, vowing to keep her wits about her.

The few precious moments she'd spent with Artyrus had helped more than they had angered her, giving her the will to focus. Of course, there was added pressure in the forthcoming round, as he would be joining her in the ring.

That wouldn't be distracting at all.

Some two dozen participants stood at varying intervals from one another, surrounded by the assorted arms scattered about the packed-dirt floor. Spying a mace through the T-shaped slit in her helmet, Rory prepared to dive for the weapon as the trumpet blared once more.

Beside her, Rory watched as Artyrus acquired a poleaxe, easily wielding the long shaft as he turned to meet a nearby opponent. Just as quickly, she found herself facing off against a Chamelautean brute, the sun glinting off the steel of his armor as he swung for her.

A wicked metal ball covered in spikes whizzed past her chest as she arched backward, her movements inhibited by the infernal armor. She pivoted to her left, spinning from his sphere of destruction before striking him in return. The edge of her mace collided with his shielded ribs, hitting with so much force that it left an imprint in his plackart.

The soldier issued a gravelly howl, somewhere between pain and fury, as he made for her again. Dodging his advance, she bent at the waist, narrowly avoiding the whirl of his flail as she stood once more, a handful of dust within her grasp.

Rory took a deep breath, holding her hand close to the gap within her damnable helmet as she blew, the cloud of dirt obscuring her opponent's face and seemingly filling his lungs in one fell swoop. The earthen fog followed him with every movement he made, looming about his head like a haze of gnats.

The man coughed and choked, clawing at his face with his hands to no avail. Tears streamed from his eyes as he suffocated, and again, Rory found herself at odds with the dream and its absurd favors. She couldn't help but watch, a strange sense of awe overtaking her as he failed before her. In a truly unexpected twist, she found that she felt sorry for him in his agony.

From behind her besieged foe, a Penzellian competitor arose, cuffing the man with a plank to the side of his skull, leveling him to the ground in front of Aurora. The hulking soldier lay in a heap, motionless before he disappeared without a trace of his presence — a phenomenon with which she would never come to terms.

The Penzellian man seemed unaffected by the Chamelautean's departure, offering only a quick bow before retreating himself. It was at once a mercy, a relief, but also another undesired favor.

"So that's how it works."

Rory turned to find Prince Philippe smugly watching as she gathered herself. Without another word, he lunged toward her, taking a swing with a club aimed at her knees. She leapt from his strike, hopping just quickly enough to avoid a devastating impact.

"You let others do the work for you. How utterly *royal* of you," Philippe chided, moving nearer still. "Whether it's this shared delusion or some minion, you always benefit to the detriment of others." He sneered, glancing at Artyrus, who was embroiled with none other than Lancelot not far from her.

Wielding her mace as a club, Rory's weapon clashed with Philippe's, the reverberation from the collision zinging up her arms and rocking her to her very core. Again and again, they struck, raining blows upon one another with unrelenting effort. But try as she might, Rory couldn't bring herself to focus entirely, her gaze drifting toward her companion as he engaged with Lancelot.

Distraction. The dream had its way yet again, utilizing the one thing, the one person who could draw her attention to bewilder her by his mere existence.

"This should be relatively easy." Philippe swung, his stroke glancing off her shoulder and dangerously close to her head. "Maybe the people won't be so angry now when I end you. They're finally starting to forget what matters. Perhaps a few more days and this place will be nothing shy of a definitive wonderland."

"You'd like that, wouldn't you," Rory snarled. "For presiding over a mindless people is likely all you could handle." She met his resistance with a ferocity she'd never before achieved, even as she ached over the truth of his words. Her time to recover her people was rapidly dwindling, and she'd not yet accomplished anything of note.

Beside her, Artyrus's battle with Lancelot had severely devolved as the two men had moved on from weaponry to hand-to-hand combat. Artyrus slapped the helmet from Lancelot's head with an open palm, only to suffer the same fate himself. The pair grappled, wrestling with their arms locked around one another's necks before issuing gut-wrenching thrusts with their fists.

Risking a quick glance about herself, Rory noted the eyes of nearly everyone gathered around her on the two sparring men, their adversarial pursuits captivating the whole of the audience as they pummeled each other.

A deafening blast signaled the end of the melee, bringing the first of two finals to a close. Rory backed away from Philippe, taking her first deep breath in what felt like hours and shocked to find that she was tired.

That was a surprising first—a sensation she'd not felt since she was awake. The realization gave her pause.

She was losing herself.

Ten participants remained on their feet, each in various states of ruin. Ten more would make their way through the melee scheduled later, only to find themselves in the tourney's final round, participating in the joust. At last, the end of her quest was in sight, but Rory knew none of it would come easily.

"We would be here for days if nobody stopped you," Philippe called to Lancelot, shaking his hand when the knight came nearer. "And you," the prince continued, indicating Artyrus, "you seem to have forgotten your allegiance is to king and kingdom. All your gallivanting about in Penzellian kilts has me doubting your loyalty. Indeed, it seems you intend to possess everything that belongs to me."

There was a lethal glint to Philippe's eyes that had Rory's skin crawling. He was ruthless, demanding — and, by all accounts, hers.

She could think of no crueler fate.

"I am ever duty-bound," Artyrus replied, though his gaze was pinned to Aurora alone. Heat suffused her from her head to her toes, the double meaning in his words thrilling her as much as they stung.

"I've no doubt," Lancelot agreed, his handsome face bearing an arrogant smirk as he moved toward Rory. Taking her hand, he led her away from Philippe and Artyrus.

The arena surrounding them faded into a forest of green, a light mist filling the air as the earthen floor transformed into a field of strawberries. But it wasn't just any field. It was the very clearing from their childhood.

Glancing down, she was stunned again to find her armor gone, replaced with her favorite blue gown from the age of fourteen, and when she touched her hair, she found it tied in a loose braid like she'd worn in her youth. Beside her, Lancelot was fitted in a crisp white tunic and buckskin breeches — the last thing she'd seen him in before he'd left Hampshire to pursue knighthood.

"How did you—?"

"A little dream trick I picked up," Lancelot said without hesitation. His willingness to acknowledge their state of mind caught Rory off guard, but she appreciated his candor.

He stopped in the middle of the meadow, taking her other hand in his. The scent of strawberries infused her senses, overwhelming her with nostalgia as she met his gaze. His confidence never failed to make an impression upon her, and though they'd not seen one another in nearly a decade, the familiarity of it all was enough to ease her weary mind.

"All right," Aurora began. "Perhaps the 'how' is a bit hazy for me. Let's try 'why'."

Lancelot's smile grew. "I was jealous."

That was not what she'd expected. She waited, knowing that more would follow, for he'd always worn his heart upon his sleeve.

"It pains me to see you look at Artyrus the way you do, though we both know his integrity would never permit him to pursue you." He stroked her chin with the pad of his thumb, his dark eyes simmering with unrestrained desire. "He is ever duty-bound, just as he said. And though I've no doubt that he cares for you, his obligations reign. They always have. His guilt would eat him alive."

She watched him, rapt by his honesty, even as the truth of his words settled deep within her soul. She knew it to be so, felt the bite of their validity, though she was certain he meant her no ill as he voiced his sentiments.

And while it hurt to come to terms with the reality therein, she could not bring herself to hold Artyrus's honorable nature against him. It would be akin to being angry at the sun for rising as it did each morning — a natural circumstance for which there was no alteration.

"I understand," he continued, "that you are betrothed to Philippe, and I would never aim to jeopardize your union. But unlike Artyrus, I harbor no such qualms where integrity is concerned. For some seven years now, I've dreamt of this — our last encounter. I've missed you, my Gwenivere."

Chapter Sixteen

It had been seven years since Rory had been there with him — a time almost as incredible as the memory Lancelot recreated for her. Every detail appeared just as she recalled it, and there were even some she'd entirely forgotten.

Crawling vines surrounded them, weaving across the earth with enough strawberries to satisfy a small village. It was more beautiful than she remembered. The princess felt her old friend's fingertips lightly graze over the back of her hand as he moved past her and tried to quell the euphoria overwhelming her senses.

"Tell me you like it." Lancelot's lip twitched, tipping up in half a smirk when he turned toward her. Aurora knew it wasn't reassurance he needed, but only to hear her praise for the gesture. He was the picture of arrogance as his eyes, dark as coal, held hers.

"I'm not answering that." Averting her gaze, she couldn't help the smile that formed.

"I despised Brecc after you told me."

Rory's grin widened with his admission as she suppressed a laugh. She hadn't heard that name, nor had she thought of the boy it belonged to since the day she last stood in the same field with Lancelot.

He was a man now, Brecc was, but had been fifteen years old when he'd kissed her behind Drustan's forge. They'd all trained together as children, and Aurora had been the only girl in her village who could wield a broadsword, thanks to her caregiver's lessons.

"Was it your intention to torture me?" Lancelot asked with a grin.

Not a thought came into his mind that he was unwilling to share, and it seemed that hadn't changed. Once, seven years ago, the princess had believed she was in love with him. Lancelot was taller now, his muscles more defined and prominent, but he was much the same as that day in the meadow.

This day.

She'd allowed Brecc to kiss her, though he was merely a friend to her. But it was the knight before her that she'd wanted, and she had, indeed, meant to torment him. For all his teasing and conceit, she needed him to see that she wouldn't wait forever.

"Oh, he was handsome, was he not?" Rory bit the inside of her cheek, anticipating a haughty retort. "Besides, you surely kept busy as well."

She knew he understood her meaning when he raised a dark brow. A wicked grin highlighted laugh lines she'd never before noticed on his face, likely developed over their years apart.

"Never," Lancelot said after a beat, his dark regard narrowing as he studied her unabashedly. "You, *Gwen*, were all I wanted." Plucking a strawberry from the vines at his feet, he sank his teeth into it like he'd said nothing of note.

He thrust his hand through his dark hair, pushing it back as he watched her closely. "You'll always be her to me...Gwenivere." The name was like velvet on his tongue. Provocative. Magnetic.

"And yet, you never once visited." She'd hated herself for waiting for him, for doing the very thing she'd sought to prove she wouldn't.

"I thought you were happy. You told me you were, that *he* made you happy, and was it not honesty we'd pledged to one another?" Something like anger shone in his eyes, but whether toward Aurora for her deception or Brecc for his disloyalty, she couldn't know. He scoffed, the enigmatic depth returning to his gaze. "Though, I suppose I broke it, too."

"We were children." Rory's words were dismissive and not entirely true, for sometimes, she wondered if she'd been more attuned to her destiny in her youth.

Time had a way of warping both perspective and will, and despite years of preparation, the princess had never believed her time to lead would come. Artyrus seemed to nurture that providence. He fought for it.

Aurora's mind drifted to her guardian, where he was, and whether she might still be with him in the strange way the dream allowed. Was he afraid for her or furious that she'd willingly vanished with a man he loathed?

I am ever duty-bound.

She wouldn't allow herself to dwell on what he said before Lancelot ushered her into lost reveries. It would be a perilous ascent for Rory and her guardian to conquer, and even if they somehow succeeded, fate would never concede so much esteem as to grant them a future together.

"Philippe would have his head before he'd ever let Artyrus have you," Lancelot said. He had always been perceptive, but *this?* She didn't want him to recognize any of it.

"How interesting." The princess seized the opportunity to change the subject, even if it meant nudging the conversation toward savagery. "I thought it was my head the prince wanted to see severed."

Lancelot cocked his head to one side, his arresting features knit in a dangerous frown. "I would kill him myself if he tried."

She believed him...always.

"You did well against him today," he continued, taking a step toward her, and the girl she once was welcomed his nearness. He smiled again as if sensing the tranquility he'd afforded through his presence alone. "I confess, it did me no favor against that keeper of yours to be so distracted as I was, the bloodthirsty beast."

Laughing, even as her heart fluttered, Aurora thought of Artyrus mercilessly felling his opponents beside her. It came as no surprise that Lancelot was a worthy contender and did not attempt to remove the threats she faced, convinced of her aptitude in matters of combat.

Favor. He'd not uttered the idea with any hint of accusation, the mention a pure suggestion of flattery, but it consumed her, nonetheless.

"Teach me how to do this." Rory indicated the field, dotted with red against a lush green backdrop. Otherlande had assisted Rory again in the melee, but she didn't want anyone or anything's help unsought.

She had no qualms about using the oddities her slumber might provide if she could learn how to wield them effectively, but she wouldn't sit idly by while the dream decided whether to help or destroy her.

"What good is this to you?" Lancelot advanced closer to her, near enough to stroke the swell of her cheek with his knuckle as he met her eyes, his gaze lingering. He was so casual in his buckskin breeches, the same Lancelot she would have followed anywhere if he'd asked. But he never had, and she had become a wholly different person in their time apart.

"Would you not rather mend our failures? Perhaps, pretend I never left Hampshire at all?"

Her voice caught in her throat, and her pulse quickened the way it always used to when he read her unspoken thoughts as if they were his favorite story. But he winked, a fiendish flicker of amusement lighting the alluring blackness of his eyes. She supposed it was an act of clemency, as she had almost forgotten what she'd asked of him or why.

"If I'm to survive this nightmare and my people are to awaken intact, I'll need to understand how to manipulate these anomalies." The validity of Rory's concern was enough to prevent the warmth from further blooming in her cheeks. "I can conjure a wheel of cheese from nothing more than vapor, but anything of use…" Frustration or, perhaps, desperation drove her appeal for help. She wasn't sure which, nor did it matter when Otherlande ruled. "Unless manifested by another, a weapon is beyond my reach."

Lancelot scoffed at her anguish, his fingers softly sweeping down the length of her neck, and for a moment, she forgot how to breathe.

"If memory serves, my darling, *you* are the weapon." The words were a low murmur in her ear, a seductive, honeyed sound so pleasing to her senses that she felt it split her resolve.

"It's simple, really, and some inborn bit of you already knows how or you wouldn't be here with me now." Retreating a step, he grinned. "You must not have wanted anything you tried before badly enough."

Lancelot knew how to ruffle her. It was affectionate and spoken with that mischievous disposition she was so fond of.

"Don't toy with me," Rory said, pursing her lips as a mirthful rumble rolled from the knight's chest.

He didn't move a muscle—not his hands, not his chest. Only mild effort shone in his focus as tulips bloomed around them, the purest of white. "For you, *Princess*." He bent, snapping a stem and cupping the freshly picked flower in his palms. He examined the manifestation of his musings, looking over pristine petals as if he'd molded each one specifically for her. She accepted the offering when he extended it to her, the feeling like satin against her flesh.

"It's about desire," he admitted, unreservedly forthright at last. Aurora held the significance of his assertion close. She felt his words and dark stare fixed upon her, claiming her, but she loved that look. She relished the intensity of his watchful gaze.

"*Passion*," Lancelot uttered, and before the princess could respond, she was in his arms, her back pressed firmly to his chest. The knight's head dipped next to hers, nuzzling the sensitive skin beneath her ear. She could scarcely think, relaxing into his warmth while his lips grazed the curve of her slender neck.

Aurora savored the sensation as his mouth skimmed over her flesh. His scent was every bit as intoxicating as his hands, slipping to her waist, tempting her will.

"Are you all right?" Lancelot gulped, though the rise and fall of his breath remained even.

Was she? Her heart beat like a war drum while the rest of her body ached to explore more of the daydreams she'd kept hidden and locked away after he'd left her behind.

And this.

He was magnificent and terrifying all at once. The ease with which he presented such vivid details from their past was enviable, but everything had always come effortlessly to him. It was, however, the first point that made her stomach flutter nervously.

He remembered all of it. Lancelot perfectly reproduced the exquisite hues of that springtide sunset when they'd watched together as streaks of golden light bled into the meadow around them before darkness had smothered its tender glow. Pinks and oranges stained a canvas of blue above them, the colors of the sky more remarkable than she'd ever seen.

All Rory had produced was a lump of dairy.

The years had passed, and she believed he'd forgotten her, but she couldn't have been more wrong. Neither knight nor princess were the type to pine, yet a spark clearly persisted. Aurora twisted in his arms, his handsome face hovering just above hers, and nodded her reply at last. "I think I missed you, too."

"*Aurora*," he breathed, her name a melody on his tongue. "I will always cherish my Gwenivere, but I knew you were destined for more." Lancelot traveled his thumb up her spine, and she sank into the indulgence of it all. He drew Rory closer still, pressing his lips to the corner of her mouth, ever the tease of their youth, then again to her brow and jaw.

She closed her eyes, taking in his scent and confidence as he inspected her with ruinous precision.

It took a moment to sort through what happened next. One moment, the princess was spellbound by Lancelot, and the next, she was merely observing from several paces away as Artyrus tightened a hand around the knight's throat.

The sky reverted to a clear, cloudless blue without warning, and the strawberries disappeared. The tulip Lancelot had given her turned to dust while the others melted back into the earth.

Artyrus loosened his grip, stepping away from Lancelot as quickly as he'd come. His breath was ragged when his eyes met hers, and a blinding fury blazed behind them.

"See?" The knight chuckled, thoroughly composed as he straightened his tunic. "Passion."

Acidic outrage roiled in Rory's gut, her anger now at both of them. Lancelot, clearly amused, didn't seem bothered by Artyrus's presence in the least. He sneered at the guardian, who looked like he might lunge for him.

"It's time to go." Venom seeped from each word as Artyrus trained his focus on the knight, while Lancelot rolled his eyes, releasing a bored sigh.

"You're absolutely right." Aurora turned from them, unwilling to say another word. She needed space and time to think, but her mind swirled with questions and tangible anger. Fortunately for Artyrus and Lancelot, Rory remained clothed in her old blue gown without her broadsword.

If she'd had it, she might well have gutted them both.

Chapter Seventeen

Aurora was being utterly unreasonable.

Artyrus wandered behind her as she made for the cottage they'd been sharing with Ffion and Petra at the edge of town. He was quickly learning that the pace of an angry woman was not unlike that of a swift horse as he struggled to keep stride. Would that she consider his perspective, at the least.

Yes, he had overreacted slightly. Perhaps he should've resisted the urge to wring Lancelot's neck. Indeed, refraining from taking matters quite literally into his own hands might've been the better call, given the dubious circumstances he had happened upon. In hindsight, his desire to end Lancelot was a bit excessive, considering his lack of clarity.

Maybe.

Or maybe he was simply an ass.

The sight of them together, and so close at that, had overwhelmed him on the spot. That, alongside the disappearing act from the arena and his ensuing search for her, had put him off, leading to what was, possibly, a lapse in judgment.

"Aurora, *please*," he called, surprised to find that he was somewhat breathless. Her retreating figure didn't miss a beat, stubbornly marching along the roadway as if she'd heard him not.

He picked up his speed, eager to make amends. It was becoming increasingly clear to him that he'd made a mistake, no matter how fitting it may have felt in the moment, and he couldn't bear the thought of her displeasure.

She reached their humble abode, entering hastily, and when he tried the door, he found it was barred shut.

So.

With a hearty sigh, he leaned against the frame, thrusting a hand through his hair. Summoning the words was a trial, for there was a small part of him that continued to feel justified in his actions. Still, there would be no sense in perpetuating the rift between them. He liked being a part of a team, even if it did mean deferring to her strong sensibilities.

"I shouldn't have…" Artyrus began, his tone deep and surprisingly remorseful. Clearing his throat, he started again. "I was out of line. Searching for you, wondering where you had gone when you simply vanished before my eyes and knowing that you were with him." He paused, swallowing his pride at last. "I'm sorry."

From the other side of the door, he could hear the friction of the latch against the knotted wood before it opened, revealing Ffion, his expression severe. "We do not forgive you." He slammed the door shut, a rush of air washing over Artyrus.

Well.

That was not the reaction he had expected, but perhaps it was deserved. Artyrus went to knock again, mustering a fresh supply of humility, when the door opened once more.

Aurora stood before him, appearing entirely indifferent, as if her beautiful crystalline eyes were looking straight through him. She lifted her chin expectantly, and he found himself bereft of speech as he took her in. The blue of her dress complemented her olive-brown skin most attractively, her elegant collarbones peeking from above the bateau neckline. A dark shock of hair had escaped her braid, framing her delicate face in a silky, raven wave.

She raised an eyebrow, and he finally remembered himself. "I let my irritation get the better of me," he admitted, taking a step nearer. "The Lancelot that I know is not a good man, but maybe he is better with you. I should never have demanded that you leave. It's not my place. You are abundantly capable. Intelligent. *Forgiving.*" He smiled a little, earning a hint of one in return. "Why did you go?" It was a thought that had suddenly occurred to him, and he'd voiced it without fully considering the repercussions.

He shouldn't have.

Rory's face fell, a mask of anger replacing her smile. "I have very few choices in my life. What would you have me choose?"

There was a challenge within her words, one that he wasn't fully capable of digesting. She held the weight of the world upon her shoulders, and he had been privy to only a small portion of the chaos she was dealt daily. The last thing he wanted to do was add to it.

"Come with me." He held out his hand before recognizing the unintentional demand in his words. "If…if you'd like to."

"I suppose," she said after a moment, accepting his outstretched hand.

Together, they made their way into town, and Rory was struck by how quickly they'd returned to their familiar routine. It wasn't that she'd forgotten her annoyance entirely but remaining sullen was of little use.

Their unusual world was already changing, becoming more outlandish in its exhibitions through each of their perceived days. Her people were forgetting themselves, just as Philippe had so gleefully pointed out. Moving forward was the only way through the chaos, though there was no way to know if her chosen path was right.

Every aspect of her dreaming existence was fraught with guilt.

The hamlet bustled with manic energy, and the wares for sale became more ridiculous with each booth they passed. Adding to Aurora's unease was the complete lack of awareness from all the citizens of what was, well, *weird* about the whole affair. It wasn't that anyone had maintained much discernment before, but the decline of cognizance was palpable.

"Are you hungry?" Artyrus asked, scanning the stalls brimming with all manner of produce, cheeses, meats. "I think I've still got a coin or two."

"Worry not. We're dreaming. Might as well embrace it." Aurora plucked a peach from amongst the bounty before bending to retrieve a handful of dirt. She turned to the merchant, offering the dust into his hands as payment. "Thank you, kind sir. Have a pleasant day!"

"Blessings to you, milady," the merchant called, overjoyed as he eagerly cradled his payment.

The princess and her guardian wandered farther into town as Artyrus snickered. "Where'd you pick up that little trick?"

"Honestly, it just makes sense," she replied, smiling. His reaction was somewhat unexpected, and it pleased her to amuse him so. "I've decided to embrace the chaos. It won't help to play by the rules of reality when this is..."

"Unreal?" He swiped the peach from her grasp, taking a bite.

Rory returned the favor, filching the fruit and eating a piece of her own. She furrowed her brow. "Can you taste this?"

"In fact, I did. What does that mean?"

"Stars only know," she replied, somewhat puzzled by the inanity of such a simple act requiring so much deliberation. "And while I'm fairly certain it's not a good thing, it is lovely to be able to taste without great effort."

Rory shared the peach with her guardian, delighting in the flavor and ignoring the nagging feeling that the dream was sucking her in more deeply with each passing moment. There was naught to be done, at any rate.

She pitched the pit along the roadside, coming to a standstill when she spied a familiar face ahead. The king of Llundyn approached a vendor, his hair as tousled as it had ever been and not unlike it'd looked in the forest of Sherwood. Indeed, if she didn't know better, he would appear to be just another simple citizen on a dream errand, not the young, newly married king of his own realm.

Yet even as she was eager to greet him, she was filled with trepidation. Was this real or another manipulation of her mind? She nudged Artyrus, indicating the king with a nod of her head. "You can see him, can't you?"

He glanced at Rory, concern written on the planes of his face. "Of course, I can. And this apparently worries you?"

She ignored his question, her mind racing. "Why is he here?"

"I imagine he's merely sleeping, though he's likely not poisoned as we are." He raised an eyebrow, earning another elbow to the ribs from the princess.

"We all do what must be done to save our kingdoms. Ric became a thief, and I've become an ever-present thorn in Philippe's side, courtesy of a poisoned spindle." She patted her satchel, where the remnant of the spindle remained, offering a wry grin. "What a privilege it is for you to be a party to such pursuits."

Artyrus groaned, even as a small smile crossed his lips.

Aurora started toward her friend, picking up her pace when King Riccard turned from the merchant. He met Rory's gaze, his eyes bright with affection. "Why, it cannot be!" He reached for her, wrapping her in his warm embrace. "How are you, my friend?"

"I can't complain," Rory replied. She pulled away, holding onto him by his forearms as she took him in. He felt like a piece of home, the familiarity between them making her ache for the crew she'd left behind in Llundyn. "How are you? How is Ella?"

"Oh, Ella…" Ric grinned, his love for his queen of shadows as evident as it had ever been. "She's wonderful. I'm a better man, a better king for the love of her. I could never do without her. Ella's instincts are unmatched, though we're both at a loss without Much."

He shimmered where he stood, his form undulating like a current in a swift river, and Rory began to panic. "What's happened to Much?"

"He's gone to Wylewoode—a mission I wished to send no man upon, but he needed it, and I would trust nobody else. The seas have changed him somehow." Ric's gaze was distant for a moment before lighting on Artyrus, an air of humor quickly replacing his troubled countenance. "I see you've survived thus far. You've even kept your head intact, though not without some effort, I'd imagine."

Artyrus laughed, a rarity for the stalwart guardian. "The lady is indeed a challenge, but every inch a heroine. I would follow her anywhere."

Rory met his eyes, dark and overflowing with unshakable faithfulness that had her near tears. Alongside the news of her dear friend Much, she was beginning to lose her grip.

"What is it, my love?" Ric asked, a faraway gleam in his eyes as though he were no longer present. A second later, he was gone, disappeared from before them as though he'd never existed in the first place. In a larger sense, he never had—their time together a brief, poison-induced interlude with news of home that may or may not have been accurate, given the circumstances.

Aurora placed her hand over her lips, her confidence shaken. As much as she struggled with the nonsense of her current state of mind, the realities that prevailed outside were every bit as troublesome. More so, in truth, with life and death consequences that far exceeded those of Otherlande.

They were *real*.

"Do you ever wish to stay here? To leave our lives outside to themselves?" she asked, her voice thick with distress.

"Never." Artyrus took her slender shoulders in his hands, watching her intently, his face hovering close to hers as he spoke again. "And neither do you. Nothing in this place matters. It's a fantasy—or a nightmare, I suppose. Don't you want something lasting? Something real?"

She took a deep breath, attempting to reconcile her contrary emotions. "Anything real brings heartache, responsibility, struggles..."

The admission was enough to break what little resolve remained for her in her ill-conceived quest and seeing Ric had only further complicated matters. Her life in Llundyn had been fruitful, and she'd felt as valuable then as she ever had in the whole of her life. She'd done something worthy, and even better than that, she'd felt *free*.

She sniffed, closing her eyes as a single tear escaped. "I want to let go."

He brushed his fingers over the length of her shoulders, skimming up her neck and cupping her jaw, grazing the soft flesh beneath her ears with his thumbs. "You won't. I know you'll stay the course, no matter the consequences. As you said, you'll do what you must to save your kingdom. Your lot has never been easy, but neither have you yielded." He sighed, seemingly deliberating. "Let me take you somewhere?"

Rory nodded, following at his side and quickly recognizing that they were headed for the arena. "What are we doing here?" she asked when they'd arrived, taking to the stands surrounding the field where they wandered amongst the shadows.

They paused, giving Artyrus a moment to carefully observe the guards at the far end, who were minding the sword Excalibur. "Wait here," he whispered before loping down the creaky stairs toward the list field.

Under constant watch by Prince Philippe's minions, Excalibur was never left alone. Though the prince himself conveyed a nonchalant indifference toward the infamous blade, his insistence upon its security indicated at least mild concern that it could be retrieved.

Would that it might be by Aurora's hand, heaven help her.

She watched from above as Artyrus spoke to the guards, his authoritative voice ringing through the empty arena as he attempted to convince them of his intent to take their places. It was strange for her to reconcile his role amongst Philippe's forces with the devoted, personal chaperone he had become to her.

After several minutes of convincing, the guards relinquished their positions, finally resolving to join the remainder of their squad at the banquet for the night's festivities. They left the arena in a huff, doubtless unconvinced of Artyrus's authority, and Rory realized how frustrating it was becoming to interact with anybody who maintained a remaining awareness.

That was, perhaps, a less than ideal attitude for one who wished to survive and exit her befuddling dreams, but there it was.

Artyrus waved her his way from below, and she was utterly blindsided as she approached.

The time is nigh.

Chapter Eighteen

Rory knew where Excalibur was located and had even been to see it as a girl. Her sword master, Drustan, sometimes brought her when he did business in town, which had always fascinated her.

In truth, it still did.

Once, she and her younger sister, Aedra—Drustan and Isolde's only legitimate child—had been permitted to touch it. Guards surrounded it as always, but for a single day, perhaps because Luther believed all threats to his throne dead, the kingdom allowed anyone who wished to touch the legendary blade an opportunity to do so.

The sun that day had been sweltering, with heat revealing itself in visible ripples undulating in fluid waves above the earth. She had still been known as Gwenivere then, the identity that shielded her from the Chamelautean king's tyrannical order until she refused to continue hiding.

The princess remembered in vivid detail how skillfully forged the weapon was. Drustan taught her all he knew of his craft, every bit the expert, yet even he admitted Excalibur's splendor surpassed his ability. All afternoon they awaited their turn, Rory and Aedra gossiping amongst themselves as they watched others approach the sword. Young boys with wooden replicas sparred, dressed as miniature knights of the court, teasing the girls for so much as wanting to make contact with the blade when it would never deem them worthy enough to pull it.

Aurora hadn't been naive enough to think she might be the one to retrieve Excalibur. In truth, she'd always thought it a ridiculous notion. It was more likely the sword would never budge than for someone honorable to claim it. But when her turn came, she had shuddered. Her reflection had shone in the unblemished steel, free of all tarnish or any indication of its age. An unforgiving sun had caused sweat to bead upon Rory's brow during their wait, but it was her time.

Instead of reaching for the hilt, the princess couldn't satisfy her intrigue over the intricate design peeking out from the stone. Upon that mirrored metal was artistry her heart already somehow knew. So little of it could be seen, with the remainder buried inside that dreadful rock, but she had been able to *feel* it. Drustan gently urged her, but when Aurora had extended her fingers to explore the soft curves engraved into the sword, the world went black.

The memory had been more lucid than any reality.

Disappointment had been her only companion for days, which grieved the princess more than not remembering touching the damned blade. She didn't want to care about such things, but it all felt pivotal somehow.

Drustan and Isolde had warned her against venturing too close to what was best left in the past, though it was still very much her destiny. Isolde, in particular, was so fearful in all the years following the butchering of Rory's family that Luther might discover their treachery and end them as well.

While Drustan had trained and prepared Aurora to fight for her rightful position, he and Isolde had advised that she embrace the new life they'd given her. It caused a rift that was yet to be mended, but she couldn't ignore the future written upon her spirit any more than Excalibur would ever yield to one undeserving.

Aurora could feel its presence now. Excalibur seemed to sing to her, a quietly hummed promise of a prophecy fulfilled. Artyrus waited for her near the mythical stone, where an ornate hilt glittered in the remaining light of day, extending from the top of the boulder where it cast a brilliant lattice over the ground surrounding it.

Her guardian had afforded her a second chance, with the guards now cleverly dismissed, but the smile he freely wore as she drew nearer made her knees nearly buckle.

Everything else fell away. The arena, the stands faded into a blur while Rory's mind became a muddled mess.

A foolhardy curse she is born to break...

"You hear it, too?" Artyrus must have understood it in her features, the foretelling that haunted her every thought, even if she didn't entirely understand it herself. He paled when he met her crystalline eyes. "Excalibur."

She merely nodded. Maybe it should have frightened her that he, too, could hear the melodic verse, but she felt the opposite.

"It belongs to you, Valkyrie. Merlin didn't have to see this for it to be so. Claim it, and we'll wake." Artyrus's earnest gaze was unyielding as he held a hand out to her, inviting her forward.

Rory shivered at his words, hesitating at first, for awakening had begun to seem more of a nightmare than remaining in Otherlande with him. And while it could be the dream inspiring her thoughts, she no longer cared.

"I don't know if I want to yet." Tears welled as the confession tumbled from her lips.

"Then don't." Artyrus moved toward her, his knuckles skimming the delicate angles of her cheek, and madness began to tug her into the same yawning chasm the dream had initiated before.

She couldn't master it, nor did she want to when it brought her to a picturesque summer day with Artyrus's strong hands at her waist as she kneaded dough in a scullery she'd never seen before. He nipped playfully at her ear, and she reveled in the affection, turning in his attentive embrace.

But before she could look into his face, she returned to herself.

To *him* and the infamous blade.

Artyrus's arm fell to his side, his features resolute and ablaze in a way that made her pulse race. He raised the hand he'd touched her with, studying it.

"*Artyrus*." Rory's voice was hoarse, merely a rasp when she spoke.

"What was—?"

"I don't know," she interjected before Artyrus could finish. His question confirmed he'd been with her, but though they'd both seen and *felt* the encounter, they'd been nothing more than ghosts. It was merely a vision that had given her an active role while withholding all control.

"You're all right?" Artyrus's words were cautious.

He'd only observed as she did, or he would not have asked. This respite was entirely different than what Lancelot had done when he'd whisked Rory away to the field of strawberries. Otherlande had shared this with them. Was it to persuade her to stay?

Instinct told her it was more as she recalled his steadying hold on the narrow of her waist and the teasing pinch of her guardian's teeth on her sensitive flesh. That was not a memory but perhaps a future of their own reckless design.

"You did nothing wrong," Aurora assured her companion. She stepped closer to him, and an echo of the prophecy sighed, proclaiming its intentions once more. Her pulse thrummed at their nearness, a dizzying sense of euphoria, as she dared lift her palm to Artyrus's chest, resting it over his heart. It hammered under her fingers, his throat bobbing with a forced swallow.

The time is nigh...

"It's a warning, Aurora." Placing his hand over Rory's, Artyrus tore his focus from her as if it was a cruel form of torture to verbalize the conviction. "I'm only an orphan with nothing of note, and you, the hope of a nation. We're tempting fate."

"Could it not be a blessing? You said yourself that Merlin doesn't have to predict something for it to be so.

He's just a man." She saw in his eyes, deep and passionate, that he wanted to surrender. The princess peered up at him through thick, dark lashes, her gaze pleading. "What if, just once, we are selfish?"

It was then that Aurora understood the struggle Artyrus had felt when his words had run away from him, unable to keep his inner musings to himself. Lancelot explained that desire ruled within this realm but neglected to mention vulnerability's role.

She was sinking, fighting for those final breaths before oblivion inevitably caught her by the ankle and dragged her under, for never would she lay bare her soul to him otherwise.

A few paces from where they stood was Excalibur in all its enigmatic splendor. The stone that confined it wore a shroud of shambling vines flecked with thorns, and somehow, this mattered. Everything in the dream bore some significance. Aurora was drawn to it, to the brambles, the blade, the boulder, the sharp nettles reminding her how it all began.

"Why should we be expected to yield to some supposed destiny, or I, an advantageous betrothal between two individuals given no say in the matter?" The princess felt for the broken spindle where she kept it in her satchel.

It was why they were there, subconsciously aware, though none of it should be possible. That poisoned piece of splintered wood had been her only means of defense when she'd arrived until her companion materialized. He'd risked life and limb to follow her, and she was grateful not to be alone.

"The Seer never shared with us any outcome. He assured no victories, nor did he mention our ruin. Alas, he told us nothing of use, and I'm done blindly abiding." Rory's growing disdain surprised even her. Contempt for the soothsayer was never something she'd foreseen, but she wondered if Merlin ever had.

Aurora moved toward Excalibur as it hummed quietly. A braid of barbed greenery provided additional security for its entrapped legend, reminding her of the striking figure left standing in her periphery. She'd managed well on her own these last years, but it was comforting to have someone who might waylay the knives targeting her back.

She felt Artyrus's powerful presence from behind her but didn't look back. Removing the spindle from her bag, the princess used one of its sharper edges, cutting a piece of the vine free. She plucked from it a few thorns before coiling the pliable stem around the broken pin, knotting it tightly.

Artyrus's face read apparent bewilderment when Aurora turned. Closing the distance between them, she reached for him with both ends of the vine in either hand. She'd kept the cord long enough to secure it around his neck, tying it at the nape. "Why not bend fate to our liking?" Rory murmured against his stubbled jaw, the tender flesh of her cheek sweeping over it. She heard his breath hitch at her words before he tugged her nearer to himself.

"Once." Artyrus's mouth tipped at the corners in an indulgent grin. Weaving deft fingers through Rory's loosely braided strands, he pressed his forehead to hers, and their eyes leveled. "Once, I will tell you that I can scarcely breathe when the wind rustles your hair. And once, I'll say that I have never been more exasperated, more...confounded by *anyone*."

Desire surged within the guardian's gaze, and he slipped his tongue over his lower lip as Aurora brushed her fingertips up the taut muscles of his back, stroking the cords of his neck. "Once," he continued, his voice rough and sensuous, "I'll confess that I've thought of nothing else, no *one* else since we met that day outside of Llundyn."

True love is the cost...

He groaned, tightening his strong arms around her waist. "We don't have much time, Aurora." Her companion's words were sobering and contradictory as he lazily nuzzled her temple with his nose. Though it was foolish, she endeavored to savor their briefly stolen bliss.

She realized Artyrus was losing himself, too, and tempting as it was to descend into madness together, it went against everything they stood for. To allow it would be an act of cowardice.

"Help me free it." Threading her fingers with his, Rory breathed the request in his ear as her heart throbbed in time to the unnerving verse rambling between them. Unseen and foreboding, the timbre shifted into something somehow darker.

Urgent.

"Move and you both will die." Philippe's threat found them before Aurora saw him, and he was not alone. On either side of him were the silver-clad knights, who she could only assume were Kaye and Ector. The same guards Artyrus had dismissed trailed them, donning mirthful sneers.

Artyrus drew his sword, and each of the others followed suit. Kaye had fought against the dream to warn his friend, but how much control might he still have? He'd warned them to stay far from the black knight, and now it appeared the wraith-like assassin and Philippe were one and the same.

Wordlessly tossing his blade to Rory, the guardian pivoted into a practiced warrior's posture beside her. The hilt was shoddy, but she'd not forgotten the damage she'd seen it inflict during the Merit Tourney. Doubtless, they were outnumbered and unprepared. Would that they might deliver enough damage to grant them a chance to run.

Gravel crunched under slowly approaching footsteps as the world seemed to regain its shape and clarity. "Come now, brother. Is it not a bit soon for a lover's quarrel?"

Lancelot.

The princess schooled her features, unwilling to show any signs of relief when the knight strode casually into the fray while Philippe rolled his eyes, otherwise ignoring his timely arrival.

"She is beautiful but a *viper*, is she not?" Lancelot drawled, undeterred by the tension.

The prince merely chuckled. "Indeed. A waste, really, of such a disarming countenance."

"I daresay the waste would be in ending her," Lancelot added with an infuriating smirk. "You must admit that she possesses a particular fire that might prove amusing in some areas."

Something low and dangerous rumbled deep within Artyrus, a growl emphasizing his outrage. But Lancelot winked at the guardian, undeterred by his obvious fury as he pushed his luck even further.

Aurora braced herself, ready for her chaperone to lunge, when one of Philippe's guards dropped to the ground. A cardinal feather protruded from the felled man's neck as his form went limp.

Before anyone else knew what had happened, the second guard slumped after a streak of crimson hit him.

Next, the one in silver, the one Rory thought could be Kaye, then his father. Philippe's eyes flashed with something like fear, but she wouldn't risk waiting to see what he would do.

Aurora glanced at Artyrus, and without a word, they ran.

* * * *

Aurora had never shared with Lancelot where their dwelling was located. Yet, the clothes she'd worn earlier for the day's melee sat alongside the sword she'd been given by Artyrus, lying neatly at the foot of the cottage doorway. Despite her assurances to that effect, her keeper had quickly dismissed himself to prepare for the evening's festivities.

And while returning to the cabin was, perhaps, a perilous choice, hiding from Philippe was not an option.

It had been a matter of hours since Lancelot had stolen her away from the tourney, since she'd seen her dear friend, Ric, but it felt like a week. Of course, there was no way to know how long it *had* been, but each passing moment made reality hazier. Rory wondered how much worse it was for those of her people who'd been poisoned days before she had been.

Petra hadn't returned to their shared shelter, and part of Rory wondered if she would come back at all. She was strange and wholly unpredictable, but had she not been at the arena, both the princess and Artyrus might very well be dead.

Perhaps the little nymph had a conscience after all.

Without Petra's aid, Rory put little effort into her appearance for the evening. Pulling her hair back into a loose, low knot at her neck, she quickly changed her mind instead, leaving it free and wavy. Managing the stays of her gown alone was trying, to say the least, yet somehow she cinched them into their customary form.

She was ready in short order and lamented, once again, the inconvenience of leaving her blade behind. Near the exit it sat, taunting her with its useless presence.

I'm sorry.

Aurora sighed, unable to discern if the whisper was real or just a figment of her imagination. Maybe she was gradually becoming one with Otherlande. Either way, she swore the voice belonged to Lancelot.

Now wasn't the time for his apologies. In truth, Rory didn't entirely believe he needed to make any. He'd been arrogant and dreadful before she'd fled with Artyrus, but he'd made a distraction of himself, for better or for worse.

It had been enough.

She made her way toward Artyrus and Ffion's shared room, finding the door cracked. Through the opening, she saw her guardian, his bare, muscled back facing her as he dressed.

While she meant to turn away, she couldn't help but watch, caught off guard by his unexpected markings. Running the length of his spine to one side was a tattoo Aurora knew, for it was one she shared, though hers was set opposite his.

The Penzellian tradition was something she'd never much considered, but the designs were magnificent. The princess couldn't tear her focus from her guardian, admiring his powerful shoulders, his narrow waist. He was ruinously enticing.

"Trying to catch flies, are ye?" Strolling to Rory's side, Ffion cackled. She hadn't heard the boy enter, but Artyrus's eyes found hers when he spoke, a surprised grin lighting his striking face.

"Mind your own business." Heat crept into her cheeks with their mutual levity, and Aurora stalked off in a huff of agitation, Ffion howling with laughter in her wake.

If she weren't so mortified, she might've laughed, too.

Chapter Nineteen

Humiliation was the last thing Aurora needed, but there it was.

And Ffion, the ubiquitous troublemaker... Couldn't he have simply let it slide with a wink and a nod in acknowledgment? She smiled a little at the thought, her embarrassment giving way to tacit amusement. The kid did as he pleased and *had* been helpful on more than one occasion.

She let it go. Besides, she really couldn't have been more obvious.

Rory wandered from the cottage toward the seaside, grateful that the evening's banquet had not yet begun. Sunset was likely some minutes or hours away. It was hard to know, with daylight an entity unto itself. Still, it was pleasing to Rory to be alone, enjoying a few moments of solitude before the endless parade of festivities continued.

It was a wonder, really, when she considered that she'd not once slept since she'd arrived in Otherlande.

Sleep had been a way of life before it became her perpetual existence, standing in stark contrast with the brutal pace they'd all been keeping. She would readily acknowledge that she tired at times there, but the never-ending activity was bound to take its toll.

Worrying over that truth was useless.

She headed up the hillside overlooking the vacant grounds, soon to be filled with all manner of revelers, and closed her eyes, taking in the mix of sea air and gentle breeze. When she opened them, she was only somewhat surprised to find that her surroundings had partially melded with a beautiful memory from her past.

Desire.

Perhaps she did understand how it worked on some level. Seating herself amongst the myriad wildflowers she'd somehow willed into her presence, she ran her fingertips over their silky soft petals, remembering the first and only time she'd done so before. A journey she'd taken with her family to a township several hours from home had seen them through the same vibrant meadow where she and Aedra had rollicked about like fillies in the brilliant sunlight.

She sighed, basking in the tranquil space every bit as much as she did the memory of her family. They'd been much on her mind of late, the nostalgia not quite overwhelming but close. Casting aside her wistful sentiments, she resolved to think of something more productive.

Rory had not yet managed to conjure her sword, despite numerous efforts. Keeping Lancelot's instructions in mind, she focused with outstretched hands, wholeheartedly meditating upon her beloved blade. She could see it in her mind's eye, feel the curve of its grip and the heft of its weight. She envisioned the delicate etchings running the length of the fuller, the bright amethyst stones inlaid within the chap and the pommel.

Yet all that materialized was a deep purple dahlia resting lightly atop her palms, its color matching the stones embellishing her broadsword. Blazes, but she was terrible with this. Either that or her desires were not in line with her heart.

"I've a shirt on now," Artyrus said, startling the princess out of her musings. She glanced up to find her ornery chaperone grinning, a hint of humor shining in his dark eyes.

"*Oh.*" Aurora laughed, burying her face in her hands before mustering the courage to meet his gaze. "I'm sorry. But even you must know you're a bit distracting."

He shook his head dismissively as he settled beside her, and she couldn't help but smile when she noticed how his face flushed. He was always so stoic, prone to blending into the background and going largely unnoticed, despite his size. Surely, he was intimidating in build and demeanor, though any superficial misgivings regarding his character vanished once his true nature was known.

Clad in the same Penzellian garb he'd donned the night before, Artyrus was anything but covert. He was also utterly unaware of his effect, his manner so unassuming as to be completely disarming. An amicable silence passed between them, their company as comfortable as her well-worn boots.

Or her favorite sword.

"I'm curious," Aurora began, giving voice to a query that had been gnawing at her since she'd seen him shirtless. "The tattoo along your spine is a strange feature for a Chamelautean knight. Where did you receive it?"

"I've had it forever," he replied, plucking the dahlia from Rory's grasp. He examined it briefly before continuing. "It is, allegedly, a noble Penzellian birthright, bestowed upon me not long after I was born. My father was a Chamelautean lord, the brother of Pelinore, and his wife was of Penzellian descent. Their union was considered a disgrace, as you might imagine, or so Pelinore explained. It mattered not, as they died in my infancy."

That was interesting. Rory had vaguely wondered if the tattoo she'd seen was a manifestation of the dream alone, but it seemed not.

The similarities in their early lives also struck her, as did his Penzellian origins. "That explains why you're so comfortable in the clothing of my people, I suppose, for you are fully half yourself. All Penzellian nobility have grace markings. It's a ceremony performed with our christening and meant to convey a blessing. I spied my mother's once, inked from hip to hip on her lower back. Others were but a small emblem branding a shoulder blade or the nape of a neck."

She paused, weighing an admission of her own. "I have a similar tattoo," she said at last. "It marks the top of my backbone to the bottom, much like yours. Perhaps they were running out of designs." She smiled at the thought, wondering how the inkings had come to be selected in the first place. "Would you like to see it?"

She leaned forward, revealing the elegant corset back of her gown. Glancing over her shoulder, she issued a subtle nod, sweeping her cascading hair from her back to give him access. He swallowed hard, reaching for the delicate gold thread that bound her in. Slackening the laces, he drew them aside, exposing the fine, scrolling lines that rambled down the column of her spine.

He traced the whorls with the tips of his fingers, his featherlight touch sending a thrill through her. "It's very much like mine, like looking in a mirror."

Aurora sniffed with a hint of disdain, her hair tumbling over her shoulder as she reclined, lying on her bare back amid the richly colored bed of flowers. "If it's good fortune it's meant to express, then it's been sorely lacking." She snatched the dahlia from Artyrus's grasp, drawing a chuckle from her companion.

He fell beside her, propping himself on his elbow, his gaze pinned to her most attentively. Indeed, he was always watching, ever analyzing their circumstances, their surroundings. She found, at that moment, that she had been remarkably dismissive of his efforts.

Would she have ever made it this far without him?

Her eyes met his, dark and soulful, holding his gaze as she slipped a little deeper into herself, her mind aimlessly drifting as she lay there. For the first time since she'd entered their unified nightmare, she allowed herself to relax.

"He never had a chance."

She turned in her dream-like state, seeing Artyrus standing on the precipice separating Otherlande from the vast sea below, the glow of the setting sun illuminating him in a burnished silhouette of oranges and purples too vivid to be real.

"I had no doubt you would win," he continued, moving toward her. They stood face to face, close enough to breathe the same air. "Your faith in yourself, in your purpose, never fails you. Your passion knows no bounds, and it will carry you through wherever you desire to go."

He smiled while she blushed fiercely under his admiration. It was, perhaps, the kindest thing he'd ever said, his unwavering confidence in her without equal. She'd never known anyone in the whole of her life who had so faithfully sought to encourage her through all her ill-advised pursuits, yet he'd never wavered.

Rory took one of his hands into her own then the other, twining their fingers before she spun, wrapping herself within his strong embrace. Their clasped hands rested over her wildly pulsing heart, and her breathing grew quicker, pacing the scuttling beat in her chest.

There was no resistance from Artyrus, despite the intimacy of their tangled hold. Though they'd frequently sparred and daily disagreed, their inability to see eye to eye didn't diminish their underlying connection. It seemed there was more between them than either had readily acknowledged, but exploring such things could never be a priority.

Turning within his arms, she glanced up at his face. He looked as serene as she felt, held tightly to his chest. In truth, he'd always been a calming presence, though his influence had likely been diminished amid their numerous arguments.

His even breaths rustled her hair as he moved nearer, tipping her chin upward with a sweep of his thumb. She rose on tiptoe, her lips skimming the sharp line of his jaw as she tightened her arms around his neck.

"Come back to me," he whispered, his low voice eliciting a shiver. "*Aurora, come back to me.*"

Opening her eyes, Rory realized she'd been...
dreaming?

"Where were you?" Artyrus asked, brushing a stray lock from her forehead. "You seemed absent."

"I saw it," she sighed. "The moments that I missed with you before. We were on the cliff. You held me, and I felt—"

"Peace?"

"*Yes.*" Her admission was spoken quietly, one tiny little word that carried more weight than she had realized.

That Aurora had been whisked away to some alter-reality while physically remaining in Artyrus's presence was unsettling, and the relief he felt over her confession was absurd.

Knowing that she now understood, at least in part, the depth of his sentiments for her was also unnerving, but he preferred that to the complete absence of that truth.

His conscience was at war with itself, the burden of their unspoken confessions hovering in the scant space between them. It would be so easy to ignore the vow he made to himself alone, to leave Aurora to her future, her betrothal. To abstain from interfering, no matter how desperately he wanted to be hers and to have her for himself.

They could live a happy life.

He wished to close the distance, for one brief encounter where their duties would not inhibit the longings of their hearts. She was everything he never knew he needed, and to have her now would be both the epitome of contentment as well as the height of tragedy. He knew it was madness, for there would be no recovery, at least not for him.

"What are you thinking about?" Aurora asked, stroking her slender fingers over the lines of his jaw, and in her eyes, he could see that it was not only he who struggled.

Artyrus was about to speak when the world around them began to glow, despite the setting sun. It seemed the banquet would begin in earnest, though attending was about the last thing he wished to do.

Even as he watched, the vast expanse was slowly beset with bountiful tables and self-suspending chandeliers, their subtle flames lighting the field in resplendent hues of gold that cut through the dusk of night.

Soon after, the revelers appeared, popping into existence and moved to merriment as though they'd been there all along—singing, dancing, imbibing. It was like they'd never left the celebration from the prior evening. Yet even more startling than the sudden emergence of the bash was the realization that it hadn't fazed him at all.

It seemed that he'd accepted the insanity somewhere along the way, and the timing could not have been worse.

In answer to her question, he merely groaned, shaking his head. What might've been, what should've been... Many thoughts to that effect were futile. They were obligated to function within the confines they'd been dealt and spending any time considering the potential alternatives would only further frustrate them.

"I suppose we're due at the banquet," he managed. "Though it might be the last place I'd like to be about now."

Nodding her agreement, Rory rose from her bed of wildflowers, thrusting her hair over her shoulder once more. Without a word, Artyrus understood what needed to be done as he set about relacing her gown in silent annoyance.

A clamor from the revelry below rang through the night, piercing through what little serenity remained. Artyrus cursed under his breath until, from above, he saw why.

The dragon soared through the twilight air, its massive figure obscuring the stars as it flew toward the sliver of sunlight resting upon the horizon. The beast paid them no mind, ignoring their very presence as it climbed ever higher, its lethal talons tucked against the armor-like scales of its torso.

The creature's body was luminescent, with purple-black skin that reflected the glow of the rising moon. Veins, not unlike long fingers, ran the length and breadth of its wings, the span well beyond the scope of what Artyrus had envisioned when first Ffion had mentioned it.

"Now's our chance," Aurora said, rising to her feet as the people in the meadow slowly recovered their senses. But she moved not toward the banquet, setting off, instead, toward the castle not far behind them.

Artyrus fell in step beside her. "Our chance for what? Where are you going?"

"The dragon has abandoned its residence. Why not have a look around? Perhaps there's a key to our exit within the palace."

He hadn't considered it, so set upon the freeing of Excalibur as the only means through which they might succeed. It was an intriguing prospect but one fraught with danger. "We don't know what we're dealing with in there. What if that beast returns?"

Aurora simply smiled. "Then we must hurry."

Chapter Twenty

Artyrus found it increasingly difficult to keep his mind from wandering. The princess was diverting enough before she'd ever tried to be, and now? He was hopeless, having witnessed her yearning and the way it rivaled his. *That* was real, regardless of the dream's duplicity. He only prayed their foolish desires would not be manipulated, forged into something catastrophic.

They took a longer route, skirting the banquet through the woods and out of sight. Rory cursed her gown when its hem snagged on a shrub as they passed. "Are men so threatened by women that we must be made to suffer so?" She swore under her breath, ripping an inner layer of her skirt away from the bush. "At least I will look pretty should we meet any peril."

Pretty. The word was an understatement, as was every other term used to define her arresting beauty. But it wasn't the gown or her obsidian hair falling in waves around her neck. In truth, Artyrus found Aurora even more breathtaking in her worn trousers and tunic. But then again, there was no world or circumstance wherein she would not command his attention.

Sense be damned.

When she tumbled as she freed herself, Artyrus steadied her at the curve of her slender waist. She groaned with frustration, kicking the folds of her dress before relaxing in his tender hold. He chuckled softly, indulging himself once more, taking in her intoxicating scent until awareness seized him.

A twig snapped from within the trees, followed by an exasperated sigh. "I thought it was safe to join you after whatever *that* was." Ffion emerged, indicating the lush hillside from where they'd come with a wave of his palm. "I haven't seen Petra in hours, and I didn't want to die of boredom at another horrid feast alone — with food that won't even take the edge off, mind you."

Artyrus, against his better judgment, was growing fonder of the pest. Ffion deserved far more than this lie of an existence, for he'd proven as resilient as he was amusing with a long life of frustrating strangers' impulses ahead of him.

"Nice of you to insert yourself, but you'll not be coming any farther with us." Artyrus's declaration drew an eye roll from the boy, who strode past him as if he'd not spoken at all.

"I found a way in once before the dragon returned to her tower. On the south side of the palace, there's an entry point. Follow me." Ffion marched on, undeterred. Artyrus and Rory were in no position to object, still desperate for answers that might awaken the dreamers. Excalibur seemed likely, but if not, it was entirely possible there was no way out.

"You've been inside?" Aurora asked.

Ffion shrugged as he swatted at branches blocking his path. "I hadn't made it very far when I heard the dragon screeching nearby. I didn't think it wise to be there when she got back." He shoved another low-hanging limb aside, revealing the castle walls yards ahead.

It looked very much the same as the last time the guardian had been there. Only then the impressive structure hadn't been covered with rambling spikes. He thought of the vine tied loosely around his neck, ignoring how it made him want to meet Aurora's gaze to see if some flicker of what he felt was in her eyes.

The boy was fearless. With thorny stems cloaking the castle, it was an ominous fortress designed by and *for* monsters—a dwelling in which one could flourish. Yet, he approached without concern, which was, perhaps, more disturbing on second thought. He was a fool, naive enough to think himself immune to Otherlande's whims. That, or his reality was far bleaker than Artyrus wished to consider.

"Here." Ffion paused, standing in front of what looked to be a solid wall. He felt around the bricks until one moved against the others. A satisfied grin lit the boy's face as some internal mechanism shifted within the stone.

Rory beamed. "How did you know this was here?"

The secret entrance grumbled as if wishing to remain undisturbed but yawned open, exposing a pitch-dark passage. Ffion should never have ventured through it on his own, but damn if his audacity didn't impress Artyrus.

"I figured something lured the dragon here, and most people don't remember the castle even exists. I'm not sure, really. I just *knew*." The boy wandered into the blackness without hesitation, where only his voice and quietly echoing footfalls guided them onward.

"It must mean something, right?" Ffion pressed, and Artyrus had to agree. There was no way to know what would be uncovered, if anything, but to disregard the possibility could be a grievous oversight.

A silvery-blue glow shone at the end of the long corridor connecting them to the outside. Artyrus saw nothing, only heard the quiet creak of metal hinges protesting as Ffion pushed. Moonlight filtered through stained glass masterpieces and flooded the dark hallway in fragmented tones of color as their remote entry brought them into the palace library. Tomes lined each wall from floor to ceiling, so many volumes that the guardian wondered if King Luther knew what half of them were.

The room felt stale and still as death, apart from streaks of glittering starlight dancing across a sizeable golden rug edged in silken tassels. It was safe to assume they were alone, judging by the way their breath alone seemed to disturb whatever strange oblivion enveloped the area.

The place was a tomb, aside from one tiny mouse skittering underfoot.

"Have you observed the creature's patterns enough to know when it might come back?" Artyrus kept one hand ready, gripped around the hilt of his tired sword.

Ffion shook his head. "I've seen her a handful of times since I've been here and twice within a short span when she'd come and gone again." He furrowed his brow, deliberating. "I thought maybe that means the beast is not truly part of Otherlande and only emerges when in genuine slumber."

Artyrus was too dismissive of the boy. He was cunning and perceptive beyond his years. The guardian never thought he'd be grateful to have been swindled by anyone, but it seemed they needed Ffion as much as he needed them.

"That may be so, but we must make haste, given how time passes here." Aurora moved gracefully through the library to an aged oak door that could only lead them deeper into the palace. While Artyrus was always one to calculate risks, doing so any longer was futile.

"My father had a strategy room." Her words were somber with the mention of the late Penzellian king. She was barely a child when her family was slain, and the few memories she seemed to treasure would surely fade over the years.

"King Luther does, too. I can lead us to it." Artyrus's gaze strayed toward the princess when he spoke, her eyes bright and eager when they met his.

He was familiar with the castle, though he'd never liked it. Something about it felt...wrong. Maybe his apprehension was purely a result of his partial Penzellian heritage, but he'd always felt uneasy around the high king of Chamelaute.

Even the rodent followed closely on their heels as they made their way out of the library with feather-light steps down a narrow access, the critter undoubtedly pleased to have company that wasn't monstrous. Ffion conjured a torch to light their path with unnerving ease, illuminating the Great Hall just beyond.

Artyrus had never seen so much as a chair askew there, but platters of picked-over fruits and cheeses, empty goblets and partially eaten loaves of braided bread in a perfect golden brown littered every surface as they passed through. They dared not linger long to investigate the spoils, but it was evident enough that the castle may well not be as vacant as it had seemed.

It was also possible that whoever had created the mess departed upon discovering a massive creature that favored luxury over the wild.

Without a word, the trio moved soundlessly throughout eerily quiet halls, quickly passing the sovereigns' private solar room and several bed chambers along their way. The mouse squeaked a few short paces ahead, shimmying through a crack under a large oak door that stood tall and proud between them and King Luther's strategy quarters.

Exchanging silent glances, Aurora nodded Artyrus forward, and he took hold of the cold iron knob. It protested softly as he carefully rotated it, and then, when it would turn no more, he pushed. The door moaned, echoing across the stone walls and floor, and Ffion stifled a giggle, to which Rory responded with one of her own.

"From whom must we cower, apart from the dragon? Are our enemies not caught up in their revelry?" Aurora asked by way of explanation for her sudden outburst. Brushing past the guardian, she offered a reassuring pat on his shoulder for his efforts, and he couldn't help the grin that formed.

"We can't be good at everything, brother," Ffion added as he passed, and Artyrus chuckled, lightly shoving the boy after Rory.

At the heart of the room was a great round table. When Artyrus was there in the past, he'd stood at the edge of the room while Luther's honored knights encircled the sizable war desk.

The king was the only one with a chair, as if everyone else was somehow lesser than he. No one seemed to mind, save Artyrus, nor would he expect them to. That was the way of things, no matter how disgusting he found it.

Upon the table lay a map, matching its surface in both length and breadth. It displayed all of Chamelaute and miles beyond in great detail, with flags marking specific territories primarily on the outskirts, while few were set within the kingdom's heart.

Artyrus had never seen a map like what lay before him during prior visits. Then, it had been a map of the whole of Fayble. Still, it was always dotted for the king's boundless greed and tagged according to his whims. The guardian always wondered about the day Luther's father had assigned one of the same small flags to Penzelle. Would that he could have been there to stop it.

His Majesty must have commissioned a masterful cartographer to customize such a showpiece, as nothing seemed to be missing. Aurora ran her fingers over some of the smaller hamlets, each of them flagged.

"They're all of a Penzellian majority." Her words were weighted with the burden of her title, a queen in her own right, trapped in sleep.

"There." Artyrus took to Rory's side, his finger pointing to Caerleon, where they'd first thought they'd stepped into a massacre.

"Do you think it possible for all of these territories to be poisoned as we are?" Rory asked, Artyrus offering little more than a shake of his head in response as she mulled other options. "But why poison a people when he has the militia to blot out Penzelle entirely?"

"To do so would collapse his kingdom. It is Penzelle's saving grace that he requires all your people provide." Spitefully, Artyrus flicked one of the small flags from its town, drawing a faint smile from Aurora.

Across the way, Ffion knelt, unconcerned with their theorizing as he extended a hand toward the mouse that had followed them. Turning his palm upward, he revealed a bit of cheese. Whether he'd wished it from nothing or snatched it from the Great Hall, Artyrus didn't know.

After a contemplative pause, Rory raised a brow. "Perhaps he means to douse any kindling before it can be ignited, while the brewing rebellion slumbers unaware. If this map is any indication, he's not informed of the stronghold in Wylewoode."

"A safe assumption," Artyrus agreed. "Philippe's presence in Otherlande alone proves Luther intends for all to awaken, especially considering the prince maintains awareness. He's here on behalf of his father to ensure all goes according to plan from within. His duty was simple before you arrived." Nudging Aurora with his shoulder, he swore he saw her cheeks heat.

"It's why Merlin was so upset when I acted on instinct. I was safer awake." Something resembling guilt flashed in her gaze.

Without a thought, he threaded his fingers through hers, bringing her knuckles to his lips. "You were safer, but your people weren't. You will save them, Valkyrie."

Artyrus's breath warmed her flesh, and the princess could still feel his kiss on the peaks of her hand. They continually forgot themselves unless, by all mercies, what they shared was real.

Valkyrie.

The word coursed through her like a war cry, and the reverence with which her guardian spoke it called upon her very spirit to answer.

"What are you doing so far from home?" On one knee, Ffion knelt at the other end of the round table, his tone affectionate when he spoke.

Before their eyes, the rodent had transformed into something entirely different, and Ffion seemed none the wiser. The boy tapped his leg, encouraging the shifted form forward. A baby crocodile waddled toward him, but he showed no alarm.

"Ffion, *no!*" Aurora attempted in vain to reach the boy, but her body failed, stuck firmly in place. Artyrus twisted and writhed beside her, unable to move beyond where he stood.

The small reptile approached Ffion, who held his hand out to it. The boy massaged between the creature's eyes with his fingertips, and it melted into his touch. Ffion seemed lost in a trance, unable or unwilling to recognize anything outside of the odd interaction, and Rory and Artyrus could offer no aid, should the situation sour.

Helplessly they watched, struggling against what looked to be nothing at all, their feet tethered to the ground. But the crocodile again became a mouse before long, and Ffion smiled as it scurried away.

Next to Rory, Artyrus's eyes glazed over as the rodent transformed once more. She touched his hand as a man materialized opposite them, noting that Artyrus's feet had been freed from their invisible shackles when he moved to meet the newcomer.

"I'm sorry I lied to you," the man said, his eyes wet with remorse.

Ffion gasped, having returned to himself, though he was now fastened to the ground. "Who the hell is —?"

"Shh," Rory hissed, waving his question away so she could better hear.

"Kaye said you were under the king's custody. Is it true?" Concern laced Artyrus's words as he grasped the figure's forearm with his hand.

Pelinore. It had to be him, though Aurora couldn't know whether he was truly present.

The guardian's uncle clasped Artyrus's arm in return and, ignoring his upset, continued as if he'd never spoken. "It was all for you and the greater good. Trust in me, I beg you." The figure disappeared before their eyes, affording Artyrus no opportunity to speak again as he became frozen in place.

The baffling critter transformed into someone new, and Rory was overcome.

"Little beauty." Her father stood before her, calling her by the moniker he'd used more than her given name. A broken sob burst past the princess's lips as her heart cracked anew with the sound of a voice she feared she'd forgotten.

The Penzellian king was as handsome as she remembered, even if memories of his countenance had begun to fade, but he was not alone. Stood beside him, her mother was also there, and it was like seeing herself from another's eyes, her hair lustrous and deepest black.

Isolde was with them, too, seemingly beaming with pride at the woman Rory had become. No disappointment shone in her delicate features, nor anger from when last they'd parted. Rory's gut twisted, tears spilling over her cheeks at the sight of them.

"Darling girl, how we've missed you." Her mother opened her arms, and Rory ran to her, melting into her embrace. "You are all we dreamed you'd be and more."

"All of Chamelaute will fall at your feet, Aurora. Your destiny awaits. You mustn't tarry, my love." Sweeping loose strands from her temple, her father pressed a kiss to the princess's brow. She continued to weep when Isolde came to her side, taking her by the hand.

"We must go now," the nursemaid urged, her other arm curled around Rory's slender shoulders. Her parents nodded, each with solemn smiles on their faces.

Their figures began to flicker, becoming one with the blaze of white light surrounding them.

"No!" The princess screamed as they faded further into nothingness. "*No!*"

Otherlande did not hear her plea, did not care when her legs threatened to give out. Somehow, she kept stride with Isolde, walking beside her, even as her soul begged to follow her parents into the blinding white. She knew not where they went, only that she ascended higher and higher up a stone stairwell lined with barbed brambles.

The vines thinned as they climbed, Isolde holding fast to Aurora as if she feared she might shrug herself free. Somewhere in the distance, voices called her name. Unclear, like a partially formed thought, the sound clawed at a dormant corner of her mind, pleading and desperate.

"Everyone thought her dead," Rory's nursemaid mumbled in a voice that did not belong to her.

Slowly, the princess remembered Artyrus. She recalled Ffion and the crocodile.

And the mouse.

At the top of the steps, a door opened. None of this was right. Isolde was not right. Yet, Aurora kept to her side, entering the circular room.

"As it turns out, His Majesty King Luther is just a dreadful liar," Isolde sneered. Her mouth twisted into something, some*one's* wicked, yellowed smile, though Rory could not quite place it. The princess followed the false Isolde's line of sight along a path of slivered moonlight.

A massive monster waited, pacing restlessly. The dragon gazed back at them, and Rory swallowed her panic, meeting its golden eyes as tendrils of dark smoke billowed from its beringed nostrils.

Her imposter nursemaid bowed by way of greeting. "Here she is, my queen."

Chapter Twenty-One

It took a moment as Rory's mind caught up with her eyes, for standing before her was the very creature whose absence had prompted their explorations.

She hadn't heard the dragon return, having been so preoccupied with the deceptive machinations of the enchantress as she shifted from animal to ancestor with such speed and persuasion that Rory had lost hold of herself.

Not that she'd had much control to begin with.

And now, the tricky woman was nowhere to be found, delivering the princess to the lofty tower only to disappear. Either that, or she was still lurking about as an ant or a fly. It seemed nothing was out of her reach.

Rory waited, watching the beast, whose massive form dominated the vast space. A long, spiky face with eyes the color of liquid gold appraised her where she remained, spellbound by the mythical giant in all its lustrous glory.

"My queen."

The enchantress's words rang in her ears, even as she wished to put distance between herself and the great wyvern. But contrary to all her natural instincts, she wasn't afraid, patiently awaiting the creature's shift into human form.

Yet the beast only endured as if she, too, was anticipating a transformation—perhaps wishing to watch the woman before her shift into a queen worthy enough to rule. Indeed, that would be a long wait if ever it were to occur at all.

Slowly, the dragon moved, her lithe body as graceful as a wave as it circled Rory. Her steps were anything but predatory as she continued her evaluation, with what the princess could only describe as a look of curiosity upon her angular face. Stepping into the subtle glow from the candlelit sconces, gemstones in an array of colors shone upon her ears, pierced with countless studs, while the flare of her nostril held a single silver hoop.

It was all rather familiar, part of a forgotten memory that wiggled free somewhere in the back of Rory's mind. She followed the limber creature's movements in search of a clue, though never had she had experience with *dragons* in her waking life.

Maybe the lost memory had never existed in the first place. Such was the reality with so many revelations in Otherlande, the constant fallacies wreaking havoc on what remained of Rory's sanity.

The dragon paused before her, smoke emanating from her nose as she scrutinized her quarry. It seemed the animal would not be taking human form, after all, further frustrating the princess. What, then, was the point of this strange interlude?

"Why am I here?" Rory ventured, earning a hearty puff of gray vapor when the wyvern sniffed in her direction.

She closed the gap, her lean body trapping Rory as she tightened her position, enclosing the princess within a circle of sharp, iridescent scales. Stretching her slender neck toward the ceiling, she glared down upon her prey through narrowed eyes.

Fear quickly seized Rory by the gullet. Had she been too cavalier? She'd felt nothing shy of calm as she'd entered the tower, but now...

The dragon blew a steady flame from her lips with a breath soft as a gentle breeze, setting the fur rug beneath Rory's feet alight. She stumbled backward, removing herself from the smoldering pelt and running headlong into the prickly scales covering the dragon's torso.

Rubbing her arms, she soothed away the sting from their touch, cursing under her breath. The damned banquet gown was nothing but trouble, leaving her exposed and swordless and effectively crippled against any productive combat.

She was at the creature's mercy, for better or for worse.

The fur continued to burn, smoking as the flames rose ever higher, while the dragon sneered, exposing a mouthful of gleaming teeth.

"I'd prefer to be eaten, if you please," Rory muttered, her mood growing darker by the second. "I quite imagine burning to death will take longer."

A deep rumble surged through the beast, sounding very much like laughter, and Rory scowled, even as she struggled to understand. Surely, she hadn't been brought to the tower as a plaything.

Another burst of fire followed, landing upon what remained of the fur rug, but this spark was different somehow. Brighter and *contained*, the edges of the pyre contorting in unnatural curves.

The dragon moved her head nearer to Aurora, her golden eyes locked upon the princess as the fire took shape between them. Two blazing circlets emerged within the confined ring of flames, hovering just above the embers — crowns fit for a king and a queen.

The crowns spun upon invisible axes, linked over a flickering heart of brilliant yellows and oranges that filtered into blue. The imagery was powerful, painting a white-hot picture for Rory.

From one queen to another, a quiet voice uttered. It wasn't audible, instead speaking directly to Rory's soul. *Your people are ready, awaiting my direction, awaiting your ascension. You need only to wake those who slumber.*

The dragon raised her chin before huffing another billowing puff of smoke from her nostrils as if she were willing the princess to understand her directive.

Understand she did, though she could not bring herself to accept what it meant for her life. Ruling alongside Philippe would be as good as not ruling at all. Indeed, she would be fortunate enough to remain alive within a union with the vile prince of Chamelaute.

But responsibility would forever trump desire. Certainly, she knew that well enough. Much like her guardian, she was ever duty-bound, regardless of how long she'd avoided it, ignored it. And much like Artyrus, she would proceed, despite the potential consequences for herself.

It was the greatest gift he'd given her, his selflessness without equal.

"Who are you?" Aurora asked at last. The creature was frightening in mere appearance alone, but her manner caused no unease—a strange truth, considering she was conversing with a dragon.

And a *queen*?

As if she'd spoken that unlikely notion aloud, the dragon recoiled, disappearing alongside Rory's next breath. The fire, too, was gone, leaving the solemn chamber at the top of the tower bereft of any traces of the beast's presence.

Spinning in place, Aurora took in her surroundings, at once relieved and annoyed. What purpose had any of that served, and who was the supposed queen to whom she'd been speaking? With the absence of the enchantress, there was nobody else to question.

Her frustration was magnified when she remembered her companions, trapped somewhere deep in the heart of the castle. She made for the passageway before remembering the dead-end at the bottom. The thought of Artyrus's and Ffion's attempts to free her from the odd errand had her eager to make an escape, to find them and head back to something known, for the castle had been one chaotic incident after another.

She took off through the only other exit she could see, though goodness only knew how many hidden passages there were within the palace walls. From the outside, the dwelling was grand, but the interior felt as if it were without end.

Making her way through one of the hallways, she came upon a narrow staircase where only a pinprick of light was visible from the bottom. It felt like stepping into the unknown, the pitch-black surrounding her as suffocating as an airless tomb.

She descended slowly, deliberately, holding fast to the wall to keep her bearings, even as she contemplated stopping altogether to rend the lower half of the infernal skirt from her body, having tripped on it not once but twice.

Mercifully, she made it to the end, shoving her shoulder into the door, only to be greeted by the blinding light of yet another length of hallway, this one with no windows to speak of. It was like a maze from hell, with intermittent doors that led to nothing and nobody, either locked or else so small as to be useless for anything other than housing a broom.

She didn't recognize anything upon the floor at any rate, which likely meant that she was on the wrong level. Either that or the whole of the castle had reshuffled, locking her in an endless loop of fruitless exploration. Anything was possible.

Turning the corner, another span of hallway stretched before her, this one featuring double doors at its end.

That was different.

Rory reached the doorway, prepared to throw the full force of her weight into opening it, but that wasn't necessary. The doors whooshed aside with a mere brush of her fingers upon the ornate panels, welcoming her into what could only be the king's quarters.

To call it plush would be an understatement. Never before had Rory been a party to such luxury, with the finest of silks in shades of amethyst bedecking the oversized bed, complete with fluffy pillows too numerous to count. A canopy in whisps of gauzy white topped the bed frame, with posts of burnished gold that nearly reached the ceiling, while flossy fur rugs lent an air of warmth to the marble floors.

To her left was a parlor of sorts, with a pair of chaise lounges set to either side of a tufted ottoman covered in shimmering velvet. Floor-to-ceiling curtains framed the numerous windows, the presence of which Rory was pleased to see. She felt as though she'd been trapped within a labyrinth with no means of escape, but perhaps there was hope yet.

Rory moved throughout the quarters, and it was evident that it had been in use, though she couldn't imagine it was the dragon doing any sort of living there. And while the creature had been docile, certainly no sane human would attempt to live within the same dwelling as the fire-breathing beast.

Just beyond the parlor, a fire burned within a gilded hearth. She was in no hurry to be near the flames, however, given her previous escapades. But something on the end of the chaise caught her eye.

The black knight's helmet sat upon the foot of the settee, gleaming in the light cast from the hearth.

Hellfire.

"Aurora."

She jumped, placing her palm on her chest to stay her racing heart as she faced him. "*Lancelot.* What are you doing here?"

He closed the distance separating them, a wily grin showcasing his straight white teeth. "I confess that I watched you enter the castle after the dragon left. Her return made me fear for you—an unpredictable monster roving about the same space as my Gwenivere..." The knight's eyes smoldered, their obsidian depths threatening to swallow her whole as he took her wrists in his strong hold. "I could never bear it if something were to happen to you."

His beautiful face conjured fond memories of their past and promised a passionate future. Aurora was rapt in his presence, captive to all that might've been in a moment that was too urgent to waste upon fantastical what-ifs. She moved nearer, despite the uncertainty lingering in the back of her mind.

"How did you find me?" she managed, giving voice to the question plaguing her conscience. "The palace is vast, and I know I'm lost."

"It's desire, my darling." The heat in his gaze could break a thousand hearts, his smile widening wickedly. "And I might also live here on occasion. Not that there's much living happening in this realm, but I always did regard myself to be a king."

He winked as though his audacious admission was perfectly reasonable, and the dismissive manner with which he referred to their state of mind was also off-putting to Rory. She looked away, reconciling the many things she knew to be true of her friend with the cursed, jet-black helmet not but a yard from her.

Lancelot followed her line of sight. "Ah, so you've heard of my illicit activities, then." He tipped her chin upward, caressing the swell of her cheek as he urged her to meet his eyes. "I did it for you."

That got her attention.

He stepped closer, resting his forehead against hers. "Philippe warned us. We three were to retrieve the rogue royal at any cost, and I've spent the better part of my time here distracting my comrades, urging them away from you at every turn."

Wrapping his arm around her waist, he drew her nearer, slipping his other hand up the length of her arm, setting her skin aflame. He splayed his fingers, lacing them through her hair, and she shivered at his touch, his affection evident in every tender stroke of her flesh.

Lancelot shifted, his mouth deliciously close to her own. "For me, there was no other choice, duty be damned. I have ever loved you, Aurora, even in parting. No edict from Philippe could change that." He took her lower lip between his teeth, tugging it gently, then said, "And neither would I share you with him."

His confession caught her off guard, and soon, she found herself pulled closer, his mouth fitted to hers. He deepened the kiss, sliding his tongue between her lips, entangled with hers.

But it wasn't Lancelot holding her body, nor was it he who ravaged her very soul. In her mind, she'd surrendered herself to Artyrus. It was his hands exploring the curves of her hips. It was his breath growing ragged as she kissed the line of his jaw. It was his heart pacing her own, his body trembling at her touch.

The light scent of strawberries tickled her senses, returning her to herself from what was a wholly imaginary encounter. She opened her eyes to find not Artyrus but Lancelot looking back at her.

She backed away, touching her lips as she furrowed her brows in confusion. "I'm sorry, I shouldn't have —"

"Forbidden fruit always tastes sweeter." Lancelot's lazy grin had returned, and while he was, doubtless, earnest in his sentiments, he was not who she desired.

Rory didn't allow her disappointment to show, instead offering up a smile of her own. She touched his face, hoping that the knight didn't notice her distress. "I must go. Your intervention where Philippe is concerned only goes so far. Perhaps I will yet see you at the banquet."

"Let it be so," he replied, sneaking one more brief kiss before she turned to go.

Peeking over her shoulder, she waved, measuring her stride so as not to appear too eager to be away from him, though she wanted nothing more than to find Artyrus.

Deeper and deeper. Rory's fantasies had gotten the better of her, leading to a counterfeit rendezvous with a man who could never be a substitute for the real one.

And, if she weren't permitted to have Artyrus in reality, she was determined to make him hers in her dreams.

Chapter Twenty-Two

In her haste to get away from Lancelot, Aurora never thought to ask how she might find Artyrus and Ffion or how to escape the palace, for that matter. None of it was his fault but hers alone as she allowed emotions to rule rather than sense.

She only hoped he hadn't noticed anything was amiss, but the handsome knight missed nothing, if memory served.

Years ago, it was all she'd wanted—to have Lancelot, despite knowing she was promised to another. Back then, it was easy to ignore fate's cruel design.

In the distance, she heard her crew. They weren't far, and she followed the sound of their shouts down a seemingly endless passageway. Artyrus and Ffion yelled, the reverberation of their struggle to free themselves ricocheting off the stacked stone walls as they pounded and beat against their rocky prison.

Unknown voices rang through the musty corridor, masking the sounds of her people, but she couldn't tell from where. The castle was a disorienting fortress, and she pined for her blade as rushed footsteps drew nearer.

But running was of no benefit when Prince Philippe's form materialized directly in front of her. Without hesitation, the princess thrust her knee into his groin. He doubled over in pain, calling curses after her as she set off down the cold hallway, her heart thudding in tandem with her rapid pace.

"*Aurora!*"

They were close now. Artyrus roared her name from behind the door that separated them, his attempts to break through the barrier seeming to grow more desperate as she approached.

Once again, Philippe appeared out of nowhere, affording her no time for evasion. He curled his lip in fury as he pinned Rory to the wall, with one hand bracing her in place by the neck. She could scarcely breathe as blackness began to spot her periphery when he let up slightly, his head cocked to one side.

"Why don't you try that again, Princess." The prince's mocking tone set her ablaze as she spat in his face. Unable to move her limbs, it was all she could manage. She'd cursed the dream for its favors, so it seemed Otherlande had chosen a new darling to indulge. Save for some miracle, this was doubtless where she would die.

Philippe raised a brow, with a fiendish smirk forming at the edges of his mouth. "Oh, what fun we might have had." He wiped his cheek using the hem of his sleeve. From either end of the passage, several of his minions closed in on them. "Bring me the others," he ordered, and they retreated as quickly as they'd arrived, not one of them daring to risk his wrath.

She saw neither the silver knights nor Lancelot among his men, and all hope for deliverance evaporated. While his hold had slackened, Aurora remained frozen. In the distance, steel clashed against steel where Philippe's lackeys pursued Artyrus and Ffion. She prayed they'd serve their adversaries all to ruin.

"I had a report claiming you'd come here, but I didn't believe you quite stupid enough to try. If it's death you desire, you only need ask, my dear." The prince's breath was cool against her flesh, brushing over the tender hollow beneath her jaw. Every part of her recoiled at his closeness, but she was bereft of any manner of defense.

"If you think me foolish for being here, it can only mean one thing." Rory clenched her lower lip between her teeth, leaning as near to Philippe as the invisible shackles would permit. "You're afraid."

His fingers tightened, threatening to crush her throat, and her vision started to blur. He sniffed in amusement at her accusation while he dug his nails into her skin. She tried to swallow, tried to gasp for air to no avail.

If this was it, Aurora would not go down without a fight.

Nearby, guttural bellows and sputters of struggle echoed through the hall. Weapons clanked together in a lethal rhythm as the metallic scent of blood penetrated her nostrils.

Artyrus wasn't dead. If she could only manage to stall Philippe for long enough, he might reach her before darkness drew her into its awaiting depths.

"*You,*" Philippe seethed, "are a disease amongst your people. You have plagued Penzelle with expectations that will never be met." The prince's hand relaxed when he spoke, releasing enough pressure for Rory to gulp in a breath. No doubt, the sadist delighted in torturing her.

"They call you the fulfillment of prophecy, but you're scum like the rest of them. How my father ever fell for one of your kind is beyond comprehension. Stories of the late Queen Maleficent remember her as nothing short of a goddess amongst women." He flared his nostrils in disgust, his lips twisting into a sinister grin. "Perhaps, if you are lucky, that's how they'll remember you after I break your pretty neck."

At once, it made sense. The dream's manifestation of Isolde spoke of Luther's deceit, of Queen Maleficent.

Mal.

The revelation betrayed her, as Philippe somehow read the surprise in Aurora's features. Her head was swimming, and she might have dropped to the stone underfoot had the prince not kept her in place with his appalling tricks.

Air flooded her lungs, painfully clawing down the length of her throat. Still, relief was short-lived as Philippe's hand moved to Rory's jaw, demanding that she meet his feral gaze. He held her chin with bruising strength when he opened his mouth. "Look at me when I speak, rat."

The sudden shift was all she needed. Aurora slammed her skull into his using every ounce of force she could manage. It was enough. The prince staggered backward, and she regained mobility while he fought for footing.

Rory bolted for the strategy room, where sounds of battle had decreased. But Philippe caught her by the arm, recovering too quickly from their collision. Trying to shrug free of his hold, the princess squirmed, pleading with the dream for a shred of compassion. He dragged her back, groaning and huffing with effort as Aurora's shoes ground against the stone.

She stumbled, falling forward to the floor when his grip on her suddenly failed. Scrambling backward to distance herself, she watched Philippe collapse, clutching his head in agony.

Ffion stood behind him with an iron fire prod in hand. His hair was mussed, his clothes spattered in crimson, but the satisfaction the boy wore was unmistakable. After Ffion struck the felled prince once more at his back, Philippe's body went limp.

"*Aurora.*" Panting, Artyrus hovered over her, lifting her to her feet. "When I couldn't get to you, I..." His words trailed, and a mix of panic and relief shone in his eyes, warring against one another when he took in her appearance. "Are you hurt?"

"Only my pride." Rory forced a smile, though all she felt was astounding relief that he wasn't wounded.

Gently, he cupped her chin, turning her face to either side, looking it over. A silent storm raged beneath the surface of his careful touch as the pad of his thumb skimmed over the place where Philippe had burrowed his nails into her flesh.

The guardian's attentive ministrations nearly broke her. Aurora sank into his chest, an errant sob bursting free. Artyrus held her, his powerful arms enveloping her in their warmth, though they could not linger. She knew the castle wasn't safe, but she'd allow herself this peace a moment longer.

She didn't hide her tears from him, for he already knew her heart. She could feel it in the way he stroked her cheek and how his lips brushed softly across her forehead. He showed her how well he understood when he drew her nearer still, folding her into the strength of his steady frame, preventing her from crumbling altogether.

Her soul had changed unalterably in knowing him, but his unwavering devotion demanded more. Aurora would die a thousand deaths before she'd ever again consider binding herself to the prince of Chamelaute or even Lancelot. Anyone else would be a travesty when she knew Artyrus would evermore be branded upon her heart.

"You'll not be safe if we leave him alive." His voice was too tender for what his words implied, but Rory could not deny their truth. "I can end him swiftly if that's what you wish."

The suggestion alone was treasonous, but for her, he was willing to run the risk.

"No."

They would never be able to stop running if she allowed the guardian to kill him. Luther would hunt them relentlessly, and Aurora had already seen the outcome of his ruthlessness. Never could she see Artyrus meet that fate for her sake.

"Neither can we linger," he continued, and it took all of her will to pull away from him. The prince would recover, and they could not be there when he did.

"Philippe is bending Otherlande to his whims with increasing ease, and countless others have begun to do the same. It will only worsen," Rory said. "As time passes, the consequences of this world grow more perilous. I cannot fail the people."

After closing the gap between them, Artyrus ran his fingertip alongside Rory's tears, watching them slip over the swell of her cheek. "You won't." He leaned in, and her chest tightened as he kissed the droplets away.

Ffion waited quietly several paces away, idly spinning his fire prod atop the cold ground before something seemed to catch his notice. "They're coming to," he said, a slight flush spreading across his features as if it pained him to interrupt.

"You'll tell me everything at the cottage." Artyrus pressed his forehead to Aurora's brow. "And *we* will find a way."

The princess nodded as he backed off, the pair sharing a meaningful look before he unsheathed his sword. He led the way then, striding toward the king's war room with Rory and Ffion close at his back.

They would find a way. Together, they would wake a sleeping nation serving justice to Luther and anyone else deserving of retribution. They'd end the tyrant's reign and never look back.

And when that was done, peace would govern.

They would choose their fates.

Aurora saw the fallout from her guardian's fury when they reached the open doorway. Only then did she note his hands and the crusted blood underneath his nails. Artyrus and Ffion had not just cut down Philippe's men but had torn the room apart to get to her.

A handful of warriors littered the floor, but they were not dead. Somehow otherwise incapacitated like their prince, their limbs twitched and guttural groans tumbled from their mouths. There were flesh injuries that would heal in time, but nothing fatal.

With how many of them might Artyrus be well acquainted? Were some even friends?

One of the heaped figures stirred before flickering out of sight. But he quickly returned, on his feet a moment later ready to continue the fight as if he'd not been incapacitated mere minutes prior.

He charged Artyrus, who blocked the knight's blow with his blade. Pivoting, the guardian evaded a second swing, positioning himself behind his adversary. Trapping the man in his hold, Artyrus dug the tip of his sword into his back.

"Make no mistake, Garreth," he snarled. "I will drive this through your kidney if you so much as blink before we exit this room."

Garreth's breaths shuttered, but he obeyed. Artyrus released him, slowly backing away while motioning for Rory and Ffion to do the same.

No sooner had they reached the end of the corridor when Philippe bellowed a curse at his men.

Swift steps followed the prince's command to seize them. The trio sprinted through the castle with soldiers nipping at their heels. Darkness was an ally as they moved quickly across the palace, never sparing a look over their shoulders to see who might be looking back.

Aurora's throat burned from exertion when, at last, they found themselves back within the great hall. Approaching the towering entryway, its doors opened unassisted to reveal a vast stairway leading to their freedom.

And to her complete shock, Briar was awaiting her at the base, grazing lazily alongside Artyrus's trusted steed, Magnus.

Rory nearly wept with relief. Perhaps Otherlande hadn't entirely forsaken her after all.

Chapter Twenty-Three

The trio made for the horses, idly nibbling what little grass was to be found amongst the thorns rambling about the courtyard. They loped down the broad staircase, the steps feeling nothing shy of endless as they descended. Under different circumstances, Rory would've stood in awe of the beauty surrounding them, the stairs reflecting the light from the moon above with a subtle shimmer while veins of gold crawled the length of each white marble step.

But the enemy was at their heels, drawing nearer with each passing moment. Further complicating matters was the perilous state of the inner court—an obstacle they'd avoided altogether when they'd entered.

"We'll never get through," Artyrus said, somewhat breathless when they reached the bottom. "I've only a single sword, and there's no way I can make a path for us."

It was true. Thick brambles covered the courtyard from one end to the other, with jagged barbs stippling the vines in a haphazard arrangement that promised pain should anybody get too close.

"I don't think it needs to be as hard as all that." Rory greeted Briar with a quick kiss on her nose. It felt like a lifetime since they'd seen Briar and Magnus, though there was no feasible way to measure how long it had been. She mounted her steed before reaching for Ffion. "Up with you," she rasped, helping him onto Briar's back behind her.

Artyrus sat atop Magnus, who appeared to be even larger within the dreamscape than in reality. He turned an anxious circle beneath Artyrus, seemingly eager to get on the move. "What's your plan, then?"

As little as Rory liked to admit it, utilizing a few of the tricks she'd picked up along the way would be the quickest road to success, assuming it worked. Closing her eyes, she envisioned the thorns parting before them in her mind's eye, forming a pathway to the portcullis unimpeded by creeping vines or prickly spikes.

Her passenger's sharp intake of breath told her everything she needed to know, and that was both heartening and unnerving. It hadn't been as challenging to conjure her whims as she'd thought, but then again, many things became easier to manifest as she fell deeper into their unified slumber.

Artyrus whistled through his teeth, a mix of awe and concern evident in his features. "Where did you learn such things?"

Rory waved a dismissive hand. "It's as simple as thought."

That much was true, though she steadfastly ignored her concern over what it meant for her state of mind. They tore off, making for the portcullis with nary an obstacle in their midst. Artyrus dismounted, hastily releasing the lever that dropped the door, turning it into a drawbridge leading to their freedom.

Behind them, Philippe and his hoard of minions poured forth from the castle, rapidly closing the gap as they made for the stairs. How they'd recovered so quickly from the thrashing they'd just taken was a mystery, but they appeared every bit as capable as before and many times angrier.

Artyrus returned to Magnus, urging the horse over the footbridge, followed by Rory and Ffion. "We'd better hurry. Can you replace the vines?"

"I can't focus!" Rory was rapidly losing her composure with the inevitability of being caught, of being that near to the vile prince once more sending her to the edge of panic. The last thing she wanted was to be weak, but the turmoil was taking its toll.

A dark form emerged on the horizon, the dragon's massive body blotting out the light from the full moon. She soared over their heads, heedless of Rory and her companions, who had stopped dead in their tracks as she drifted toward the castle. To say that the sight of her was impressive was a vast understatement, her presence garnering the attention of everything that drew breath as she circled above.

But she didn't make for the tower, instead diving toward Philippe and his men. She swooped toward them with a bloodcurdling shriek, breathing hellfire from her mouth in an endless stream of flames.

The contingent dove for cover, with cries for mercy and howls of anguish emanating from the men as she made a second pass. Her ruthless pursuit saw two knights into eternal slumber as each was burned to ashes in a matter of seconds. The others were nowhere to be seen, including Philippe, who had quickly sought refuge by leaping from the mezzanine overlooking the staircase into the mess of thorns below.

Would that he might have met his end at the bottom. It was Rory's most fervent hope.

"Come," Artyrus pressed, spurring his steed onward. "We've wasted too much time already. Who'd have thought that beast would be a godsend?"

Rory knew. Indeed, the creature was much more than that, but that conversation would have to wait.

They headed for the woods, away from the castle, far from the revelers who continued with the banquet in earnest. It felt like a piece of home had arrived as they rode, the familiarity of her horse a blessing amidst the chaos.

Unusually bright moonlight made their escape easier as they approached a clearing of sorts on the far side of the forest, the rhythmic beat of their horse's hooves soothing away some of Rory's frayed nerves. They'd put a fair amount of distance between themselves and the rotten prince, though she was certain it would never feel like enough.

"Is it safe at the cottage?" Rory asked as they slowed slightly to a trot. "It has been so far, but I guess after tonight..."

"We gave 'em hell," Ffion replied, his confidence never wavering. "I doubt he'd be willing to go through that again."

Rory couldn't help but smile. His youthfulness was evident in his assurance, for she harbored no doubts that Philippe would be back for more.

"Allow me to—" Artyrus's words fell away as he glanced skyward, focusing on something far above them. "Is that—?"

"Petra," Ffion finished. "I haven't seen her in days... I think..."

It had been earlier in what would've been afternoon that they'd seen her last, but time was a blur in Otherlande. She coasted past them, hovering on the wind currents in the open air above them, only something seemed wrong.

As if to confirm that sentiment, the girl plummeted from the heavens, tumbling headlong toward the earth with no signs of attempting to stay her fall. Her body crumpled, her limp form plunging with ever-increasing speed.

"Yah!" Artyrus took off like a shot, racing toward Petra as he prodded Magnus to a new, impressive pace. Rory and Ffion quickly followed, arriving just as Artyrus leapt from his horse, positioning himself beneath Petra. The girl dropped like a rock into his waiting arms, the pair collapsing to the earth under the force of her fall.

Rory dropped to their sides, pawing through Petra's wild mane as she sought to find their covered faces. "Are you all right?"

Artyrus groaned, easing himself onto his elbows, while Petra remained motionless, rolling off the guardian. "I'll do. Is she all right?"

They clustered around Petra, finding that she was at least breathing. Her eyes were open but vacant, a distant gleam shining in her glassy gaze. "The shadow," she whispered.

Ffion watched, his face a mask of confusion. "What shadow? We have no shadows here."

Was that true? Rory wracked her brain, irritated that she'd taken no notice.

"I've not seen one," Artyrus agreed, amplifying Rory's annoyance with herself. She'd have to be more observant.

Petra rose to her feet without warning, backing away from her companions as her eyes grew wider, frantic, staring at something beyond them. She clutched her head, wrenching her hands away as tears streamed over her cheeks. "Leave me! Just go!"

Rory turned, startled to find a darkened figure standing not far from them upon the hillside. It had no face, no distinguishing features other than its slightly elongated form, distorted by the glow from the moon.

The shadow didn't move, only spied from its perch upon the ridge, and it was then that Rory realized how long it had been since last she'd seen one. Further mystifying the princess was the presence of such visible darkness at eventide, for it retained a distinctly human outline, even as it held no depth.

It flickered in place, rippling under their scrutiny. Stepping backward, the dusky figure moved once more, slowly retreating into the woods as though it couldn't be bothered to care about being surveilled.

But then again, they were observing a shadow with no discernible origins.

Artyrus sprang off the ground, mounting his horse and moving toward Rory. "I'm going to follow that...*shadow*." His voice was low, so only she would hear, the absurdity of tracking a non-human entity written in his features. "I need to know what sort of a threat it is, and I want to clear the cottage. Perhaps you can see to Petra then meet me there?"

"Yes," Rory agreed, offering a tight smile. She didn't wish to see him go, but they'd accomplish more apart than they could together.

Artyrus reached for her, cupping her cheek. "Please be careful."

"You, too." She placed her hand over his, the pair sharing an anxious moment as they parted. Rory backed away as he took off, following him with her gaze until he disappeared into the forest.

"There's something wrong with her," Ffion croaked, his voice thick with concern. Rory turned to find him fussing over Petra, who was curled up on her side, her knees tucked to her chest.

The vacant mien had returned, her features drawn and devoid of color. Her wild hair was coiled about her head in a tangled puff, one hand resting in Ffion's as the other clutched her chest.

"She doesn't even know her own name," Ffion continued, a tear slipping down his cheek. "I think she's been here too long. She's losing herself." Sniffling, he stroked his free hand over her head, his faithfulness cracking Rory's heart in two. The boy had come here because of Petra. She could only imagine what her condition was doing to the young lad.

Rory moved to her side, taking her face between her hands. "Speak to me, Petra. Who is the shadow? Why are you so afraid?"

The girl thrashed, eyes widening with the mention of the shadow. "The huntsman," she whispered. "The shrouded kingdom will have my heart."

Rory balked. Yes, Otherlande was absurd, but at least it was real. "The shrouded kingdom is a myth. You've nothing to fear."

"Who told you that?" Ffion demanded, catching Rory off guard with his accusatory tone. "The shrouded kingdom is as real as Calaise or Llundyn. The fallacy that it doesn't exist enables those who dwell there to get away with all they do."

She watched the boy, deadly serious in his assertion, and wondered how far gone he was. Her allies were rapidly failing, their minds ever more fraught with the fog of what felt like a never-ending reverie. Aurora shoved aside her misgivings, refusing to succumb to any further deterioration herself. She would do what she'd come to do.

Stars only knew if that were possible.

In a moment of unexpected clarity, Petra's eyes focused, narrowing on Rory. "The boy is safer with you. Take care of him, and see him freed of this nightmare, just as you said you would." She shuddered, flickering where she lay before reappearing. Gripping Ffion's hand, she met his gaze. "Stay alive, you little troll. Perhaps I will see you in another life."

Smiling, she flittered away, leaving only the imprint of her slight form behind in the crushed grass. Ffion gasped, covering his mouth with his fist as he stared at the void she'd created. He worked desperately not to break, but his distress was as visible as the eventide moon. Rising to his feet, he set his jaw, determination marking his features.

Rory stood, moving toward him. "Is she —?"

"*No*," he hissed, raising a warding hand. "Petra is too great a force to simply die. She fights. She always has, and this is no different. She'll be back. You'll see."

Nodding her assent, Rory was anything but sure. She'd watched people filter away in much the same manner when they'd received a mortal blow in the arena, and they had never returned. In those instances, they were almost certainly dead.

"All right," Aurora managed as she moved to mount Briar. "Until then, we must find Artyrus. He may need our help with her shadow."

* * * *

He loathed leaving Aurora behind. And to chase a being made of darkness and air no less, like following nothing more than vapor. But the girl, Petra, had been nearly catatonic due to its presence, and to treat it without seriousness would be a grave violation of his duties as a knight. For now, he considered the shadow a threat.

But a new obstacle presented itself as he wandered through the woods. What good were his tracking skills when he was chasing a phantasm? For all he knew, it was merely a mirage, a distraction. Perhaps he'd just played right into somebody's hands, leaving the princess behind and unguarded.

He was a fool.

The darkness of the forest surrounding him hampered his pursuit, with little light to speak of finding its way through the thick canopy of leaves sheltering him from above. It was an errand for a stooge…nothing more.

Artyrus was about to turn around when he heard a faint crack not far ahead. Dismounting his steed, he moved toward the disturbance on foot, unsheathing his sword and creeping through the brush beneath him as silently as a ghost himself.

Another crack. He was getting closer.

A small gap in the glade before him felt like something of a trap—an opportunity for failure. He paused, observing the small expanse from the cover of fronds.

It was no shadow. It was the black knight, and he was anything but unaware. The armored figure sprinted his way without missing a beat, picking up speed with each step. He reached Artyrus in a matter of seconds, affording little time to prepare for the assault.

The two men brawled, broadsword against broadsword, with the intensity of his opponent rocking

Artyrus to his core. He hadn't been unprepared, but he'd treated the whole of his errand with contempt, leading him to complacency, damn him.

Sparring in the spare open space, Artyrus had a sudden realization.

He'd done this before.

His adversary was not unknown to him. Indeed, they'd scuffled that very day in the melee, though that run-in felt like a lifetime ago. They had similar techniques and had always evenly matched, leading to clashes of ego alongside their physical showdowns.

Artyrus was, admittedly, surprised, having previously determined the black knight to be Philippe. But there was no mistaking his opponent for the sniveling prince.

"Why not resolve our disagreements once and for all, *Lancelot*," Artyrus snarled. He backed away, throwing the black knight off balance when he lunged for Artyrus's throat.

"So you've solved the riddle," Lancelot jeered, casting his helmet aside, revealing a face red with exertion. "Would you like a prize?"

Artyrus tossed his sword to the ground, eager for a more hands-on approach. "Only a fair fight. One on one, weapon free. That is, unless you're afraid. You always were a shoddy grappler."

"Ah. Weak taunts from a poor excuse for a knight." Lancelot chuckled, jabbing his sword into the earth before removing his gloves. "Fine. Strangulation will suit my purposes every bit as well as running you through with a blade. Either way, you'll be dead."

He wore a wicked smirk that told Artyrus their battle would be anything but fair.

Then he disappeared.

Chapter Twenty-Four

Artyrus cursed himself, never having considered the black knight's other possible identities sooner, especially after Kaye had risked warning him.

Of course, it was Lancelot. The black knight had been too formidable, too cunning to be someone as half-witted as Prince Philippe.

Lancelot reappeared, ever the calculating weasel he'd always been. His black suit of armor was gone, and he squared his shoulders, wearing a serpentine sneer. "It's a bit cumbersome, really." He rolled his head in lazy circles, first in one direction then the other, addressing his casual attire. "Philippe has always been a bit dramatic, though the armor did afford me new admirers. You know, you've made it increasingly difficult to avoid killing you. Tempting as it may be, I can't be sure it wouldn't result in a particular *consequence* I'd prefer to bypass."

"You're bold enough to assume you could?" Artyrus raised a brow, his sword at the ready. Pomposity like Lancelot's was rarely supported by action. He was skilled in the art of combat, to be sure, but was not one to sully himself performing another man's dirty work, royal or otherwise. "I confess you have my attention, brother. And if I'm to die at your hand anyway, why is it you deign to do so?"

The knight sighed, picking an errant speck of what looked like ash from his tunic. Would that the tedium of conversation might soon find him at rest in an early, unmarked grave.

"I and your wearisome keepers have been tasked with pursuing a rogue royal—and so I have." His gaze narrowed on Artyrus, daring the guardian forward. "The question that consumes me is whether or not the fulfillment of Merlin's prophecy would be achieved or eradicated by your death. Would it nullify the poison and awaken a rebellion?"

Artyrus sighed. Lancelot always talked too much, but there was a chance he might yet learn something from the self-important jackass, even if it involved a bit of goading. "Luther never meant for the poison to last. His son Philippe would not be here if he had."

Scoffing, the knight swiped his blade through the air as if testing the weight and feel of it. "Very astute. But who convinced him to use it in the first place?" He grinned, leaving no room for question that it had been him.

"Once I demonstrated how one might wake themselves from this dreamland, he thought it all rather brilliant, assuming anyone put under willingly could also wake at will as I had managed. I didn't know if that were possible and didn't care, in truth. Luther is a foolish man, bless him. A sovereign ruler shouldn't be so naive, wouldn't you agree?"

Artyrus remained silent, all the while burning with indignation over the callous machinations so flippantly employed by Lancelot. These were people's lives he was messing with, and he didn't care.

"But then I realized nobody outside of my dream knew what had happened within," the heartless knight continued, heedless of any judgment from Artyrus. "Not until Lief's cousin, Ordel, reported his untimely demise did I become fully aware of all that could be accomplished. It was purely good fortune that I'm so adept at manipulating this remarkable fantasy."

"You killed him."

"Sacrificed, yes," Lancelot corrected as if it made any bit of difference while making no effort to conceal his apathy. "I wanted to test how distant subconsciousness is from the reality we think we know. They aren't so different, it seems. Only here, I won't be charged for my offenses, while in reality, it appeared that Lief passed in his slumber. I win on all fronts."

The knight took a leisurely step toward Artyrus, madness plain in his devilish stare. "I'd hoped you and the princess's face-off with our dear prince would have lightened my burden, but alas, I presume I'll have to end him myself as well. Such are the woes of one with aspirations so lofty."

Artyrus knew Lancelot better than to believe he intended to assist Penzelle. No, he was incapable of any action that didn't somehow benefit his personal objectives. Philippe's death would leave the throne vulnerable, with no heir.

"And what of His Majesty, the king? I suppose he will die in the throes of battle?" The possibilities of Luther's passing were endless.

Lancelot sniffed. "Too valiant. I will instead weave a tale of his weakened heart failing him while asleep."

"How unfortunate."

"Indeed." The knight strode nearer Artyrus, his relaxed posture tensing as he clenched his fists. "But his crown will suit me well."

"It's regrettable that you'll have gone to such great lengths only to find that Luther doesn't sleep with his crown atop his head." Artyrus shifted his weight, securing his footing as the assertion settled. It was never wise to be the first to strike, especially when met with a crafty opponent. Thankfully, Lancelot never required much provocation. "Would you like to kill me now, or is there more burdening you?"

"Shut up," Lancelot shouted, only to rush Artyrus.

He braced himself, anticipating the hit when his adversary struck a blow directly to his side with blinding fury. Pain shot through him like a bolt of lightning slicing through his rib, but it had left Lancelot exposed.

"*What*? Did you think I would be *impressed*?" Artyrus grabbed the knight's wrist, wresting his arm as he threw his fist into Lancelot's jaw.

Lancelot's head jolted backward with the impact of Artyrus's powerful hook. He retreated a step, and the guardian pursued him without a moment's hesitation, dealing a second punch to his stomach.

Lancelot doubled over before Artyrus slammed his knee into his hunched form, again and again, holding him in place. But he knew better than to think his opponent would ever surrender. Once more, the guardian thrust his knee into Lancelot's middle when suddenly, he'd taken hold of Artyrus's waist.

With a grunt of straining effort, the knight brought him to the ground. The struggle continued as they hit the earth, each grappling for any advantage over the other.

Artyrus could not let him win—not for pride or glory, but because he would never let the bastard near Aurora again. He could tell she trusted him, and though he knew not the details of their shared history, Lancelot would have to breathe his last for her safety and Penzelle's future.

Sweat and dirt stung the guardian's eyes while they wrestled atop a cold, woodland floor. Fatigue slowly settled over both men, but neither relented.

Lancelot's elbow made contact with Artyrus's temple, and he growled with white-hot frenzy. The knight didn't miss his opportunity when Artyrus's vision blurred and darkened, quickly shoving him off before slamming the guardian to the ground.

Artyrus was pinned, with his chest and stomach fixed to the earth beneath him, sputtering bits of dust from his mouth. Lancelot took him by the hair, yanking his head backward with brutal force before driving it into a fragment of stone.

The world went black. Sheer will kept the guardian from slipping into blissful nothingness, for he alone prevented his foe from pursuing Aurora. Warmth trickled down Artyrus's forehead as he fought to stay conscious, the world swimming around him.

Certain agony rescued him from the brink of oblivion when he felt his arm wrenched backward at an unnatural angle. His shoulder blazed, and his mobility floundered, but he couldn't give in to the pain. He wouldn't give in to *him*.

Lancelot groaned, releasing ragged, wearied breaths. Artyrus sensed his lurking, murderous presence hovering above him as he twisted beneath the knight. He gritted his teeth, pushing past the ache radiating through his chest and arm. With his remaining strength, the guardian slammed his boot into Lancelot's knee with crippling force, clearly rupturing the joint.

He collapsed with a howl of agony, dropping to the ground, and Artyrus kept his writhing frame in place, pinning the knight under his weight.

Lancelot sneered, even as Artyrus tightened his grip on his neck. Blood coated his teeth from their encounter, dripping slowly from the edge of his mouth. He would die with that wicked smile, though the guardian delighted in no man's death.

"My only sadness in your demise will be informing the princess of your betrayal." It grieved Artyrus to be forced to share such things. He hoped against all hope that she might understand he'd been given no alternative but to end Lancelot. Aurora was reasonable, but history and emotions could give way to warped perceptions.

Artyrus felt Lancelot's breath thinning as his fingers crushed his windpipe. He thrashed about to no avail until the life in his black eyes dimmed.

Then he was gone.

Artyrus fumbled, his hands empty and still warm from their fight. The knight's disappearance was every bit as unnerving as the first time he'd witnessed someone blink out of existence, never to reawaken from this hellscape.

He let himself sink to the earth, with aching muscles and bones protesting against his every movement. The only relief from one wound was another crying out, reminding him how close he'd come to meeting the same fate.

Artyrus's thoughts were incoherent and muddled by all his opponent had revealed, but what to make of it was entirely unknown. While he'd eliminated the immediate threat, Philippe and King Luther lurked about the fringes of this cursed tapestry of greed, and he was in no condition to face them.

"What happened?"

The guardian considered whether he was further losing himself when he heard Aurora's concerned voice calling to him. He listened to the earth crunching beneath her quick steps as she made her way to him, with even lighter footfalls trailing her own.

"Artyrus—" Falling to her knees beside him, she clutched his arm, forcing him upright. Rory's brows knit together, her distress over his condition apparent when he winced.

How bad must he look to worry her so?

Ffion emerged from behind her petite frame, his bright eyes pooling with moisture. "This wasn't Philippe or his stooges, or you'd still be fighting."

The boy's innate confidence in his ability made Artyrus's throat tighten. He'd nearly lost his life more than once that night, but Ffion's faith never wavered. "You're right. It was the black knight."

Aurora gasped. "*No.* Lancelot did this to you? Oh, Artyrus…" His name was a whisper on her tongue. She moved nearer, stroking his arm. "I only just learned at the palace that he donned the armor. He claimed it was the only way he could protect me from Philippe, but I should have—"

"What would it have changed?" Artyrus was surprised by his admission, but how could he be upset with her for not sharing her knowledge when they'd barely begun to catch their breath?

"Very little." Clipped syllables drifted toward them, a wraith of impossible doom materializing near enough that they felt the air shift with his sudden arrival.

Lancelot smiled, a mirthful sneer that instantly had Artyrus on his feet, despite the searing pain pleading for him to surrender. No sign of injury shone on his foe's form. It was as if he hadn't almost become a memory.

Dawn broke through the surrounding trees, followed by horns blaring in the distance. The knight sniffed, indicating the beginning of The Merit once again with an outstretched hand. "Philippe grows impatient. It seems he's as eager for you to die as I am."

"Why are you doing this?" Aurora's voice cracked as she rose to stand at Artyrus's side, while Ffion joined them on the other.

"Your *plaything* can fill you in while I hunt him in his real-life slumber. But fear not for yourself, Princess. I cannot reign without a queen. How much more poetic that it shall be you who rules beside me?" Lancelot displayed no insincerity when addressing her, leaving Rory clearly dismayed in his presence.

He'd saved this final detail of his plan for her hearing. Perhaps, had he successfully killed Artyrus, he might have shared the rest of his musings with her alone, only to learn that ruling was never a desire but a sentence for her.

"The burden of Luther's crown would crush you as it will him. You're a fool to wish for such affliction. Chamelaute is failing, but you're too stupid to see it,"

Artyrus seethed, his condemnation laced with intensity over everything he loathed about the self-serving wretches in leadership.

"You truly don't know, do you?" The knight cocked his head to one side, disbelief evident in his scrutiny.

"Spare us your manipulations, Lancelot," Aurora grumbled, her lithe figure trembling with frustration.

"Very well." He straightened his tunic with an indifferent brush of his palm. "Then it would seem you're late for the joust. Good luck."

His well wish was delivered as more of a curse, and with it, he was gone once more.

And if he meant what he'd said, he'd left their present nightmare altogether to hunt a slumbering Artyrus.

Chapter Twenty-Five

The Merit Tourney would have its way, come hell or high water, announcing itself in a moment of utter desperation.

It was the last place Aurora wanted to be, her flagging spirit desiring nothing more than to take Artyrus back to the cottage and see him to better health. He was in no shape to participate in the joust, arguably the most dangerous challenge they'd have yet.

There were too many variables, and that even without considering the nuisance of the dream's random interventions. Then there was the simple truth that Rory had never participated in such things. She'd done her best to pay it no mind as they'd made their way through the previous rounds of the competition, and now that the time had arrived, she was not only unprepared physically but mentally as well.

The sun continued its stubborn ascent, rising in the distance as the trumpets sounded once more. It seemed the entirety of Otherlande was against them, hustling them against their will into a situation that felt fraught with danger. They were running short on time and woefully unprepared for the chaos that lay ahead.

Ffion examined the vacant space left behind by Lancelot, his curiosity seemingly without limit. "Surely there's another way. At the end of the day, it will be Princess Aurora versus Prince Philippe, and he will never allow you to remain alive. You'd have to kill him first."

"I will." While Rory may have lacked confidence in her jousting skills, she would never allow it to shake her faith in her ability to do what needed to be done. "It didn't have to be this way, but if it's him or me…"

She shook off the sense of foreboding that was threatening to strangle her. It did her no good to entertain all the fantastical scenarios that might emerge. Taking Artyrus's injured arm in her hands, she tested its range of motion. He sucked in a sharp breath as she moved it, grimacing when she lifted it above his shoulder. "I think it's out of joint."

He was unusually quiet, the brutality of his skirmish with Lancelot seemingly taking a toll. His face was strained, with a fresh, jagged gash marring his forehead, while the blows the two men had rained upon one another likely had him exhausted and in pain, though he made no complaint.

"Why not just pull the sword without jousting?" Ffion demanded. His eagerness to find an alternative was well-meant, but for Rory, there was no substitute for action.

"I'm no coward. My participation is the only way to prove to my people that I'm worthy of leading them. I want to be someone they deserve."

"You already are." Artyrus gritted his teeth as Rory rotated his arm, knowing what was coming next. She wrenched his arm toward herself with a hearty tug, a sickening crack echoing forth from the socket. The guardian groaned, rolling his shoulder.

Rory ran light fingers over its curve, knowing there was nothing more she could do for him. "Better?"

"Better, yes. And as much as I hate to admit it, you're right." Artyrus supported his injured arm at the elbow as though it hurt to straighten it. "You need to do this as much for yourself as for your kingdom, and for that, I stand in utter awe of you. Your resolve, your courage is beyond admirable. But Philippe will play dirty. He's lost to this place, and he'll use the dream against you, so do what you must."

She bristled at the prospect of involving any sort of illusions, especially given how challenging it was for her to wield control over them. In truth, it would be more of a distraction than a help. "The tourney is all about merit. Does it not stand to reason that I should compete with honor?"

"If you won't use the blasted dream to your advantage, perhaps I'll have to do it for you." Artyrus stepped before Aurora, his features grim. "You'll have a hell of a fight on your hands. I don't suppose you'd allow me to assist you?"

"I'm afraid not." Her mind overflowed, with all the tumult of the day's events surfacing in his presence. "Do you suppose he's really left this nightmare? Lancelot, I mean. Much like Petra, I guess we can't know for sure."

"What's happened to Petra?"

"Nothing but the usual. She likes to be alone a lot," Ffion piped up, idly picking some wild blueberries.

Rory didn't miss how he soured with the mention of her, turning from the pair to his own pursuits.

Rory met Artyrus's gaze, a silent understanding passing between them. She reached for him, grasping his tunic in her fists. "There is so much we need to discuss."

"Later." He took her face between his hands as he kissed her brow. "It's time to focus on the here and now." He kissed the tip of her nose. "No distractions."

Resting his forehead against hers, he paused, sharing a brief moment of peace. He dropped his hands to her waist, pulling her nearer, and she reveled in the moment, so achingly close to the most unexpected of lovers.

"My Valkyrie," he breathed. "You're so strong. It's my most sincere desire to be somehow worthy of you. When we find our way out of this, I'll endeavor to prove myself. I know it should be the last thing I want, that it's the furthest thing from rational, but—"

The trumpets sounded in the distance, the third and final warning that the trials would again begin.

"Unless you plan to miss the games, I suggest we get a move on." Ffion glanced over his shoulder before taking off through the trees, safely betting that Rory and Artyrus would not be far behind.

Artyrus sighed, seemingly frustrated by the interruptions. "Is he all right?"

"He will be. We need to get out of this dreamscape for all our sakes. Even more so now, for Lancelot could very well be hunting us while we slumber, and I'd prefer to be there to take him on in both mind and body when he tries."

"Don't worry over that now." He placed a featherlight kiss upon her forehead before stepping away, their never-ending duties taking precedence, just as they always did. Reaching for her hand, he threaded his fingers with hers, a genuine smile lighting his handsome face. "Now, let us show Philippe how foolish it is to challenge this mistress of blades."

* * * *

The first several rounds of the joust had been difficult to watch. Brutality was an anticipated element of such pursuits but being so close to the action and knowing that her participation was on the horizon had Rory's stomach in knots.

Watching Artyrus's turn in the event had been equally challenging, though for a wholly different reason. He was in pain but refused to forfeit as a matter of honor — the very same reason she herself had given him not long before the competition.

It was maddening, his insistence that he contend at all. Yet attempting to talk him out of it was a fool's errand, just as it would be for him, should he consider asking the same of her.

Despite his somewhat vulnerable state with a cracked rib, untold bruises and a sore shoulder, Artyrus succeeded in his bout, besting his adversary in the second of three rounds. A sight to behold, and one that Rory watched with bated breath, the guardian separated his opponent from his steed without breaking much of a sweat.

"Let's hope I will have as much success as you managed," Rory said, greeting Artyrus as he exited the list field. Her champion was tired but, surprisingly, no worse for wear, having avoided taking any severe shots during his trial.

"I have no doubt." Artyrus grinned, battle-born zeal shining in his gaze as he made his way toward her. He wrapped his arm around her shoulders, kissing the top of her head, and she smiled in return, amused by his unforeseen enthusiasm.

"To witness your disregard for your duty, king and kingdom in such close proximity is truly shocking," Prince Philippe chided. He appeared before them without warning, his arms crossed over his chest. Glancing at Rory, his face was a mask of disgust. "For the supposed savior of a bygone people, you don't seem to treat your obligations with the slightest bit of urgency. It's a shame that Penzelle was saddled with someone like you."

His eyes were wild, a frantic quality tainting his every movement. It was safe to say he was lost, a victim by choice or by consequence of their never-ending nightmare.

Perhaps it was callous, but Rory couldn't bring herself to care. The man was a tyrant, just like his father and grandfather before him, and if their interactions were any indication, there would be no altering that.

Philippe scoffed, indicating the pair with a waggling finger. "And this... For how long have you, a *betrothed royal*, been gallivanting about with this sorry excuse for a knight? You're to be my queen, and yet—"

"And yet I have my own mind and make my own choices," Rory spat. "I'll not take orders from you or anybody else. I choose *me*. Indeed, I'd rather die than marry you."

"So you shall," Philippe replied, taking a step backward when Artyrus lurched toward him. Aurora held him back as the prince laughed. "Chain your mangy beast. I'll see you in the arena." A delighted chuckle escaped him as he walked away, leaving Rory feeling cold inside.

"Well, that's certainly no accident," she uttered.

"*No.*" Artyrus seethed, shaking with fury.

Rory took his hand in hers, working to remain calm, even as she felt she might lose her cool altogether. It wouldn't do to succumb to such whims, especially given her impending bout against the prince.

"This is for the best. If I'm to prove myself in combat, who better to face than the most treacherous amongst the competitors?" Rory was pleased to find that she'd managed to suppress the tremor from her voice, though she trembled within. She straightened, drawing Artyrus along beside her as she made for Briar. "Help me prepare, won't you?"

He stopped mid-stride, holding her hands between them as he faced her. "You need not do this. You've proven yourself over and over again. He will not yield."

"Neither will I." She smiled, hoping to ply him with some of her counterfeit confidence. "It was always meant to end here — prince versus princess. Everything else, all the other matches, the chaos of the dream, the trials — it was all mere pretense. My time is now."

Artyrus took her in his arms, his long fingers threaded through her hair at the nape of her neck. "Come back to me, Aurora. I am lost without you."

She shivered at his touch, at his words, drawing comfort from his strong embrace. The rapid pulse of his heart was at odds with his quiet directive, and she knew he was every bit as anxious as she.

But she would not fail.

They reached Briar a few moments later, where Ffion dutifully awaited them with Rory's armor and lance. The boy was busily outfitting Briar in armor of her own, with a spiked chanfron for her face, a peytral for her chest and a crinet that covered her neck in segmented metal plates from her poll to her withers.

The barding wasn't particularly heavy, but it did appear cumbersome, causing Briar to stamp her hooves in displeasure each time Ffion approached with more dressing.

"I feel the same way," Rory cooed, stroking her mare's face. She stepped away then, outfitting herself in the bulky metal suit that would, God willing, preserve her through three rounds of jousting. The plating was inordinately warm, at times singeing her fingers as she reached for more, but she refused to give voice to her discomfort, having vowed to make do. Besides, it didn't seem to bother Artyrus as he handed her piece after piece.

It was unnatural. Something about the heat reeked of sabotage, whether the dream itself or Philippe's machinations, she didn't know. But she would not speak of it, eager to deny either of those two entities the awareness of her discomfort. She'd gut it out.

Artyrus met her gaze as he fastened her pauldron in place. "Are you ready?"

"As much as I'll ever be." Rory jumped in place several times, stretching and moving in the uncomfortable armor as she tested its mobility. Her skin burned beneath the layers of cloth and metal, sweat dotting her forehead as she stepped toward Briar.

Artyrus bent with his hands clasped, offering Rory a boost onto the back of her steed, the horse champing at the bit as they awaited their turn. "Remember," Artyrus began, handing the reins to Aurora, "you can unseat him for immediate victory, else earn a point for each lance you shatter. Aim for his shield or helmet to gain the most points."

"Don't forget your lance!" Ffion scurried toward her with her shield and first lance in hand. The sun gleamed off the shield, nearly blinding Rory with his approach, while the lance was covered in swirls of white and sapphire blue. On the tip sat a coronal of gold, splayed into four separate prongs to diffuse the force of impact.

Rory took the shield in hand before reaching for the lance. Its weight nearly took her arm from its socket, dropping it to her side under its mass. Struggling, she attempted to lift it again, growing frustrated as her arm shook uncontrollably. "Why is it so heavy?"

Ffion glanced at Artyrus, who watched the princess with growing concern. The boy shrugged, shaking his head. "I didn't notice."

Artyrus took the lance from her, testing its build for himself. "It feels no different than usual to me, unless..." He turned, watching something in the distance.

She followed his line of sight, her gaze landing upon Philippe, who wore a vicious smirk.

More sabotage.

His horse was more dragon than steed, massive and black with smoking nostrils. He would be formidable even without cheating, but of course, Philippe would leave nothing to chance, intent upon proving himself the rightful ruler even in spite of his deceptions.

"Lash it to my arm," Rory said, raising a hand to ward away Artyrus's emerging protests. "*Please.* I can manage well enough if I no longer need to worry about dropping it."

She willed her words to be true, desperate to achieve all she'd set out to do, even as she ignored the anguish of her scorched flesh and deficient strength. Never had she expected it to come easily, and stars knew a fair fight would never suit a fraud like the prince.

That would only make her victory all the sweeter.

Chapter Twenty-Six

Briar galloped into the ring, her gait steady and sure. Would that Aurora might share her confidence.

The princess' chain mail and suit of arms seemed heavier, blazing upon her slight frame like it might melt onto her body. Her mount circled the end of the tilt separating them from the feral prince, whose steed was kicking at the gravel and eagerly huffing as Rory stayed their position.

Tightly clutching her lance, Aurora's palms began to sweat despite the straps digging into her arm. The anticipation alone would likely drive the princess to madness if Otherlande didn't seize her waning sensibilities first. Opposite them, Philippe waited astride his colossal beast, who looked ready to charge at any moment.

Sparing a glance toward the base of the stands, she found Artyrus. Ffion was at his side, neither of them tearing their eyes from her. The guardian offered a nod of encouragement, though she knew he felt every bit as anxious for her as she had for him.

Try as she might, she could not settle her racing heart. Her nerves were a bundle of kindling awaiting a flame when the starting flags finally dropped, signaling the onslaught.

Aurora and the prince took off, facing one another from either end of the jousting lists. Both horses hurtled for the center point where the riders would clash, with a cloth tilt guiding each broad stride.

Rory watched through the slit of her helmet, ignoring how the steel cuisses and fauld threatened to brand her flesh. She'd never attempted to fight with bulky armor, let alone wield a lance. It was cumbersome, to say the least, and grew more painful with every breath, but Philippe would never drop his pursuit.

The gap narrowed between them, thundering steps pounding in tandem with Aurora's pulse in a rhythm of certain doom. She would not blink, would not so much as spare a thought toward what might happen should she be unsuccessful. The burden of her weapon weakened her posture, making it even more unlikely to level a hit.

He was in front of Rory before she could position herself to attempt any offensive action. Philippe was just a blur, moving so quickly that she barely had time to react, pivoting in her saddle. She saw the coronel of his lance, and it became clear he'd tipped it, no doubt taking advantage of Otherlande's influence on the spectators' perceptions.

The sharpened end penetrated her pauldron, its effect brutal and nearly felling her, but Briar eased to a canter, affording Aurora the chance to regain her hold.

Her chest and shoulder throbbed as she heard the prince's groan of frustration when he passed. Though his desire was unmistakable, he'd achieved nothing more than a surface wound.

Two more rounds.

She was not too proud to understand the impossibility of withstanding the full force of his attack but refused to cower if she were ever to be a worthy queen.

Her gaze fell upon Artyrus as he sprinted for her from the opposite side of the arena. There wasn't much time before the next round would begin, a few minutes at best, to prepare for her second run.

If she was to give herself any shot at victory, she couldn't continue with the inferno blazing upon her shoulders. It had indisputably preserved her, but how much more had it cost? Rory shrugged free from the breast and backplates, slipping off her vambraces, revealing singed, ruby-stained forearms. No part of the cursed metal remained once she finished stripping away every shred of intended protection.

Concern marked the guardian's visage when he reached the princess, his comforting touch finding the small of her back. Aurora threw the armor to the ground, where it turned to nothing more than a heap of smoking ash. "Tell me how to win," she demanded before he could speak.

"You don't mean—"

"It's the only way." The princess would not relent, even when Artyrus's throat bobbed, swallowing back the protest she saw stirring in his dark stare. There was no time to explain herself, and he never asked it of her. She knew he understood what drove her and why she had to meet the challenge, even if it killed her.

He took Rory's hand, pressing his lips to her knuckles. "You will win by bringing him to the ground." His gaze remained pinned to her, his urgency obvious. "Philippe will aim for your heart as he did just now, and you will wait until he believes he's won. Fall back the moment he expects to make contact then strike with every bit of force you can summon. He won't have time to recover before you make your move. Don't hesitate."

His words had barely registered when Ffion arrived, panting at Briar's side. He patted the horse affectionately, though his features were grim when he acknowledged his friends.

"The prince has coated the tine with something. I just heard him tell his men he'll not be leaving anything to chance. We must find another way." Worry rang through the boy's voice as he exchanged a meaningful look with Rory's faithful companion.

Artyrus answered with a partial shake of his head as if his response warred against soundness of mind.

"You can't be serious. It's suicide, Rory!" Ffion's plea nearly broke Aurora's tenuous resolve. While she still had much to learn about their young ally, he'd become as dear to her as any sibling or trusted confidant.

Her throat tightened when a trumpet sounded, signaling the beginning of the second round. Rory blinked back tears, refusing to meet Artyrus's eyes, for if she did, she would surely lose her nerve.

Philippe's demon steed reared when the princess advanced to the starting line, dust billowing in a mass of clouds beneath his hooves as the flags fell. Briar didn't wait for Aurora's command to attack, lunging forward with momentous speed.

She told herself she would see Artyrus again and that she would carry out her promise to provide for Ffion once this damned dream was over.

This isn't how my story will end.

Clutching the lance to her side with every ounce of her strength, the princess watched her betrothed's vicious pursuit. His tread was easy and calm, like he wasn't the least concerned about failing.

Fear crept up Rory's spine as she fought to set her weapon, the weight tugging painfully at her shoulder. She only hoped she wouldn't tumble from Briar's back as they made for the prince.

At once, he was before her, his lance aimed at Aurora's heart. Her thighs strained against Briar's saddle, bracing her firmly to the mare's back. The leather ties held, preventing Rory's weapon from slipping out of her grasp, and while they cut into her skin, the bite paled in comparison to the impact Philippe's weapon would have.

The prince leaned forward, directing his hit.

Aurora waited.

He drew nearer still, angling himself for the most devastating strike, the sharpened tip of his lance mere inches from her chest. Rory clenched her legs against Briar's sides before bending backward at the waist, narrowly dodging his attack.

Adrenaline pumped through her veins, summoning the merciless warrior lurking within the depths of her spirit. The princess raised her weapon, willing her aching limbs to comply.

A mighty crack echoed throughout the court, the brutal force of their collision shuddering through her like an earthquake, rattling her bones. But in her hand, the lance remained, its end splintered and split to the core.

All around Aurora, the gathered crowd erupted with cheers. Thunderous roars of excitement resounded through the arena before she could make sense of what had happened. Righting herself upon her mount, the princess steered Briar back to face the field.

Philippe had fallen.

The prince glowered, his ire for Rory alone. He dug his fingers into the earth, dragging himself closer to where she sat astride Briar, a sword materializing in his hand. The promise of vengeance burned within his focused gaze.

Staggering to his feet, Philippe sprang forward, and the princess's mare reared at his approach. Aurora clung to Briar's reins, but the weight of her lance ripped her hold away.

Somewhere nearby, Artyrus cried out to her as she fell. His voice was all that mattered, and it was the last thing she heard before the stadium fractured and fell away. His fierce countenance was the last thing she saw before Otherlande faded to black.

Too far.

Artyrus would never reach her in time.

Briar reared when Philippe lunged for Aurora, murderous intent in his pursuit as he lifted his blade.

The guardian cursed himself for obliging when Rory had demanded he strap the lance to her, let alone competing stripped of her armor. He'd known then that it was foolish to do so, but what choice did he have?

Rory tumbled from her horse's back to the solid earth, her head hitting the ground so forcefully that she didn't move. Her limp form flickered in and out of existence before his eyes as he ran for her.

His desperation didn't matter. Like treading through mud, he made for her in what felt like slow motion, but she was gone by the time he made it to the place she'd fallen. The dirt was displaced where she'd been only seconds prior, but she was nowhere. Disappeared.

Artyrus knew what it meant.

A roar escaped from him so anguished and sorrowful that Otherlande cracked. It could've been his grief, his fury, that caused the ground to split. Or perhaps the sight of the prince yet clutching his sword as Briar struggled against whatever snare the wretched dream had manifested.

None of it made any difference.

The guardian watched the fissure in the earth's crust expand, extending to the end of the arena before it finally stopped. He followed the path it forged, heedless of the world around him until he stood at the foot of Excalibur. Nobody stopped him. No one dared.

He saw nothing but red when he took hold of the legendary hilt, cool to the touch. If desire ruled, then the sword would be his, for he wanted nothing more than Philippe's life for the one he'd taken.

Centuries-old steel shrieked against the stone as he raised Excalibur from its ancient prison. He sensed a unified intake of breath and heard murmurs of shock all around him, but there was no time to think about what he'd done or the destiny he'd stolen from the woman he would never be given a chance to love.

Aurora was gone, and Otherlande had won because of the prince.

Philippe would never taste victory again or see a world outside this hell. The guardian was neither a fool nor naive enough to think avenging Rory would bring him any solace, but he knew, with absolute certainty, the wretch would die.

Artyrus had never felt anything like it. Grooved metal melted into his hold, his fingers and palm tingling as he tested Excalibur's weight.

Flawless.

Mere paces away, he saw him. The prince met Artyrus's merciless stare, his eyes blazing as he brandished a sword and gladius in either hand.

Philippe was a formidable opponent, skilled but also a cheat. It came as no surprise he'd be unwilling to face Artyrus without some advantage. He could bend the dream to match his violent designs and manipulate steadfast warriors to do his bidding, but Artyrus would never let him leave Otherlande alive.

"Such a shame, isn't it? All that beauty wasted," Philippe taunted, inching ever closer. The guardian tried in vain to disregard his flippancy, but internally he seethed.

"You're mad if you believe you won't answer for what you've done." The prince was not alone, and something savage shone in his eyes when Artyrus spoke. Philippe's men came to his aid, with Ector and Kaye amongst them.

Death didn't alarm the guardian and never had. He feared for Aurora's safety alone, and without her, he would cut down every soldier in his path before seeing her sacrifice made in vain.

Penzellian onlookers seemed to share Artyrus's sentiments, quickly making their way into the arena from all around the stands. Some conjured weapons while others braced for hand-to-hand combat.

Rory would've beamed with pride to watch them rally against the tyrannical order that had slaughtered her family and destroyed her countrymen's livelihoods. While Penzelle yet slumbered, the princess had not failed. She'd awakened dormant spirits and full-scale revolt through her fearlessness.

Aurora was a spark that would set kingdoms ablaze.

Fights began to break out near Artyrus between Philippe's knights and Penzellian loyalists. Chamelautean blood would undoubtedly blemish Otherlande, heavily outnumbered on the field.

Metal clashed, still too soon for any warriors to fall, and in all the chaos of bloodshed, Artyrus's focus never once strayed from the prince. For the first time since he came to know Philippe, he saw what looked like terror flash through his eyes when he moved for him.

Wielding Excalibur, Artyrus at long last believed the legends surrounding it. Whetted steel sliced through the air, and Otherlande rippled for a fractured second. If there were still a way out of the nightmare, it was impossible to determine how awakening would look or feel. Perhaps these subconscious lands would crumble and cease to exist entirely.

The prince was quick on his feet, maneuvering nearer as battle sounded around them. Behind him, Kaye faced off against a fellow knight, his statement clear, with Ector taking up arms close by. In every sense, they were his family, even when reality grew murky. Artyrus prayed that discovering their true allegiance would not affect Pelinore, wherever he might be.

Philippe bounced from foot to foot, eager for the fight to begin, his features dripping with disdain. "None of it's real, the sword and the Merit. When we awaken, no one will remember. If we awaken at all, I suppose."

"Then nobody will remember it was I who killed you. I'll admit I did not revel in the idea of facing a guillotine." The guardian turned Excalibur over in his hand, admiring the craftsmanship. Vague recognition dawned, but it was no time to examine the artistry engraved upon his weapon.

A foolhardy curse she is born to break, alongside a soldier with equal stake.

He didn't have to look more closely to know what it was. The truth sang to his blood, drawing him in. He'd seen it with the princess time and again since they'd arrived, but until that very moment, it hadn't made sense.

Two souls and one heart unite royals lost, inscribed upon flesh, true love is the cost.

Excalibur.

The sword itself was the heart of which foretellings spoke, an unmovable force beating throughout centuries, awaiting those whose love ran so profoundly.

The prince's gaze turned wild, narrowing on something over Artyrus's shoulder. "Killing a curse breaker has proven more trying than I thought."

It couldn't be, but Lord, let it be so.

He'd seen her form flicker out of existence and knew she was gone. But if somehow she fought her way back to him and her calling…

It could be a distraction, but Artyrus was unable to help himself. Yet, when he followed Philippe's line of sight, she was there. Aurora's presence was solid and unwavering.

She was alive.

An errant sob escaped from deep inside when he saw her before searing pain cut across the width of his mid-section.

Artyrus pressed a hand to his wound, turning to answer the assault. Blood flowed unceasingly through his fingers, pooling where he stood. He lurched forward, meeting the prince's hideous sneer, and raised Excalibur with a savage roar.

At once, he sprang toward Philippe, ripping the splintered spindle from around his throat. The cord of brambles snapped free, and Artyrus lunged at his target with unrelenting speed, despite the slash to his abdomen.

In one fluid motion, the guardian drove his blade through Philippe's middle, plunging the spindle into the hollow of his neck. Surprise and anguish contorted the prince's countenance, his limbs flailing when he yanked the fractured pin from himself as realization crept in. He swayed on his feet, but there was no mistaking the aftermath of his injuries.

Artyrus collapsed, blood flowing freely from him as he lay on the ground. His vision blurred, but Aurora was there. Even in death, he wished for nothing more than to look upon her face, his sleeping beauty, and the missing piece of his soul.

She was alive, and Philippe would not harm her.

They had won.

Chapter Twenty-Seven

Rory could only describe how she felt as 'awakening'. The moment had come and gone quickly, and she'd been out for some seconds — or days, for all she knew. Philippe had been there taunting her, inciting Briar, until suddenly, he was nowhere to be found.

What she'd felt upon impact wasn't painful or even memorable, and the oblivion that followed her collision with the packed arena floor had been devoid of any sensations at all — no fear, no regret. Nothing.

But waking was different. Her head ached, a relentless throbbing radiating from behind her eyes alongside spasms running the length of her back and shoulders. She trembled where she lay, working to recover herself enough to rise, but her body was nothing shy of uncooperative.

Absently, some small part of her realized that she had, perhaps, died, or at least been close to it. But she was surrounded by chaos once more, locked securely within the confines of the never-ending dream yet again.

Philippe was there, staggering backward, his complexion graying with each step. It was as if he were rotting before Rory's eyes, his movements becoming increasingly labored. Her temporary vanishing act had seen her missing something pivotal, and she struggled to catch up, taking in the various bouts that had erupted between knights and villagers.

What in the blazes had happened?

The prince fell, clutching his neck as he collapsed without making any attempt to protect himself, his body splayed awkwardly over the earth beneath him. Only then could she see what lay beyond.

"*Artyrus.*"

His name was less than a breath from her lips, thin and desperate as she wrestled with the realities taking shape all around her. He wasn't moving, his large frame a heap of muscle and bone stagnant in the center of the list field.

What had transpired between the prince and the guardian readily evaded her — likely a duel for the ages with an outcome that threatened to leave her bereft of her greatest desire.

Aurora rolled to her side, ignoring the ceaseless hammering in her skull as it thrummed in tandem with her aching heart. She crawled across the dirt, her head spinning as she made her way past Penzellian warriors who were engaged with Philippe's minions.

Not far from Philippe's felled body were Sir Ector and his son Kaye, each clashing with their compatriots in solidarity with Artyrus. It was utter chaos, with her beloved lying in the midst of it all.

She spared the prince only a passing glance as she scrambled by him, noting no visible wound. He was breathing despite the sickening pallor of his skin, and she wondered what could have befallen him. In truth, he rather looked near death—a surprising turn of events, to be sure. She'd seen an unfortunate amount of that in her time and recognized the signs for what they were. But while she had momentarily ceased to exist, how was it that he continued to survive?

It didn't matter.

She was single-minded in her pursuit, coughing away the clouds of dust that permeated the air. And though she was moving at the pace of a snail, she was nearly there.

Having him within her sight did her heart some good, for he was, at the very least, alive. Nearing his side, she was startled to find a concerning amount of blood pooling around his inert body.

Rory dragged herself through the crimson sands surrounding him, holding her tears at bay even as the life-giving fluid stained her hands. His skin was warm, still full of life, as were his lungs, though his breaths were sharp, anguished, with each intake seemingly causing further distress.

He reached for her, winding his fingers into her hair as his lips tipped upward in a heartbreaking smile that jeopardized her composure. "*Aurora.* I thought you were lost to me."

"What happened?" Rory whimpered, curling herself around him before stroking his paling face. Her gaze traveled from his head to his feet, searching for a wound and landing upon a wide gash on his abdomen that was flowing at an alarming rate. She pressed gentle fingers to it, testing for discomfort, and when he didn't flinch, her heart dropped into her stomach. "Can you feel my touch?"

"If only." He tipped her face toward himself, eyes shining with moisture. "Do you know that I love you?"

Tears streamed over the swells of her cheeks, her gaze meeting his in earnest. "*What*?"

"I didn't always," he admitted, a sheepish grin pinned to his face. "You were a trial in the beginning — a nuisance. But *oh*...I love you desperately, Rory. I needed you to know."

"Stop this!" She sobbed, clinging to his chest. He drifted his fingers from her neck down her spine, eliciting a shiver as she reasoned her way through any means of restoration. He was only somewhat coherent, his heavy eyelids drawing him nearer to a slumber that was likely permanent. She pinched his chin between her fingers, forcing him to look at her. "Artyrus, please —"

A pair of combatants tripped over their entangled feet, teetering away as they continued their battle, but it was all too close. There were assailants with flashing swords and flying fists in every direction that could only further endanger the idle couple.

With merely a hint of a thought from the depths of her mind of an imagined structure composed of twisted thorns, a prison of her own choosing sprouted from the earth in a mess of prickly vines. They rose around them, splitting the ground as they broke through layers of rock and soil, forming a web of knots as they fashioned a makeshift enclosure, not unlike a birdcage.

Alone within the heart of the cage, Rory and Artyrus lay, free from the escalating chaos as the world around them crumbled to bits. Artyrus lifted his gaze, taking in the canopy of nettled fronds with wide eyes. "How did you—?"

"I only pictured it." She sniffled, tucking herself nearer to his side. "Everything here has become too strong. The people are lost—a simple thought causes untold levels of destruction. We are done for."

The clamor of swords rang through the arena, followed by screams as the people began to stampede. On their heels was none other than the dragon—Maleficent—wreaking havoc on the remaining knights of Chamelaute as she breathed trails of fire in their wake.

Her distress was palpable as she razed the arena to the ground, chasing Philippe's goons from the list field as she circled above their flowering refuge. More than once, she dove toward them, her eyes locked upon Artyrus as he began to falter.

"I did something ill-advised." Artyrus shifted, pulling a sword from his side. He clasped it to his chest, regret evident in his features. "This was yours to free, and in my grief, when I thought you were gone, I pulled it."

Rory examined the blade, awed to find that it was, indeed, Excalibur. She traced the etchings running the length of the blade, the same ones she'd seen a hint of in her youth, finding something oddly familiar in their delicate scrolling. "I know this…"

Closing her eyes, she forced the memory to the surface of her addled mind. "It's you. It's you and me, our tattoos. Two halves of the same design." Stroking the subtle whorls emblazoned along the flawless silver metal, they suddenly took on new significance.

"This belongs to us," Artyrus declared, brushing Rory's long hair away from her face. "Do you feel it?"

She did, a faint reverberation humming through the blade alongside the fading whispers of the prophecy that seemed always to reveal themselves in the presence of the sword Excalibur. "I'm so pleased you've done it, but we're still here. I thought—"

"We need to get you out of this place." He heaved a labored breath, even as his mind seemed one step ahead, always strategizing for her benefit. "All hell rages around us. Take Ffion and hide until this chaos ends, for you may yet free your people with this."

Artyrus pressed the hilt of the sword into her hand, their fingers interlocked upon the grip. "I can see things for what they are, wish as I may to finish this adventure with you. You'll succeed, Valkyrie." He smiled sadly before his head began to loll, though he managed to recover himself.

"Don't you leave me!" Rory cried, her tears freely flowing as she nestled her head into his chest. "What kind of life could I possibly lead if you're not in it?"

"The life that you must," he said simply, stroking soothing fingers through her long tresses, his chest rising and falling beneath her cheek.

Fire had caught within the stands, causing onlookers to dive from their seats, only to bolt from the havoc wreaked by Maleficent, who roared in agony as she apparently struggled to sight the pair inside of their thorny refuge. Just beyond them, Ector and Kaye continued their traitorous battle, having turned on their fellow knights to shield their brethren, casting worried glances in Artyrus's direction as they narrowly avoided the blades of their compatriots.

The commotion surrounding them would have been overwhelming to Rory had she not been in the midst of such utter devastation. Artyrus had somehow become her heart, a constant source of strength that never failed to shore her up. He sustained her through her doubts and allowed her the space to be the woman she was called to be. He believed in her, pushed her and somehow, despite it all, *loved* her, too.

How could a valiant soul such as his ever cease to be?

She lifted her head, cupping his cheek as her gaze met his. He was fading, his eyes glassy, even as they held boundless regard for her. Rory trembled, her teardrops leaving trails as they fell, washing over Artyrus's grimy face. "I will never do without you. Please don't leave me." She closed her eyes, resting nose to nose with the man who was her soul.

Tilting her head, she closed the distance separating them, fitting her lips to his. He pulled her nearer as she deepened the kiss, his response as heartening as it was devastating. Her tears mingled with his as she drew closer still, their tongues tangled together as she breathed him in, hoping in the depths of her being that she might will him to remain with her in body as he ever would in spirit.

Time stood still, the bedlam all around them melting into the recesses of Rory's consciousness as the sword clutched between their linked fingers began to glow. Subtle at first, its light was soon rivaling that of the mid-morning sun overhead, drawing their attention with its brightness and its inexplicable warmth. The prophecy thrummed through Excalibur, sonorous and powerful as the blade pulsed within their adjoined hands with a heartbeat all its own.

The tumult beyond their barbed sanctuary slowly subsided as one disappearance became dozens before her eyes. The people of Otherlande flickered away, their absence quickly diminishing the strife within the arena as they left behind nothing but fire and brimstone.

Ector blinked away before Kaye, who paused mid lunge to observe the exodus of humanity. He turned to watch Artyrus, his countenance troubled—a brother in every sense of the word—before he, too, was gone.

"You've done it," Ffion cried, his face visible just beyond the briers where he stood in sober understanding. A listless smile crossed his lips as his eyes filled with moisture. He bowed his head, only to depart a handful of seconds later.

"I knew you would succeed," Artyrus whispered, his labored breaths cleaving Rory's heart in two. His discomfort was evident, even as he beamed with pride. "My Valkyrie."

"It was never meant to be me alone. We were always one—two destined souls. Our fates were written on this sword for centuries." She glanced at their linked hands, noting that while hers was vanishing, his was very much intact. "*Artyrus…*"

He pulled her close, wrapping her in his strong arms. "*Go.*"

* * * *

A burst of blinding light hit her face, the intensity in its warmth so authentic that she could only be conscious. She opened her eyes, immediately regretting her foolishness as the direct sunlight scorched her retina. Throwing a hand in the air, she shielded herself, taking a moment to catch her breath.

She was off-balance. Tucked tightly into a cot of some sort, she felt bereft of any understanding. Her thoughts were a jumbled mess of waking and dreaming, the lines utterly blurred as she attempted to discern the difference between what was true and what was, apparently, nothing more than fantasy.

Was any of it real?

Her head no longer throbbed, and her shoulders didn't ache. All the things she'd felt mere moments ago had evolved when she'd awakened, leaving her with a gnawing hunger in the pit of her belly and stiff muscles from doing nothing more than lying in bed for some, what? Days? Weeks?

She hadn't been alone. Her first coherent thought was of Artyrus.

Her eyes flew open again, and this time, she took in everything around her, ignoring the discomfort it caused. It was nothing like she remembered — the strange interior of Merlin's cottage replaced with a tent not so unlike the one she'd visited in the heart of Wylewoode where Maleficent dwelled.

She shifted beneath the confining blankets, straining to see beyond the sheer panel that separated the tent into semi-private rooms.

"*Artyrus.*"

Thrashing to free herself, she was suddenly consumed, desperate to reach him where he lay unmoving in a cot not a half dozen feet from her.

She rose from her bed, stumbling as her head swam, her muscles protesting with her restless movements. Flinging the gauzy curtain out of her way, she fell at his side, relieved to see he was still breathing and fearful because he had not awakened.

It had been real, for better or for worse.

But what kept him in slumber? She closed her eyes, trying to recall all that had transpired as she'd been subject to the whims of her subconscious.

The tourney. The prince. The helplessness and triumph—every bit of it had felt like life and death were at stake, and perhaps, in the end, it was true.

Artyrus had been there with her through it all, even unto battling his own men, his own sovereign.

Philippe.

Aurora gasped, her mind filling in the blanks so quickly she could not readily keep up. Yanking the covers from his torso, she examined his abdomen, relieved to find no wound while also feeling crazy that she'd expected to see the gash when it had been delivered within the dream.

Outwardly, he appeared to be whole, healthy, strong. He was everything that she loved. Rory climbed into the cot, her body flush with his as she lay beside him, tucking her arm carefully around his ribs. She rested her head upon his chest, leaving circles of moisture on his tunic as silent tears fell. "Come back to me," she whispered. "*Please* come back to me."

"You've returned!"

Rory jumped, the sound of Merlin's chipper greeting grating on her nerves as she sought some semblance of peace. She raised her head to find the Seer standing alongside Archimedes and Mal.

"We knew it to be true when all the slumbering Penzellians began to wake." Merlin was undeterred and seemingly unconcerned over the plight of Artyrus. "And yes, I did see it," he continued, answering a question she'd asked just before she'd been lost to the poisonous slumber. "I saw all of it, and it went according to plan, thanks to you, even if it did take your doubting me. And while I wouldn't have stabbed myself with a spindle, it did get you to where you needed to be."

Aurora furrowed her brow, working desperately to keep up with the Seer's assertions, fatigued as her mind was from waking so abruptly. "What is your meaning? I don't understand."

Merlin smiled, his jovial demeanor annoying her to no end. "If you had pulled Excalibur in reality, it would've broken the curse. But you hadn't yet accepted your birthright, so never would it have budged. Your dreaming was the only way, as sub-consciousness frees both mind and ability in a way that most have not harnessed in full consciousness. You've done it!"

"Yes," Rory agreed, clinging to Artyrus. "And it cost us everything."

Chapter Twenty-Eight

Mal stepped around the two men, her gaze cast upon Aurora as she tended Artyrus. "You love my son."

It was a statement rather than a question, and Rory had an unexpected realization as she looked the woman who'd been breathing fire in Otherlande in the face. "You were there. You're Maleficent, the former queen of Chamelaute."

"*Exiled,*" she corrected, her tone sharp. "And my son is—"

"The rightful heir of the Chamelautean throne." Rory was aghast as reality struck. The prophecy had been unfolding before her eyes, with revelations occurring all around them that had defied her comprehension, even as they fulfilled the words foretold so many centuries before.

A kingdom from stone and steel will soon rise,
Preserving their kin from fated demise.

A foolhardy curse she is born to break,
Alongside a soldier with equal stake.
Two souls and one heart unite royals lost,
Inscribed upon flesh, true love is the cost.
The war will be won in a tower high,
As centuries foretold, the time is nigh.

Artyrus had had every bit as much at risk in their pursuit of freedom from the tyranny of King Luther — perhaps even more, given his lack of understanding of his lineage, his future, and now, his very real royal obligations.

Blazes. He was a prince of Chamelaute.

The epiphany hit like a mace to the skull.

She turned toward him, taking in his still form as she shot up a silent prayer for his recovery. The discovery didn't change anything, not really, at least not with regard to her feelings for him. It was pivotal, though, and likely in ways she could not yet comprehend.

"Somehow, despite all the occurrences outside of my foresight, we seem to be on the path to victory, for all is now known," Merlin said, his near giddy delivery causing Rory to bristle with anger. "It hasn't been easy, what with having to move the two of you from Caerleon to Wylewoode to protect you from King Luther's raids, but — "

"But *nothing!*" Rory shouted. "Your blasted prophecy has cost us everything! And this, right here, is the result!" She gestured toward Artyrus, peaceful but absent all the same. "Weeks of slumber and — "

"Weeks?" Merlin chuckled softly. "Why no, dear girl. A mere two days have passed since first you fell prey to the poison."

That brought her up short.

Two days?

It felt like a lifetime had been lived as they toiled and waited and ran for their cursed existences. They'd met friends and slain foes. They'd lost tremendous ground, only to emerge victorious.

Two days... The reality puzzled Rory, though perhaps it shouldn't have, for her arm still ached from her self-inflicted wound, bound and bandaged in fresh gauze. She squeezed Artyrus's hand, reconciling all the confusing memories of the dream with her present ones when she felt a squeeze in return.

Her gaze flashed to his face just in time to see him jolt, bolting upright in his bed as he gasped for air, his breaths coming in short, panicked spurts. Glancing downward, he searched himself, probing his abdomen with his free hand, undoubtedly searching for his dream wound.

"You're alive," Rory whispered. It was all she could manage before she was wrapped in his arms, his strong hold never faltering. Indeed, he seemed as vital as he ever had, burying his face in her hair as he pulled her impossibly closer.

"You were my singular thought — the reason I made it out of that pit of despair," he said, pulling away only enough to look her in the face. "We still have so much to discuss."

"You have no idea." Rory averted her gaze, overwhelmed by the truth in his words. She glanced toward the entryway, uneasy with all the onlookers. "Would you please excuse us?"

Artyrus followed her line of sight, startled to find they were not alone. Three pairs of curious eyes stared back at them, each full of untold questions. "Oh..."

"I think it best for the truth to come from me," Maleficent said, her features softening as she took in the impressive specimen that was her son. "Would you give us some time?"

Doubtless, she'd missed much of his life. What must it be like for her to look upon a stranger and know that he not only belonged to her in a way but also to a people? Rory wondered over the conundrum facing Mal but was beyond uneasy at the thought of leaving Artyrus.

In truth, she never wanted to do so again.

"Forgive me, but who are you?" Artyrus began, his tone polite and even, as though he hadn't just awakened from a nightmare.

Silence fell as Merlin and Archimedes quickly excused themselves, each offering a bow, while Mal gazed pointedly at Aurora, who hadn't moved a muscle.

"She stays," Artyrus added, drawing the princess to his side with an arm wrapped tightly around her waist. His insistence upon her presence set Rory's mind at ease, even as she harbored concerns over Mal's looming revelations.

"Well, privacy certainly has its merits where familial business is concerned, but we'll make do." Mal took several steps nearer, stopping shy of the cot where she pulled up a nearby chair. Her tone dripped with irritation, matching the annoyance that shone in her eyes as she appraised the pair of royals poised to change the course of two kingdoms.

She sighed, seemingly making an effort to suppress her discontent. "Long ago, I reigned alongside Luther as the future queen of Chamelaute. And you, Artyrus, are my son."

Mal's conjecture was preposterous to Artyrus, flying in the face of everything he'd known. He'd been raised by his uncle and become a knight. His parents were dead.

He was an orphan...not a prince.

Artyrus shook his head, a wry grin forming on his face. "Forgive me if I'm skeptical of your absurd assertion. I knew no parent, aside from Lord Pelinore and Sir Ector. They helped raise me with the aid of Kaye, who remains an older brother to me to this very day. Those three saintly men were godsends, without whom I would've died a beggar's death upon the streets."

"Indeed," Mal agreed. "You were placed within their hands purposefully by none other than Merlin himself upon your birth."

"*Merlin.*" Artyrus scoffed. "Is there no realm beyond which his reach will extend?"

"I will start from the beginning." Mal folded her hands in her lap, maintaining her composure, despite his obvious disdain. She pinched her lips together, taking a deep breath as if she meant to gather her thoughts.

"I once had with someone what you seem to share." She glanced from Artyrus to Aurora, her gaze briefly lingering on their adjoined hands resting in the prince's lap. "And however fleeting those entanglements may be, they certainly feel like forever in the moment.

"King Luther and I were very much in love, finding our purposes in one another in a tiny pub within the heart of Penzelle. I knew not who he was, only that he was a soldier from Chamelaute, for he neglected to share that he was heir to the throne." She paused, her mind seemingly lost to the memories. "We fell madly in love, and only after we had married in secret did I discover who he was, that he'd made me his future queen.

"I was thrilled, believing in vain that our union might subdue some of the animosity between our nations, that perhaps after so many centuries of brinksmanship, we might finally exist in peace, but I was wrong.

"Luther's father, King Archibald, was furious over our secret marriage. He tolerated my presence for a time, but all pretense of acceptance was lost when I fell pregnant with you."

"I think I've heard about enough," Artyrus said, his words brisk. Her tale was all so *fantastical*, and, truth be told, he didn't want to believe it.

Aurora sighed from beside him, wearing an encouraging smile. "Let's hear her out. Stars know we can handle the unthinkable with ease after Otherlande."

"You're right," he agreed before kissing her forehead. And that was all much easier to handle with the princess by his side. "Please continue."

Mal shifted, wearing a mask of scarcely concealed displeasure. "As it turns out, Luther had a well-stocked bedchamber, with an abundance of courtesans to keep him company. In King Archibald's eyes, any of them would be far better as queen, given their Chamelautean heritage. I was shuttled off to the east tower, locked away. The town heralds decried my losing my mind over the loss of my pregnancy, even as my belly grew larger by the day with a strong, healthy boy.

"But I'd already been replaced, with Luther having selected one of the ladies of the court as his new bride upon reports of my demise. You know her now as Queen Maerwynn."

"Prince Philippe's mother," Rory muttered.

"He is no prince!" Mal's eyes flashed with anger, her fists tightly clenched as though she maintained little control. "He's an interloper, just as his mother is, for the real prince and heir sits exiled in Wylewoode alongside his mother!"

Artyrus and Rory remained in stunned silence, watching the woman before them fall apart with recollections of scorn and heartbreak.

"The day of your birth arrived, and I bore you alone, trapped within the turret walls with no assistance to speak of," Mal continued in earnest, a single tear slipping over her cheek. "I made no sound and worked desperately to keep you quiet and calm so that you would not be taken from me. I had miscarried many months prior for all they knew, having hidden my pregnancy to preserve you.

"A day after your birth, Merlin arrived — the one and only visitor I was permitted. It had been the first day the door within the tower had opened since my imprisonment, with everything else coming and going through a small hatch. His relationship with the Crown allowed him privileges not granted to others, and I was grateful beyond words.

"Of Penzellian descent himself, Merlin sought to assist me, escaping with you, with my son, doing his part to protect the prophecy. Nobody was any the wiser. He took you to the Penzellian artisans at my request, ensuring me that you would receive your grace marking, given your royal heritage, despite the foreign blood running in your veins. It was the only gift I could impart to you other than your very life, a blessing due to every noble of our beloved country.

"I remained within that lonely spire for another four years, biding my time as I awaited Merlin's prophesied sign—a vague directive that assured me I would one day be free of my prison. But the slaughter of Penzelle changed everything for me, evil King Archibald's final act before he handed his crown to his son.

"In desperation, I scaled down the tower wall, using the thorny vines that had climbed their way to the turret. It was a suicidal act, but I was beyond caring by then, prepared to be free of my prison in one sense or another." She sniffed, her emotions nearly getting the better of her, but she was well-practiced in controlling her sentiments.

"From there, I vowed to raise an army, to rally our people to the cause for Penzelle. I knew the lost princess was out there somewhere, though Luther foolishly bet against Aurora when he offered his firstborn son in marriage, thinking you couldn't possibly be alive. And now, my life's work dwells in this encampment and many others like it all across the outskirts of Chamelaute. When the time is right, all will be won."

Artyrus was speechless, his mind working to process all the unbelievable details Mal had disclosed. Certainly, it was all possible, and lying seemed too audacious considering their circumstances. Then, there was the prophecy in which he put little stock, but even he couldn't deny the ease with which all the pieces of the puzzle were falling into place.

"Why have I never seen you before?" The thought had suddenly occurred to him. Indeed, the first time he'd ever laid eyes upon her had been on his journey through Wylewoode. "I knew nothing of you, thinking instead that you were dead."

"It was the only way. Any interaction with me would've surely seen you perishing. I did it for you and for Penzelle." Mal met his gaze, seemingly attempting to convince him of the soundness of her decision.

It mattered not. His past was what it was, as was hers.

"You're very brave," Rory said at last. "I don't know how you managed all these years."

"A woman does what she must." She glanced at Aurora, with something strictly feminine seemingly passing between them in the silence that followed.

It was clear to Artyrus that the women were somewhat at odds, the discord palpable in the small space they shared, but somehow, they'd reached an accord. He would leave it at that, eager as he was to keep from fanning any flames of contempt between them.

The woman who'd helped take him hostage on his first visit to the hidden outpost poked her head into the tent. "You're needed, my queen." Adelyce spared a quick glance for each of them, disdain evident upon her face.

Well, there was no love lost there, though he couldn't fathom her problem. Perhaps it was as simple as their presence, with the return of not one but two royals, two heirs, come to claim their thrones.

Blazes, but he would never come to terms with that. Suddenly, Aurora's reluctance to accept her role as the Penzellian queen came into stark relief. The burden, the sacrifice… Was he prepared to face the same fate?

Not alone. He'd been blindsided by obligation, none of which he had ever given even the most indirect of thought. But with Aurora by his side, surely he could handle the responsibility to his people.

Maleficent nodded, rising from her seat. "Would you excuse me?" She offered a halfhearted bow before following Adelyce through the tent flaps, the cloth flopping closed behind her.

Artyrus turned to Rory, grateful to be alone. "I won't pretend to understand what just happened there." He smiled, tracing the outline of her cheekbone with the pad of his thumb. "Care to enlighten me?"

"I don't trust her," Rory whispered. "And she is doubtless of the same mind where I'm concerned. We will never see eye to eye, I think, especially when it comes to you."

Artyrus sighed. While he wasn't familiar with the inner workings of a mother-son relationship, given his lack of a mother for the vast majority of his life, he was keenly aware of the struggles that arose between powerful women. His greatest wish was to remain free of such intrigues, though it was likely too late.

"There's another thing," the princess continued, her eyes bright with moisture. She exhaled heavily, seemingly preparing for the worst. "I want you to know that you're under no obligation to me. Our supposed betrothal— We resolved in Otherlande to choose our own fates, and there is nothing I want more for you than that. You must choose the desires of your heart, not have them dictated to you by a father you do not know."

"Indeed. It would be devastating to marry the woman I love." He grinned, meeting her gaze. Taking her hands in his, he continued, his tone becoming serious. "I know it's what I want, but your desires matter, too. Never would I deign to make your choices for you."

A breathtaking smile formed on her lips, and he knew without question he would never want anything more. A life with her was greater than he'd ever dared dream, and it lay before them. He wanted a future committed to her, because of her and for her alone, not due to some random betrothal or age-old prophecy.

"We must see him," came a voice from beyond the tent walls, one Artyrus recognized as Ector. "Is he alive?" The sounds of a minor scuffle emerged, only to be cut off by none other than Adelyce.

"You're not permitted," she groused.

More scuffling.

Artyrus could picture it in his mind's eye, Ector and Kaye squaring off against the surprisingly stoic right-hand woman to Maleficent. He hadn't realized they were under guard, and it wasn't necessary, but it seemed that Adelyce treated her duties seriously.

"Begone!" she shouted, drawing some indistinct grumblings from the two men as they continued in their quest to see the prince.

"Let them in," Artyrus shouted, pleased to find that his request was honored. A moment later, the pair of men sauntered through the doorway, eagerly making their way toward Artyrus, and sat in his cot alongside his princess.

"Thank God you're alive! Oh—" Ector dropped to one knee, his fist clutched to his heart as he bowed his head. Kaye followed suit, kneeling beside his father as they honored their sovereign.

Artyrus balked, flustered by their deference. "Rise. Nothing has changed."

"Everything has changed, sire," Kaye said, the last of his words spoken with a subtle smirk. Doubtless, he understood the absurdity of their circumstances and, like any brother would, saw the humor in the unease of his kin. "For not only are you the future of Chamelaute. Lancelot has sworn to end you, seeking you even now. And doubtless he'll have King Luther's blessing, distraught as he is over his son, who remains in slumber."

"It's simple," Rory declared. "We must cut Lancelot off at the knees. Never can his deceptions and his ambitions be permitted to stand."

The two men looked from Aurora to Artyrus and back as they rose to their feet. Understanding dawned, each of them failing to mask their delight over fate's wily designs.

"I like her," said Kaye, his stage whisper drawing an eye roll from Artyrus. He turned to Aurora, bowing deeply before her. "Sir Kaye, Your Highness, and my father, Sir Ector. We're humbled to be at your service."

Chapter Twenty-Nine

Perhaps they would never see eye to eye.

Aurora trusted Merlin about as much as she did Mal. Once, she'd revered the Seer's foresight, but now he seemed to be nothing more than an egotist. His certainty in himself and his purported visions was beyond reproach, at least in his own mind, making discussions of strategy tedious beyond words.

Maleficent was cordial in her dealings, but Rory sensed the scorned woman's bitterness with every word she spoke. The former queen held herself in high regard, exuding an air of superiority that didn't sit well. And, despite their lack of titles or claims to the throne, neither she nor Merlin seemed the least bit willing to consider any outside counsel.

Narcissism, to the princess's knowledge, did not win wars.

"Now is the time to strike. We'll act while the king licks his wounds." Sir Ector was unrelenting, with his position on the matter clear, aligning with both heirs.

Artyrus nodded his agreement, working over the strategies their provisional unit put together. "The longer we wait, the more time it gives him to recover and for Lancelot to discover your stronghold." Thus far, he'd refused to acknowledge Merlin's presence, directing the statement toward his mother.

How the princess hadn't seen the resemblance between them before was unthinkable. The forgotten prince bore an uncanny likeness to his mother and father. Yet, regardless of their abounding flaws, he was more honorable than anyone Aurora had ever known. Watching him shift from a lionhearted knight into the rightful inheritor of Chamelaute took her breath away.

And he was hers—not by some betrothal established through greed or bribery, but of their own choosing. Artyrus's eyes met Rory's, dark and intense as if he sensed the musings of her heart. Since awakening, they'd barely had a moment to themselves, with Mal's scouts and messengers constantly coming and going.

Her guardian's lips twitched in amusement when he noticed the flush he'd caused blooming up her neck and into her cheeks. Aurora forced her focus away from him, for their plans wouldn't make themselves.

Across the tent, Maleficent's beautiful minion, Adelyce, huffed her disapproval. "You do realize Her Majesty has spent countless months preparing for this. She knows Luther better than anyone else in this room."

"I think you're failing to remember others play a vital role in your *queen's* and Merlin's schemes. Lives are at stake—lives that we both nearly lost defending." Rory indicated Artyrus, unable to hold her tongue any longer. While she'd never considered herself royal in any way but heritage, the princess found it increasingly apparent that Adelyce didn't either.

"Do not forget yourself, dear," Maleficent chided, rebuking the golden-haired hellhound, who dared roll her eyes. "I only meant to aid the prophecy. It has nearly been realized, and all that remains is to unseat my husband. Penzelle will be restored in short order, but we are not ready...not yet."

"Indeed, preparations are being made, even as we speak." The soothsayer was unyielding in his conviction, but so had he been when Otherlande took hold, seizing an entire people as hostages.

"We're to trust you?" Balancing the tip of a dagger in his palm, Kaye scoffed before snatching it out of the air. He plunged the knife into Mal's table, his imposing form hovering over its smooth surface. "Make no mistake, *Seer*. I speak for my father and Pelinore as well when I say we will always be grateful for what you did to protect the prince, but don't think anything you claim will impact the course of this war or where we portion our confidence. Either you don't know as much as you pretend or you're a self-serving bastard. I've yet to decide. For why else would you withhold your insights?"

"Divulging too much can alter the natural paths of fate. It—"

"Enough, Merlin." Artyrus dismissed him with a sweep of his hand. "You were either wrong or lied. Still, you keep your visions to yourself, even after Aurora proved we were meant to break Luther's cursed slumber from within it. You both swear we must wait to take Chamelaute, but why? My father will never suspect an attack, nor will he wish to fight when so many of his best knights perished at The Merit."

Rory could hear her beloved's disdain for his father and the Seer when he spoke. And while she was of the same mind, even they, the embodiment of ancient prophecy, should not wield so much control over a kingdom. "We'll put it to a vote. Remember... We're gathered here that our nations might thrive, whether together or separate from what they were forced to become."

Mal shook her head. "This will not end as you hope. I know these people. They are *my* people. Do you think for a moment I'll stand by and watch them march to their death after all these years?"

"*Yet*," Aurora snapped, "you were willing to watch them be subjected to nearly two decades of despotism after their king and queen were murdered by your husband's army. Do not think me so naive as to believe you were waiting for me to stake my claim all that time?" Something resembling pride shone in Artyrus's eyes when they met hers once more, her hands shaking with frustration as the words spilled from her mouth.

She didn't regret them.

It was not the time to remind Maleficent that she was no longer queen and never would be again, but oh, how the princess ached to tell her. She was never meant to rule Penzelle but placed herself upon a throne of her ambition, despite knowing it was her son's birthright to lead Chamelaute and believing the curse breaker had survived Luther's massacre.

Rory didn't want to be queen. In truth, she wished to lace her fingers with Artyrus's and run from everything tethering them to this so-called destiny. But to leave Mal in charge with Merlin whispering in her ear would only mean further devastation for Penzelle.

The princess swore she saw the dragon lurking behind Maleficent's stare when she lowered her head in deference. "As you wish, Princess. A vote. All in favor of strategizing a siege once the dust of this disaster has settled, say aye."

"Nay," Ector offered without hesitation, followed quickly by Aurora and Kaye. Artyrus answered with a shake of his head before verbally confirming his decision to act swiftly.

"Aye." Merlin's accusatory gaze moved over them as he cast his vote, though he knew it to be futile.

Adelyce bit her lower lip, sighing, as she threw her arms up in a fit of annoyance. "This is a farce. I'll be on my way now to prepare to hunt that wretch skulking about our borders. It's only a matter of time before he finds us and tells his king our secrets or kills you both. I'll leave tonight." Straightening the weapons at her hips, she turned on her heel, avoiding the poll altogether.

"Lancelot has aspirations devoid of any loyalty. He'll not harm the princess unless we force his hand, but everyone else is fair game, including Luther." Artyrus moved to Aurora, sliding an arm protectively around her slender waist. "Be ever on your guard."

"He may possess information that could serve us well," Ector added, slowing Adelyce's hasty departure.

"You shouldn't go alone. Lan is a devil willing to do anything to get his way, always has been." Kaye readied his satchel, tossing it over one shoulder before he continued. "I'll accompany you, and we'll take him alive."

"You'll do no such thing. Thank you, but I'm fully capable of ensnaring a Chamelautean knight."

It was precisely the retort Rory would have made during those initial days she'd spent trying to rid herself of Artyrus, and she was unable to hide her amusement when Kaye winked in response.

"I've no doubt." His eyes sparkled with humor as her eyes narrowed. Adelyce curled her lip in distaste, dismissing the warrior's blatant advances and immediately setting off for the fringes of Maleficent's vast encampment.

"Tomorrow night, we take Chamelaute." Artyrus's declaration cut through the tent, the implications of such actions weighing heavily over the gathering.

"You can't be serious!" Merlin scoffed, his brow red with fury when he looked to Mal for backup.

"Very well, my son." Her tone was grave, but she didn't object. "Then it is Penzellian tradition we feast this night like so many ancestors before us on any eve preceding battle. I'll make the appropriate arrangements."

Maleficent set off without further ado, ripping the flap of her tent open upon her exit. Merlin trailed her, issuing no final words of caution or backward glances.

"Eat. Drink. Be merry, brother, for tomorrow we steal the crown." Kaye clapped Artyrus on the shoulder with a wry grin. The knight nudged Aurora with his elbow. "We'll have a new one fashioned for you as well, sister."

* * * *

Eventide fell as it should, but after his time in Otherlande, Artyrus still felt disoriented from his poisoned slumber. Aurora had not yet emerged from her tent, and the minutes seemed to crawl.

Penzellians gathered in the center of their Wylewoode fortress, laughing and imbibing as if the prince had not only hours earlier declared war against his own kingdom. He was anything but alone while he awaited Rory's company, with men and women alike, all donning traditional plaids in various forms, approaching him at every turn, questioning him about what they'd witnessed in the dream and offering fealty.

Kaye made himself scarce, undoubtedly enjoying the company of some Penzellian beauty, but Ector remained close, watching over the prince, as always.

"I was hoping we might be allowed to speak before tomorrow."

Artyrus heard his mother's voice from over his shoulder, uncertain whether or not it would be a conversation he was willing to have.

Gracefully, she maneuvered around him, her eyes gentle and pleading when she stood before him. It was strange to see her — the former queen of Chamelaute — and more peculiar still to come face to face with someone he'd always believed to be dead.

"I wanted to...*apologize*." Maleficent's words were cautious as she reached for his hands. Moonlight reflected softly off the silver rings and studs adorning her hands and face, her appearance almost other-worldly. Flames from the surrounding torches danced in her pupils, reminding the guardian of how fiercely she'd guarded him in the arena while he was yet lost to sleep as his blood pooled around him.

As if sensing his discomfort, she gently squeezed his hands before letting them fall back to his sides, pain evident in her gaze. "Merlin said giving you up was the only way I could protect you. Doubtless, he was right, but that didn't mean I couldn't have found a way to know you."

"I'm not angry. Luther is ruthless, and I would never have survived had you not brought me to Pelinore. For that, I'm grateful—equally for everything you've done for Penzelle in these years of exile." Artyrus took a step away from her, his feet acting on instinct.

"Merlin is wrong about wanting to delay, though, just as he is regarding many other things. So, too, are you." He swallowed hard, meeting her gaze. "I do not wish you to believe I think ill of you, but I know nothing of your true character apart from the loyalty you've amassed. And that, at least, speaks well of you."

Her features hardened, even as she smiled. "Someday, you may understand the complexities of war, Artyrus, but if you allow your princess to carry out this reckless strategy, you'll be complicit in the ruination of Penzelle."

"I don't *allow* Aurora to do anything," Artyrus clarified, clenching his jaw at the unabashed condescension lacing her words. "The Penzellians are ready and willing to fight. We saw it ourselves in Otherlande when we freed Excalibur."

"That was a dream, son." Mal looked at him almost as if he were slowly losing his mind.

In some ways, it felt like he might be, though her insinuations irritated his sensibilities.

"Is that all?" His words were growing more venomous by the second. His mother was no villain, but someone so ignorant was as unfit to rule as the reigning king of Chamelaute. "The prophecy itself spoke of the poison curse. I never believed it until I held Excalibur and saw the markings etched into its blade. Only then did it become clear. The time is nigh."

Maleficent's words were seemingly stuck to her tongue as murmurs of awe circulated through the gathered crowd. Artyrus followed their stares, excusing himself from his mother until, pushing past the revelers, he saw her.

Aurora dazzled when she arrived at last. She made her way toward him, lacking only a crown atop her head, with everything else about her ensemble nothing shy of breathtaking. Wearing a gown unlike any he'd ever seen, its colors blended from brightest amber inching up the lower portion of the princess's skirt before transitioning into the depths of midnight cerulean at her middle.

The bodice was a masterpiece of crocheted knots, revealing bits of flesh beneath before blending into the iciest of blues at her bust, matching her eyes flawlessly. Sheer, feather-light sleeves of the same colors cascaded to the earth on either side of her, rustling alongside Wylewoode's gentle breeze.

She was magnificent.

Artyrus took her hand, guiding Rory off toward the nearby woods before anyone could distract her away from him. Too long, he had waited for a moment alone with her when so much had transpired.

Together they veered into the tree line, swerving through shrubs and around boulders. Dipping under a low-hanging limb, the guardian wrapped her in his arms, drawing her close to himself. Aurora gasped, her palms pressed to his chest.

Artyrus's heart thudded wildly against her delicate hands as the princess' silvery gaze fell upon him, her painted lips tipping at the corners.

Neither spoke a word to the other, their pulses thrumming in tandem with eyes fixed on one another.

Aurora's exposed back felt like satin beneath his calloused fingertips when the prince trailed them tenderly up the length of her spine. She shuddered at his touch, clutching his tunic within her tight fists.

Artyrus brushed her collarbone with his knuckles, her skin shimmering with soft, golden dust as if the stars had caressed it. He tipped Rory's chin upward, smiling. "For you." He lifted his free hand, presenting her with the splintered spindle that had started their adventures knotted within a thin strip of leather, not unlike the necklace Rory had made in Otherlande for him. "A promise — that I will ever abide by your side. May I?"

Rory nodded and he tied it around her neck. It made for a strange charm, to be sure, but for them, it was symbolic of all the things that mattered — their loyalty, their courage, their passion.

The princess looked at him through thick lashes. "I love you," she whispered, her eyes shining with tears. "I love you so much, and when you didn't awaken, I — "

He kissed her then, their mouths colliding in a rush of desire left unmet for centuries.

Two souls and one heart.

Weaving his fingers through Aurora's long, raven tresses, Artyrus deepened the kiss, desperate for more. And when a sound of profound rapture escaped from her, the prince was undone.

Rory clung to him, but they could never be close enough, never explore each other so thoroughly as to settle their longing. Tugging at the hem of his tunic, she freed it from the waist of the prince's kilt. Her nails grazed over the length of his grace marking, the tattoo that mirrored hers unmistakably, and he growled wickedly at her touch.

He nipped at her ear, and she giggled, a melodic gift in the mess of the terrors awaiting them. "I love your laugh," Artyrus breathed, fitting his mouth to hers once more. His hands navigated the swell of her hips with dexterous precision, pulling her as close as he dared.

"And?" Rory teased, taking his lower lip between her teeth. She scrunched her nose, looking at him before continuing. "What else do you love?"

"You, my Valkyrie. You're my soul, and without you, I'm nothing." Artyrus pressed a kiss to the princess's temple, and she smiled up at him.

He'd never seen someone so radiant, and somehow, she was his.

"I wouldn't be here now if you'd not called me back to you." He tried in vain to explain the void between Otherlande and waking, falling short. "I felt your hand in mine. Though you were no longer there, I felt it, and I heard your voice when you begged me to wake."

"And tomorrow we provoke the beast who set the trap we narrowly escaped." Aurora rested her head on his chest with a mournful sigh. "Are we wrong to pursue Luther so soon?"

Artyrus had asked himself the very same countless times since the question arose.

"No." His lips found hers once more, an unwavering assurance that this moment, hidden in the heart of Wylewoode, would not be the last.

* * * *

The feast remained in full swing when they returned, and the princess only hoped that no one would note the flush of passion that surely colored her cheeks. Artyrus led Aurora through the merriment, her hand in his as the music swirled around them.

Raising a brow, her guardian grinned. "Would you like to dance?"

"Oh, indeed!" Rory smiled, throwing herself into the prince's awaiting embrace as a new song began. It was strange and familiar all at once, dancing with one so beloved to her.

They moved about the makeshift dance floor, laughing and whirling through the hosts of Penzellians. It was a heartening experience, a celebration of life and filled with hope for a future free from tyranny. They need only survive the chaos of the day to come.

A piercing scream shattered the joy of the gathering, so grave it brought the upbeat tune to a staggering halt.

Squinting, Aurora made out a form not far away, retreating into darkness and out of sight. Her eyes wandered to the source of the cry, finding Mimi standing before the long table, set for a banquet to rival any kingdom's best. Maleficent was at its center, where none but a crowned sovereign would be seated, a crimson slash across the column of her throat. The scorned queen's head lolled as ruby-tinted streaks fell to the white cloth covering the surface in front of her.

It was there that the princess saw it. She ran, holding her skirt with sweating palms, stopping when she reached what she didn't want to believe.

Plucking the lone, white tulip from the table, she knew beyond any conceivable doubt who the fleeing figure was.

Rory took a fortifying breath, willing herself to keep calm in the presence of her people even as the faint scent of strawberries filled her senses.

Chapter Thirty

The events following Maleficent's horrific death were anything but restful. For Aurora, however, sleep was the last thing for which she wished.

Once Mal's body had been wrapped and cared for and the Penzellian citizenry had dispersed, Aurora and her guardian found solace in one another's arms.

Neither dared to dream, nor did they speak.

Images of the former queen slumped in her chair with blood flowing freely from the wound at her throat surely kept Rory from any attempt to slumber. It was difficult to conclude whether returning to Otherlande might be worse, but oddly enough, fatigue never plagued the princess as she worked to prepare for the day ahead.

A soft golden glow cut through the entrance to the princess's tent, and a strange sense of relief overcame her. Artyrus shifted behind Rory, her body nestled tightly against his, with his strong arms wrapped around her like a shield.

"We need to prove to them we can win." Aurora's voice broke the silence preserving them against the impending chaos.

Artyrus released her, propping himself onto his elbows. "My mother contended Otherlande was no more than a vivid reverie." He shifted, straightening the kilt he still wore from the night before.

Rory felt the warmth of him on her skin, yearning to remain in his sheltering embrace, but alas, the prophecy beckoned. "She's wrong. You know she is, and so do I, for we lived every moment of that forsaken dream. We only just survived."

Artyrus rose from their shared cot, draping the spare plaid of his ancestors over one shoulder. "Then we'll verify before Fayble awakens this day that together, we are the ancient foretelling personified."

"You mean to retrieve Excalibur," Aurora breathed, taking the guardian's extended hand, her gown bunched and twisted when he drew her to himself.

"Beautiful and astute," he said with a faint smile, though behind his eyes, Rory perceived distant mourning for a woman he would never know.

They moved quickly, shrouded in unremarkable cloaks borrowed from a chest filled with clothing and other essentials in Aurora's shelter. Their trusted steeds had been brought to Wylewoode when the two royals had themselves been relocated—a sight for sore eyes and a precious shred of normalcy.

Together atop Artyrus's beast, Magnus, they galloped into the borough of Caerleon. Aurora was weighed down with the weaponry Otherlande had so stingily withheld from her throughout their time in those derelict lands, with the transition back to order jarring, to say the least.

Her beloved's horse slowed to a canter as they approached what had become a dilapidated arena after decades of neglect. To the princess's knowledge, it had been continually under guard throughout the duration, even over the course of its abandonment, with King Luther unwilling to risk Excalibur being freed.

A handful of individuals shuffled about town, none of them sparing a glance for the prince or princess. Caerleon was very much the same as it had been in sleep, apart from the legendary court. The tournament field had appeared almost brand new there, unaffected by inattention's decay.

Artyrus dismounted, lifting Rory from Magnus's saddle. Fastening the leather reins to a nearby beam, they wasted no time before descending into the heart of the arena. Its lists and tilt were time-worn, but in the center was a fissure within the earth so deep it could swallow a man whole. Any guards had since abandoned their posts inside The Merit stadium, leaving no one to prevent them from the sword in the stone.

"It was all real." Artyrus gulped, his voice hoarse when he spoke. "I knew it was, that somehow it mattered, but to see it here, the cleft *we* created... That didn't exist before."

"Because Excalibur was always meant for us. You're the foundation, the immovable rock that will secure a virtuous rule." The princess proceeded toward the blade, and it shimmered subtly, though no rays of light reached it.

"And there's you," Artyrus added, stepping up behind her. "You're the symbol of hope and strength through which Penzelle will flourish, your resilience cleaving a new path for your people."

A kingdom of stone and steel will soon rise.

Aurora stood before Excalibur, overwhelmed by the responsibilities that would result from its retrieval. Artyrus reached for her, intertwining their fingers as she leaned into him, her shoulders pressing into his chest.

He snaked an arm around her waist. "Together." His breath kissed her neck, warming her chilled skin from the brisk morning air. She rested her head on his collarbone and closed her eyes, nodding against him.

A friend and lover, the prince had become her cornerstone. As one, they extended their joined hands for Excalibur, taking hold of its hilt.

The ground trembled underfoot, widening its division with a deep, yawning rumble. The existing crack further fractured the earth, hastening toward them and splitting the stone in half. Excalibur broke free, and they stumbled, tripping backward.

They had succeeded, a beacon of ancient lore in their hands for all Fayble to behold.

Artyrus grounded them, finding his footing as Aurora staggered into him when an amused chuckle sounded nearby from the shadows. Rory knew the laugh the instant she heard it, a sound from her past, once endearing and seductive.

"Did you like my gift?" Lancelot crooned from the darkness cloaking him. "It was, I suppose, a bit much. I should've been more courteous with the table linens."

He stepped into the swelling illumination of dayspring, his striking visage becoming the very face of depravity. Artyrus pivoted, entrusting Excalibur to the princess as he rooted himself between her and the childhood friend she'd lost long ago.

"Think of what we could accomplish, you and I. We were not born to lead simple lives, *Princess*." He brandished the title as if it would somehow compel her to join him, ignoring the guardian standing between them. "Maleficent would have continued to be a thorn in your side throughout your rise to power. I took her life for your benefit, Gwen—" The beautiful knight cleared his throat, recognizing his error before correcting himself. "Aurora, that is."

In the months following Lancelot's departure from their village, Rory had envisioned a reunion much like they shared in Otherlande. But seasons turned, as they so readily do, and her soul's musings had wandered. She had never been in love, having instead mourned the idea of what they might've been with a man who'd never understood the essence of devotion.

"You assassinated her for selfish gain. Either you seek Luther's favor, or she was a nuisance to your ambitions, but you did not slit her throat for me." Aurora words were clipped, outrage rising at her core.

"It's true." Lancelot shrugged, his face a mask of utter indifference. "I had tired of her. At first, it was thrilling to sneak away with her night after night. *Dangerous*… If Luther had discovered our dalliance, we'd undoubtedly have faced the guillotine." His admissions of a forbidden romance with the scorned queen of Chamelaute were both unexpected and plausible. A serpentine sneer crossed his features when he noted the royals' mutual bewilderment.

"Don't seem so surprised. Did you never consider why the dragon failed to turn me to ash when I found you at the castle? How I knew precisely where her encampment was located? Only the old woman was aware of our...*meetings*. I won Mal's trust and removed her from the equation after she grew too needy."

Again, Aurora believed every word. Lancelot was cunning but no liar. Not a word he breathed was false, but there was always more stirring beneath the surface of his careful artifice.

The man before her was one she no longer recognized. The naivete of youth had long since faded—a point at which she thought, perhaps, he'd absconded with her heart. How many more had he stolen in the seven years separating them from that field of strawberries he reimagined so flawlessly in their dreams?

It was of no import, for he was only a stranger to her now. Lancelot's compulsive hunger for influence would forever taint treasured memories of their companionship.

Artyrus drew his sword. "I think I've heard enough."

Lancelot quickly matched his stance, his blade rasping against its sheath. "Let's not pretend you'll ever sacrifice your virtue enough to run me through."

"It would seem you know little about me, if that's what you believe." The prince's muscles tensed, preparing to lunge, when a dagger flew past him in a blur of polished silver, embedding itself into a crevice in an ornamental archway that had safe-guarded Excalibur from the elements for centuries.

Lancelot's countenance paled when he glanced behind the princess and Artyrus.

"Must we, gentlemen?" Adelyce strode casually toward the gathered trio, unruffled by the unfolding chaos, her long, golden hair rustling gently in the morning breeze.

Dropping to his knees in her presence, Lancelot was wholly stricken.

"I've grown accustomed to this sort of reaction from men, but I admit, I didn't expect it from you." Her countenance was the very picture of disgust, staring down at him through narrowed eyes as she reached into a deep pocket in her breeches.

Lancelot gaped at her, his features bewildered, when she yanked his head back, tipping the knight's face skyward. Adelyce popped a cork from the tiny glass bottle she'd retrieved, using her teeth and spitting the stopper out.

She smiled. "Thank you for making this so easy." Between slender fingers, she pinched the container, sweeping it beneath Lancelot's nostrils.

He didn't attempt to fight her or speak another word before his body swayed, coal-dark eyes wide with wonder at the woman standing before him. His substantial frame sagged until, at last, the deviant's consciousness gave.

Adelyce tossed aside the container, its contents spilling over the earth. She nodded over her shoulder in a non-verbal command for assistance. With the toe of her boot, she pushed Lancelot's comatose figure to his back. "Don't fret. He's still alive. Help me move him, and I'll ensure he's adequately detained."

* * * *

They returned to Maleficent's stronghold before noon, the heat of day causing a trail of sweat to slip down Rory's temple. Artyrus held her close, the princess's back firmly pressed to his muscular frame as they rode into camp.

Murmurs followed them as they made their way to the center of the refuge, where horrors from the previous night yet hovered in the atmosphere. But Penzelle did not cower, its tyrannized citizenry coming together despite their mourning.

Astride Magnus, the heirs watched as a people assembled before their eyes, with far more present than those who had, for years, called the sanctuary of Wylewoode home. In silence, they waited — a crowd of warriors prepared for their call to arms.

"Show them." Artyrus's words were a breath in Aurora's ear, causing the hairs of her arms to stand on end.

Her hands trembled as she reached for the ancient weapon strapped to her waist. Steel shrieked when she pulled it from its casing at her thigh. When she raised Excalibur to the sky, her people, at long last, witnessed the prophecy personified.

Cries of exultation erupted, the triumph of a subjugated people so profound that tears streamed freely from Rory's eyes, her throat tight with emotion.

Amongst the grouping encircling Aurora and her guardian, familiar faces emerged. Too much time had passed since she'd seen them, with many words left unsaid.

It was Isolde who approached the princess first. Her cheeks were wet from the sobs still bursting from her lips. Drustan was with her, his hand placed tenderly at the small of her back — ever the compassionate husband and father Rory knew him to be. Pride shone in the swordsmith's gaze when his eyes fell upon her, and Aurora wept at the sight of them, only to find Aedre was there as well, stepping out from behind her parents. They had come, knowing all along who she was.

The lost princess of Penzelle.

For most of her life, they were the three who had protected and loved her. Drustan had taught her how to wield a sword, unaware of the blade she would one day carry. Isolde was the princess's nursemaid in infancy and rescuer from slaughter. And Aedra had ever been a confidant—the truest and most supportive of sisters.

Artyrus took Excalibur before easing Aurora to the ground, her legs unsteady and shaking. She ran into Isolde's welcoming embrace, the two women weeping as they held each other. Aedra joined them, draping an arm over Rory's narrow shoulders while Drustan drew them all closely to himself.

They were a family in every sense but blood.

"We love you," Drustan told Aurora as Isolde retreated a step, kissing her brow. The princess nodded, unable to speak, her tears revealing the sentiments anchored deep within her soul.

A revolt against the crown would soon rise—a nation primed to end an oppressive reign.

Artyrus dismounted, his nearness bringing Rory solace amid the surrounding chaos when he made his way to her. He was soon followed by Mimi, who made her way through the assembly, her eyes dark with fatigue.

The aged woman lowered her head in deference before them. "The Seer has not been seen since your unanimous decision to pursue Luther. And while Maleficent was wise and led this encampment well, she lost sight of her role over time. Merlin has never had the stomach for conflict in the first place." She met the eyes of her sovereign, her features filled with determination. "I've sent messengers to the outer villages. Penzelle will take up arms with you this night."

Mimi's gaze shifted to Artyrus, her fist pressed to her chest as if she meant to convey her allegiance at last. "Your Chamelautean brothers have gone to spread the word of your lineage, telling tales of the sword you now wear upon your belt. The time is nigh."

Chapter Thirty-One

It was a risk they had to take.

Chamelaute was quiet, with most of its populace either fast asleep or tucked away in one of countless pubs or brothels still conducting business hours beyond day's end.

They found much to be as it was in Otherlande, adrenaline coursing through Aurora's veins as they approached the secret place Ffion had revealed during their poison slumber. There was no way to know if the passage existed, but it would doubtless improve their chances of successfully removing Luther from the throne.

Though few soldiers patrolled the premises, a rolling tempest acted as an active guard over the palace, promising a deluge of rain and whipping winds. Rory wasn't foolish enough to believe they might easily take control of the castle, but her cunning friend's discovery of the forgotten entry would undoubtedly catch the king unaware.

Merlin's absence was yet another infernal question hovering in the back of Rory's mind. The Seer was an enigma, and the princess thankful that neither her guardian nor she had divulged their knowledge of Ffion's find in his presence.

Would that it might be real.

"This is it." Her voice was less than a whisper, carried away by a whirling gale, chanting vows of the imminent storm brewing in black, ominous clouds overhead.

Drustan rested a reassuring hand on her shoulder, the mantle she wore flapping wildly around her. It was a wall like any other she'd stood before, and dread struck like a thrashing whip.

"Here, let me help." Ector fell at Aurora's side as if he sensed her concern, mimicking how she tested each brick one at a time. Artyrus joined, followed by the swordsmith and Kaye as a flash of blinding light cracked through the night sky.

Thunder rumbled while their hands moved from brick to brick until a rock shifted suddenly behind Rory's palm.

"Artyrus," she murmured breathlessly, her disbelief clear. Struggling to force the rock any further, she gulped as droplets of rain began plummeting to the earth in increasing measure. Rory wiped the moisture from her brow with the hem of her cloak, blinking away the rain, even as it persisted. "I can't move it."

Artyrus stepped toward her, pushing the stone, slick from a heavy downpour. His body tensed, straining as he pressed his weight into the wall. It shifted just enough, grating past the surrounding bricks. Bits of mortar crumbled when the prince turned, forcing the passage open with his broad shoulders, a grunt of exertion freeing the aged hinges that protested their use after decades of oversight.

Catching him before he stumbled into frigid darkness, Kaye gripped the prince's forearm, hauling his brother upright. "Shall we?"

"Now or never, I suppose." Artyrus led the way, followed by Rory, with each eager to see if the interior would also match the dream castle. It was surreal walking through the same tunnel in the same shadows, though Ffion's absence was profoundly felt.

To her great relief, the library was unoccupied when they entered and dark as it had been when last they'd seen it in their dreams. Laughter sounded from the hallway outside, with several voices conversing casually in what Rory could only assume was the Great Hall.

"I'll make for the dungeon the moment we clear the corridor. I only pray Pelinore is unharmed." Malevolent stillness suffocated Ector's hushed words, the vacant room home to their last moments of peace.

"And we will welcome the rest of our guests," Kaye added with a nod to Drustan, who grunted his approval in answer.

It was no small miracle to see Penzelle rally that day behind a princess they'd believed in earnest would return, along with countless Chamelauteans who recognized Artyrus as the rightful heir to the throne. Word of Excalibur had spread rapidly through the boroughs, garnering loyalty amongst unexpected allies, and together, they would fight for liberation.

Their strategy was simple, but the execution would be a feat of stealth and endurance.

"Be careful," Aurora softly demanded when Drustan took her hands in his. Pressing his lips to her knuckles, he inclined his head.

"I'll abide at your word." Lifting his eyes to meet Rory's, he offered a sly smile. "Remember what I taught you."

"Always." The princess kissed Drustan's cheek in farewell, a promise of victory plain in her gaze.

Goodbyes had never been her way and seemed only to encourage heartache. So, none were made, even if death were to wrest her into its awaiting embrace, leaving only a silhouette of abandoned hope and futility.

Kaye proceeded toward the door separating their band from prophetic triumph, and Aurora's pulse thrummed with anticipation.

The knight and swordmaster slipped out of the library first, followed soon after by Sir Ector, departing without a word with the fate of a people suspended precariously at their fingertips.

Rory and her beloved stayed their positions, awaiting the signal to act. It wouldn't be long, with Kaye and Drustan moving silently for the main entrance. Allies would soon flood the palace, understanding not what was at stake but what might be gained should their efforts prevail.

"We must make it to the tower, no matter the cost." The prince folded Aurora into his arms, his instruction firm but calm. "Luther will be there."

Rory pulled away from him enough to appreciate the angles of his face and the flecks of honeyed amber in his devastating eyes. She forced a smile. "Try not to die again."

"I should say the same to you." Artyrus brushed the tip of his nose over hers, his thumb skimming the line of her jaw. "Together, we'll return him to dust."

A war cry broke out in the Great Hall, a battle igniting within the palace walls. The guardian brought his mouth to Aurora's, sliding his tongue over hers, eliciting a sigh of utter contentment amidst the growing chaos. She tugged him closer, his frame pressed against hers as she wove her fingers through ash-blonde waves, which fell to one side of the prince's striking face.

Rory's impulse to remain with him there was the very thing that made her pull away from him once more. The half-smile he wore when she did confirmed what she already knew to be true in her heart.

They were ready and would not fail. The princess's proof rambled up the lengths of each of their spines, inscribed on a blade that had not been moved in centuries.

Artyrus's voice was raw, his words but a breath sweeping over the princess's temple. "Don't let them forget who you are, Mistress of Blades."

He unsheathed the swords set upon either side of her hips, presenting both to her. Excalibur and the trusted blade Drustan had forged years before fit flawlessly within her grip as she tested the feel of each.

It was time.

The reverberation of clashing metal and groans of agony energized her wearied spirit. Aurora had not slept since awakening from Otherlande, but her body was unwilling to comply, even while her essential being craved rest. Sleep would come in time, though the idea frightened her more than the war at hand.

Artyrus knew the turns and passages that would deliver them to the eastmost stairwell, guiding them swiftly through the palace. They moved silently, avoiding guards as they maneuvered their way eastward, but once they approached the stairway's base, there was no time to waste after one of the king's men spotted them.

Together, they began their ascent, the stairs leading directly to the central tower, with steady, urgent footfalls echoing closely at their backs.

The war will be won in a tower high, as centuries foretold, the time is nigh.

And if Luther wasn't there...? The thought had crossed Aurora's mind countless times as they worked over their strategy. The king could've escaped the moment he heard sounds of bloodshed, but to second guess their plan would surely see them dead. Faith alone prevented Rory's focus from further venturing into notions of failure, for the prophecy had already proven itself more than once. The ancient foretelling never mentioned a king, but instinct told her she would find him waiting. That was, if his guards didn't seize them first.

Higher they climbed, the princess's muscles burning as they scaled the infernal steps. Sweat trickled down her neck, her head throbbing when Luther's remaining men found them progressing upward, higher and higher, without stopping. The knights were not alone, with evident carnage ensuing below the heirs' seemingly endless ascent.

"They're gaining on us," Artyrus huffed, bracing himself between narrow stone walls. "I'll hold them off."

"*No*, Artyrus." Rory was gasping for air, her desperate plea only a rasp, scraping against her throat.

"You have to go." He hesitated a beat as voices began to ring more distinctly beneath them. "Now!"

The princess nodded, her throat tight with emotion. She knew he was right, though her chest ached when she watched her beloved descend into the fray.

A soldier with equal stake.

Aurora halted at the top of the stairwell when she heard the king.

Luther was, in fact, there, but so was another.

Outside, a storm raged, with wrathful explosions of thunder making it challenging to hear, but the king's words were clear enough. "You *will* find a way to awaken him," he demanded. "The others can slumber until their bodies fail. I care not, but Philippe cannot remain like…*that*."

"Archimedes is working tirelessly to do as you say."

Merlin.

The princess could scarcely believe it.

He had no stomach for conflict, yet he'd planted Luther precisely where he needed to be. After the Seer revealed to Rory the truth of his majesty's poison hold over Penzelle, she'd thought him spineless. Aurora would never agree with some of his chosen methods, but at least he'd not failed in this.

Every nerve in her body was aware of the gravity of the moment. Generations came and went, never knowing when the famed prediction would be realized or if it was even true.

When the princess had been a child, Isolde read the story of a woman who changed the lives of her people. In the age-old account, the courageous woman, a queen, knew approaching her land's sovereign ruler on their behalf without summons would likely result in death.

"Perhaps you were born for such a time as this," the woman's guardian in the tale had encouraged.

Aurora had never forgotten those words, resonating in every crevice of her warrior's spirit. The queen in Isolde's book did, in fact, triumph, and so, this night, would she.

Opening the solid tower door, King Luther turned when he heard it creak, his eyes narrowing on the princess standing in the opening with a sword clutched in either hand.

Rory found both of his sons looking back at her in His Majesty's face through Luther's wild, fury-filled eyes. Sparing a sideways glance at Merlin, he clenched his jaw as the betrayal dawned.

"Oh, the lies you've spun in all our years together. And now, you seek to end me, is that it?" The king's words were venomous, but Aurora sensed his fear lurking within them.

Merlin said nothing, his gaze never wavering as he stared back at Luther. Leaning onto his staff, the soothsayer didn't so much as blink.

Maybe travel-worn or stricken by grief from Maleficent's sudden demise, his pallor was wan in comparison to his standard golden complexion.

"You knew well before turning over Pelinore that my first-born was alive, didn't you? And all this time, where my Maleficent had fled. You told me they were dead. *Both* of them!" Thunder matched the king's fit of outrage, causing the high tower walls to tremble and shattering the massive window in which Mal's dragon had once perched in that strange, parallel consciousness.

"The queen was murdered just one night past by your man, Lancelot." Merlin's tone was grim, but what he revealed in his statement was not lost on Aurora. He'd seen her death and permitted it through omission. And by his own hand, Luther had learned of Pelinore's role in raising his true heir, all to meet a purpose the Seer believed to be greater than the lives of people who had trusted him.

To stoke revolt.

Luther stalked the venerable deceiver, kicking his staff from his hands when he grabbed for his throat.

Aurora ran for them, Merlin stumbling backward over shards of glass, glittering with flashes of silver light from violent bolts ripping through the blackened sky. Deafening rumbles again rattled the isolated spire as the Seer struggled to regain his footing, but Luther was resolute in his bitter pursuit.

Merlin tripped. Too close to the fractured window, and Rory too far to stop him from toppling over the cold, wet sill.

Dropping her swords, the princess lunged, extending an arm out to him as she braced herself over spikes of broken glass. Slivered bits dug into her flesh when the Seer caught Aurora's hand, her slight frame jolting forward from the force of his fall. She grappled against the stone under her, struggling for inches as she commanded every ounce of her strength to comply.

Merlin's grip began to slip as rain poured over them, drenching them both until the princess lost her hold. Rory screamed, the Seer's visage contorting into one of unadulterated terror as his body flailed, plummeting to the earth far below.

The princess scrambled, pushing herself from the vast opening, her shoulder blazing from the weight of

Merlin's suspended figure. She panted for air, her breaths coming in short, frenzied bursts.

She clutched her chest, turning from the window when she saw him. Luther's eyes were glowing with certain victory as he raised Excalibur against her.

There was nowhere to go and hardly a moment to react before the blade sliced Aurora's way, slashing the inside of her leg as she dove, followed by instantaneous, searing pain.

She collapsed to the stone floor, cold as winter's pernicious sting. But the king's lethal blow never came as shadows crept into her vision. The tower swayed, or maybe it was she who could not prevent her surroundings from spinning.

Either way, the darkness beckoned, pulling her under as she lost all consciousness.

* * * *

Artyrus hoped he was not too late, praying the princess's wound was not fatal, though her mien had already begun to pale. He couldn't tell where all the blood originated, with a crimson pool filtering into cracks between the bricks underneath Aurora's shuddering form.

"I wondered when I might see you, my son," Luther crooned, a vicious tilt to his lips.

"You've made a grave error." The prince lifted his sword, still dripping with another man's blood. Artyrus wiped the steel edges, staining his tunic without a thought as he moved for Luther.

"Had I known you'd lived—" The king retreated with every step Artyrus advanced, his hands visibly shaking. "I can't believe I never saw it for myself."

The guardian raised a brow, narrowing the distance separating them. "Would it have changed anything?"

Luther scoffed. "I would've killed you sooner."

"Is that why you pull away from me now? Because you're so unflinching in your wrath? Your hands tremble, even as you threaten me." Artyrus's nostrils flared as he stepped closer to his father, a ruler he'd never respected nor desired to serve. "You're a coward."

Luther sprang forward with his accusation in a maneuver Artyrus evaded with ease, ducking out of his reach. The prince twisted, pivoting to the king's back when he hooked his neck from behind, choking him with his forearm. Luther sputtered some intelligible profanity as Artyrus tightened his hold, tugging his wrist toward himself as he slowly crushed the sovereign's windpipe.

Luther fumbled for release, his movements growing more sluggish and careless as he thrashed.

"*Sleep*," the prince growled into his father's ear. The king sagged, and Artyrus let his body fall into a heap. He spared the man only a single glance, ignoring all thought of what his life might've been had he not been relieved of his station from birth.

Aurora's breath labored nearby, her exquisite face void of color. Artyrus dropped to his knees, scrambling toward her as the rise and fall of her chest became harder to distinguish. Drawing his beloved to himself, he shredded the hem of his tunic, binding the gash upon her thigh. Her wound showed no sign of clotting, but Artyrus held her close, warming her chilled, wet frame against him.

He brushed soaking strands from the princess's face, fitting his mouth to hers in a desperate plea for her life.

"Come back to me, Aurora." A sob burst from the prince, his fervent request evaporating into the merciless night. "Come back," he pleaded, his tears mingling with the pooling blood beneath her cradled form.

Artyrus pressed his lips to her forehead, to her temple, grazing his nose over hers before kissing her once more. His hopes faded with each of her strained, shallow breaths until her eyes slowly opened.

Aurora's ice blue eyes fluttered, and his heart soared with relief. She peered up at him, neither healed nor whole, but she was alive.

He wept into her hair, his fingers combing through the silky locks in long strokes. "I love you," he wheezed.

She cupped his face, wearing a subtle smile. "I love you, too."

Chapter Thirty-Two

It would take time to recover from the impact of their recent losses.

Aurora felt it daily, a ripple left behind by the late despot of Chamelaute and his passionate former queen. How different might things have been for the ambitious couple had they not ignored the musings of their hearts amid the thirst for power?

And while Merlin inspired liberation through his insight, the gravity of his choices was not without consequence. Authority had been given without accountability, a circumstance in which morality is often stifled.

"The arrangements have been made, Your Majesties. A garden will be planted in Maleficent's honor beginning next week," Pelinore said, his advisory role suiting him well. Rory grew to love him more with each passing day, though she would never grow accustomed to her new title.

King and Queen, they all called them. Together, Aurora and her beloved guardian laughed about it, even as the burden of what it meant was not entirely understood in the short time they'd been established.

Artyrus nodded to him. "Thank you, Pelinore."

The king's relief brought tears to Rory's eyes when he and his caretaker were reunited. She was still recovering when Ector and Kaye delivered Pelinore to Artyrus — her faithful companion having never left her side as healers closely watched her wounds. Pelinore had embraced Artyrus as one would a son, the king's father in every sense that mattered.

The sovereigns and their new counsel, consisting of advisors and knights alike, were seated as equals in what once had been Luther's war room. Each member had been handpicked by the king and queen, with their decisions made independently of one another.

Meetings were to occur weekly to prevent any sensitive matters from going unnoticed, along with larger monthly assemblies to include as many of the combined citizenries as would fit in the Great Hall. Their people had been deprived of input for too long, but no longer. Indeed, a new nation had risen, one which might provide its populace with just opportunity.

"And the prince?" Aurora addressed Archimedes this time, his countenance still pallid after the Seer's earthly departure.

"Philippe is as well as can be expected, given the circumstances. He's not yet awakened, but I've found a way to sustain him in body while he yet slumbers." His skills were as impressive as his ability to avoid eye contact. Archimedes kept his gaze from both king and queen at all costs.

From loathing or introversion, they knew not. And while Artyrus had expressed no interest in coming to know his half-brother, Philippe, neither he nor Aurora thought it right to leave him to die while his consciousness endured at Otherlande's fickle whims.

"You've done well, Archimedes," Rory said, though his gaze lingered upon the vast round table separating those attending the intimate conference.

There was a certain informality about the environment they'd created that made a space to foster artifice and strategies for war somehow less intimidating. Would that it might remain so.

"Preparations are being made as we speak for tomorrow's banquet," Ector offered in what was likely an attempt to remove persisting attention from Archimedes. A favor, indeed, as Adelyce's sharp glare bore into the introverted scholar as if she might somehow think him complicit in Maleficent's untimely death.

Mimi looked askance at the knight, her serpent-like tongue running across yellowed teeth. "You think they'll want to celebrate with ye, eh?" Penzelle had not forgotten the running tensions between themselves and those of the former Chamelautan rule, nor should they. But Aurora hoped, given more time, the kingdom would reconcile, for it was Luther who had subdued them through tyranny.

"Should they not wish to witness one of their own be sworn into knighthood?" Rory answered, observing the embittered woman. While Mimi pledged fealty to the new leadership openly, she was far less amenable to implementing much-needed changes behind closed doors.

They were grateful for her wisdom, nonetheless, with Mimi's knowledge of the outermost lands and its people unrivaled by any but the following night's honored guest, Adelyce.

"We wished to acknowledge your accomplishments privately before the ceremony tonight," Aurora said, turning to face the brave young woman. With bewilderment in her striking features, she raised an inquisitive brow.

"You have earned your knighthood, if not through merit than your dealings with Lancelot alone," Artyrus added, picking up where Rory had left off. He laced his fingers through hers atop the table, squeezing her hand a bit with the mention of her childhood friend.

But she had accepted that Lancelot was no longer the boy she'd once known. There was a seat for him at the round table, though he would not often be escorted there. Still, as Philippe's trusted confidant, the information he'd gained might someday prove valuable. Until an occasion momentous enough arose, however, the knight would not be permitted to leave his cell beneath the palace.

And it was the beautiful woman warrior's duty to manage him.

Adelyce flared her nostrils in distaste. "I do hate him," she sighed, though a wry smirk formed on her bow-shaped lips. "I'll accept the commission. Thank you." She inclined her head to Aurora, and the queen stood, returning her sentiments.

Artyrus rose beside her, their hands still joined. "We'll see you all tomorrow."

Adelyce smiled, bowing to her chosen family before she departed. The council slowly dispersed behind her, until only Drustan remained. "Still no word of the lost boy," he said, his countenance troubled.

Aurora's heart sank. She'd promised Ffion when first they'd met that she'd repay him for all he'd done to help them in their time together. In truth, she couldn't bear the idea of him somewhere in Wylewoode, alone and hungry. They'd learned little of his circumstances outside the dream, but Rory prayed, night after night, that he was all right — that he was *safe*.

"Please keep looking." Artyrus snaked his arm around the queen's waist when he spoke, a gesture she considered maybe comforted him as much as her. Each of them had a stake in finding the boy, who had quickly become as close as a brother.

"We'll do our best," Drustan said, squeezing Aurora's shoulder. He offered a nod of farewell to the king before he departed.

Artyrus pulled Rory closer, his face nuzzled against her neck. "Ffion is strong."

* * * *

They had learned to sleep again.

For days following the mass awakening, they'd feared laying their heads down to rest. Each night they'd returned to Otherlande, strangely aware that the subconscious existence mattered just as much as what most people would refer to as reality. To them, there was little difference between dreaming and wakefulness.

Not a night passed in which Artyrus failed to stay with Aurora in her chambers, though no longer did she thrash or awaken in a terrified, cold sweat. It was not until they found each other in sleep that it became welcomed again. To dream was not as rejuvenating as it once was, but it afforded the couple an escape from their duties presiding over the court and provided precious spare time alone together.

The initial struggle resulting from their inability to wield control of their nightmares at last decreased, giving way to secret trysts. That was, at least, when they could find one another. Their capacity to do so improved as time went on, but a natural slumber would never permit the same level of mastery as their poisonous interlude.

Aurora awakened to slivers of golden sunlight peeking through finely threaded satin curtains. The queen's quarters were magnificent but nowhere near as breathtaking as the man who held her in his strong embrace. Their entangled bodies were a jumble of linens and limbs draped carelessly over one another, and Rory could find no other way to describe it than absolute bliss.

Next to her, Artyrus opened his eyes, shading the morning beams from his face with one eye closed, squinting the other. "I didn't see you in there last night." Tugging Aurora to himself, he gently brushed his lips over hers. She'd also looked for him in Otherlande but had instead seen something far more disturbing.

"Should I believe you sought me out, or did you, perhaps, find another queen to whom you might whisper roguish sentiments?" Rory worked her fingers through the king's messy waves, and he nestled into her touch. He groaned, a lazy, devastating sound, nipping the sensitive flesh just below her jaw.

"Is it a war you seek, Valkyrie?" She could sense his smile, his voice low and rough from slumber. He smothered her giggle away, their mouths colliding in a rush of desire that would be her undoing.

The queen couldn't comprehend how she'd come to be so blessed but vowed never to take this gift for granted. "I had the strangest dream," she admitted between eager, fevered kisses. "A nightmare, rather..."

"Tell me." His words rustled her hair, gentle and laced with understanding.

"I saw the shadow again," she began, trying to remember the details and ignoring the shiver accompanying her recollection of the dark, lurking figure. "Petra was so afraid in those final moments we shared with her that I never noticed the hook at the end of its limb. It was as if it was looking back at me, almost like somehow it...*knew* me."

Artyrus stroked the length of Rory's arm, pressing his lips to her temple. "Did it attempt to harm you?"

Aurora shook her head. While she knew not everything in the dreamscape bore significance outside its confines, the shadow seemed as tangible as the man next to her.

It mattered not and was futile to be swept away into fantasies concerning something over which she had no control.

A knock at the queen's chamber doors drew her back to the present, with thoughts of Petra and all her demons dissipating as Artyrus rose from the bed. He strode toward the doors, cracking them open just enough to receive a letter bearing King Riccard of Llundyn's royal seal.

Aurora couldn't contain her excitement when Artyrus broke the note open. "Please read it."

Clearing his throat, her beloved began.

Dear friends,

I hope this letter finds you well, as Ella and I found our diplomat's reports most alarming. For it seems we were thieving about Llundyn with none other than the famed lost royal of Penzelle – a shock if ever there were one! In short, we wish to congratulate you and your king on your recent coronations and look forward to further unifying efforts between our respective kingdoms. You are deeply missed.

Be well,

Ric & Elle

Tears misted Rory's eyes as her guardian read the note, the time she'd spent with her friends feeling like a lifetime had passed. Her world, her hopes and dreams had since changed irreversibly. But as Aurora watched Artyrus, both imposing and steadfast, she knew her heart was, at long last, whole.

She smiled, reaching for him. "Come back to me."

Artyrus took her hand, returning to the warmth of his queen as he lay beside her. He kissed her bare shoulder, tucking her close to his chest. "As you wish," he growled, earning a sigh of contentment from his beloved.

And so it was and always would be.

Want to see more from these authors?
Here's a taster for you to enjoy!

Chronicles of Fayble:
Daughter of Neverwoode
Britt Cooper & Erin Dulin

Coming Summer 2023

Excerpt

There was something inherently risky about roving the streets of Llundyn in the dead of night, regardless of efforts to bring the town into submission under an honorable reign. Doubtless, the queen would have their heads if she knew of their pursuits, but she'd have to find out first.

"You need not accompany me. Stars only know the hell there'll be to pay upon your return to the palace." James Much wasn't wrong, his eagerness to be on his way overriding his unrivaled civility. The pair scuttled past pitch-black alleyways and decaying shanties lining the seafront, the creaky boards beneath their feet making each step an agonizing exercise.

For all their efforts to traverse in silence, they may as well have announced themselves to the waterfront. It was no matter. They were nearly there, and they'd seen nary a soul, the eventide surf crashing ashore all around the harbor providing at least some semblance of cover.

"Ella is nothing if not forgiving," King Riccard muttered, his words carried on the ocean breeze toward his companion. "She'd have to be, given our union. Imagine being married to me."

"Yes...imagine." James smirked, running his only remaining hand through the dark, tousled waves of his hair. The loss of his left had been a hefty blow, with the former sheriff of Llundyn having removed it by force with a saber and a smile, his devilry leaving the young sea captain abruptly bereft of usefulness.

Certainly, James had found his place, readily pillaging from the wealthiest of Llundyniens with Ella and her merry men. It had been the adventure of a lifetime—and a fulfilling endeavor at that. But something more had gone missing alongside his hand.

He'd always found purpose in the workings of them, having performed the duties of a carpenter at Locksley Manor for a large portion of his life. Indeed, they were his livelihood, and while he knew that he would never be on his own, never be left to fend for himself, the last thing he wanted was to be served.

Ella, the newly coronated Queen of Llundyn, had been his most faithful friend, their comradery carrying them through tragedy and triumph. She'd been there on that fateful eve, cared for him, bandaged his wounds. She'd blamed herself for his predicament, though it had had nothing to do with her. His decisions were his and his alone, rendering her guilt pointless where he was concerned.

What followed had been the epitome of success, with the pair having seen the starving citizenry return to prosperity, even as they helped preserve the rightful king through an attempted coup.

But those harrowing months had evaporated into monotony with order restored. King Riccard was just, ruling alongside Ella, who'd easily maintained her humility, despite her lofty new position. His bandmates had found their places within the palace, quickly achieving success in their most unexpected endeavors and readily adapting to their ever-changing roles.

James, however, had sought refuge far away from the confines of the castle walls. He'd been apprenticed to a sea captain and had quickly risen within the ranks, performing each of his tasks in prompt compliance and earning a sterling reputation as he went. It didn't hurt that he'd been raised upon the waters as a boy, having seen much of the continent of Fayble with his late sea-master father as they skirted the coastline.

A figure in the distance brought the pair up short. They'd been largely ignored until then, the slumbering town proving to be an easy companion with which to travel incognito. She was stood upon the wharf facing the ocean, her cloak fluttered in the air. It was almost as if she'd materialized out of nothing, but then again, that was Ella's way.

She turned as they approached, a knowing smile upon her lips. "Two of my favorite boys galivanting about without guardians. How did you manage to slip away unnoticed?"

Ric took to her side, grinning from ear to ear when he slipped his arm beneath her mantle, pulling her nearer as he encircled her waist. "Perhaps I'd ask the same of you."

Doubtless, their lack of guards was potentially dangerous—perhaps even stupid. But the king and queen of Llundyn had loathed giving up the freedoms of Sherwood Forest for the shackles of courtly responsibility. Even so, *this*—their endless love and adoration for one another—had always seen them through their duties and sustained them in uncertainty.

James shifted his weight from one foot to the other before looking away. The pair never flaunted their affection for one another. It was merely the natural state of things, and he'd be lying if he weren't to admit that it had him mildly jealous.

"We were to celebrate your upcoming voyage this evening, but something told me you wouldn't wait," Ella said, withdrawing from her king enough to look at James.

"You know that's not for me." He gazed at the water, his heart full of conflicted longing as he wished to be on his way, but leaving his friends caused a bitterness he couldn't quite describe. A celebration of his impending departure would simply be too much to bear.

Ella nodded as if that was the response she'd expected. Of course she had, for she was there, awaiting his sneaky escape from Llundyn. She knew him, perhaps better than anybody else in the whole of Fayble. "You two have become quite the conspirators of late." She poked her husband in the ribs. "How will you ever do without him?"

"How will you?" Ric returned.

"You speak as if I'm to meet my end," James added. "I've every intention of returning unscathed."

"We know nothing of these people, these *pirates* of Wylewoode." Ella grimaced, her features pinched with worry.

The threat had revealed itself in only a week past when James and his crew had been targeted by what they'd later found to be a large iron ball, launched from the foreign ship by an explosive charge that had left a sizeable hole in the heart of his vessel. The siege had taken them all by surprise, if for no other reason than that Wylewoode was not known to harbor many citizens, let alone seafaring ships.

"I must go, Elle." James's eagerness for a new adventure quickly surpassed his desire to continue on in the familiarity of his Llundynien routine as he strode down the pier to his beloved vessel with Ric and Ella at his heels.

He could feel every ounce of their trepidation as they moved down the length of the dock behind him. Never would they force him to go. Hell, they hadn't even asked him — but somehow it felt right.

Ella paused, eyeing the mammoth ship with wide, bright eyes. "Your crew…"

James could finish her sentence, even as he felt the disquiet churning beneath her polite exterior. His sailors were rough around the edges, with some old and some mere boys. They were surly, bitter, *lost* — some of the last people with which one would expect to endeavor around the continent. "They're a sorry lot, I admit." He grinned, offering a shrug. "But for some reason, they fall in line. We manage to make a way. Maybe we aren't all that different in the end."

The trio fell into silence, with Ella averting her gaze. He hadn't meant for his words to seem spiteful — only that he felt he finally belonged, leading his very own band of misfits on a dubious journey with an outcome that was anybody's guess.

And he would return knowing that he'd given the voyage his all. Putting some arrogant pirates in their place along the way was an added benefit, allowing him to defend his kingdom, to prove himself worthy of the inherent trust from his beloved sovereigns.

"Well," Ella managed, "I'd be remiss in sending you on your way without a little something." She reached beneath her cloak, presenting him with a wide, flat box tied shut with a hunter-green ribbon. Plucking the cords with delicate fingers, she opened the case, offering the contents to James, her expression bashful.

"A hook?"

"I felt silly," Ella continued, pulling the gleaming silver crook from the velvet-padded box before handing it to Ric. She cradled the curved metal appendage, smiling at last. "Still do. But I've seen them used all over, both on ships and around the harbor, and I thought..."

James shook his head, floored by her foresight. "It's perfect. I admit I'd never considered the possibility before now, but to have the use of my hand — or my hook, rather? It's ingenious."

"As ever," Ric beamed. "If there was any doubt about the wisdom behind the Crown, it was laid to rest by this Queen of Shadows."

"Doubtless," James agreed as Ella moved toward him, rolling up his shirtsleeve. She attached the polished hook to the brace covering his forearm, a task simpler than he'd have guessed. He held his arm up, the moonlight bouncing off the contours of the hook as he shifted it. "It's effortless. Shall I test its usefulness on Sheriff Dane?"

Ella furrowed her brows, biting her lip to suppress a smile while Ric laughed openly. It was reassuring to James, their ability to see the humor in his remark, even if it was a little dark.

"Ahoy there, Captain!" came the familiar voice of his quartermaster. Second in command, William Smee was an eccentric sort — a man James had known for the whole of his life as he'd served in the same role for

James' father. He made his way down the gangplank, blowing the wild springs of his salt-and-pepper hair from his face with a hearty puff of air.

"Mr. William..." Ella breathed as recognition dawned. Not long ago, he'd been the very man who had prepared her tiny band of heroes for the ball that had been their greatest strike against tyranny.

"Alas, I'm no longer a purveyor of borrowed goods, Your Majesty." Smee bowed deeply, first to Ella then to Ric, his face an unabashed mask of delight as he clapped James on the shoulder. "I always knew we'd set sail again someday! Your father would be proud."

"This feels wrong." Ella glanced from Smee to the ship behind him, her countenance troubled. "We know nothing of a people in Wylewoode, save that it's where *criminal exiles* are frequently sent to live out their days. And goodness knows there can't be many remaining, given the dangers lurking within that savage territory. There's a reason those lands are avoided at all costs, and we don't even know if any of this is real! It feels like you're chasing a ghost, Much!"

James moved toward her, wrapping her in his arms as she angrily wiped her eyes. She always worked to control her emotions, to be the unflappable rock upon which the kingdom could steadily thrive. Her concern for his wellbeing was nearly enough to have him second-guessing himself, but the prospect of leaving his country exposed to the dangers of what did, admittedly, feel somewhat like a phantasm...

Well, he simply couldn't justify it.

"It felt real enough to me," he whispered to her alone. He took her by the shoulders, looking her in the eyes. "The hole in my vessel was no accident, and the enemy ship? It appeared out of nowhere, and —"

"And I can't lose you." She fisted his cloak, choking back her tears. "*We* cannot lose you. Your kingdom and your people need you."

James took a deep breath. Ella was as dear as the closest of sisters, and he knew she meant only to keep him safe. "I must go. This threat to Llundyn cannot stand. Whether it's a figment of our own minds or a legitimate menace remains to be seen, but one way or another, it will be dealt with. I'll return before you've missed me."

He kissed her cheek before backing away from his beloved friends, offering a wave and a smile in parting. Ric saluted him, taking to his wife's side as they watched him make his way up the gangplank behind Smee, whose steps bounced with obvious expectation.

When he reached the deck, James refused to turn around. Moving forward was the only way. "Haul out!" he cried to his crew, and as the ship came alive with the tumult of departure, he finally found peace as he was lost to the chaos of the sea.

About the Authors

Britt Cooper

Brittany has been a cosmetologist for over a decade, an occupation that continuously explores fresh avenues of creativity and beauty. She is a new mother, learning to balance the reality of what it means to be a mom, wife, stylist, and author. Reading has always been one of her passions and writing an endeavor she refuses to leave behind.

Erin Dulin

Erin is a wife and mother who loves spending time with family. She's an enthusiastic fan of all things sports, experimental baker/chef, and amateur gamer in her free time. Writing has been a passion since her childhood, and while finding peace and quiet in which to write never comes easily, she knows it worth every ounce of chaos when the stories take shape.

Britt and Erin love to hear from readers. You can find their contact information, website details and author profile page at https://www.finch-books.com

Sign up for our newsletter and find out about all our romance book releases, eBook sales and promotions, sneak peeks and FREE romance books!